I0587412

BLUE SKY, DEADLY SECRETS

A Psychological Thriller

BLUE SKY, DEADLY SECRETS

A Psychological Thriller

Don Beere

CARDON BOOKS

Blue Sky Deadly Secrets

©2019 Donald B. Beere. All rights reserved.

ISBN: 978-1-7321106-1-8
Printed in the United States of America
Cover and interior design: n-kcreative.com

Published by:
Cardon Books
400 S. 14th Street
Suite 1001
Saint Louis, MO 63103

*Dedicated to victims of torture,
violence, and suffering*

CHAPTER 1

The year: 1986
The month: August
The day: Wednesday, the 20th
The time: Midafternoon

I come to a standstill, shocked. Students swirl around me while I ponder what happened.

I was approaching the Student Union, having just said good-bye to two graduate students, and was walking toward the full-length glass doors that serve as its main entrance. I noticed the curly, blond hair first, and next the red plaid shirt. Then I saw Rick through the doors. He was striding, almost running, to reach them.

I doubled my pace, eager to hear about his research and to talk about our good news. I was ten yards from the entrance when he burst through the door as if it blocked his way. He paused for a second to twist and peer behind him into the building. I stopped short, puzzled by his actions.

Rick wrenched his body forward, hunched his shoulders, and jammed his hands into his pockets. He marched ahead, as if racing, and bumped a startled young man whose glasses popped off his nose. This forced a second student to step aside. Rick was thinner than I remembered, and his face looked haggard, as if he had not slept. Is he sick? His rapid pace quickly brought him within speaking distance. Frozen where I stood, I wanted to say something. But what?

"Rick—"

"I sent something to your office," Rick whispered. "If anything happens . . ." His voice was taut, impersonal, urgent. He didn't turn or glance at me.

Then, right after he passed by, he stopped and stared at his feet. As if to the cement, he whispered, "Tell not one person."

He rushed forward and vanished among the mass of students.

I had never seen Rick this way. He was not acting like someone just back from sabbatical. It was as if he was barely here and struggled to say anything. My first reaction is to feel hurt and disappointed at not being able to share our good fortune. If he is going to be so remote right when we are supposed to start our project, how can we work together? I'm dismayed at my irrational and self-centered response; then I'm alarmed.

"If anything happens," he said. If what happens?

Why did he say so little? Why "tell no one"? Tell no one what?

After this troubling encounter, my delight has faded. I notice students bunch up, trying to get around me where I stand. Their muttered complaints now reach me. I force myself to move and continue toward my office. The books I am carrying from the library will help me finish the work I planned for this afternoon. As I thread through the crush of undergraduates, I realize that I can find answers when I call him later

Rick is a complex and sometimes difficult person. Over several years, I have developed fondness and respect for him. Today's interaction brings back my earlier mixed feelings. The first time we met, I misjudged his positive reaction to my proposed tai chi workshop as a genial and easygoing style. I later discovered he was competitive, "superior," and challenging. Yet, at other times he could be accepting and thoughtful. We laughed often . . . but his humor could be cutting.

The second time we met was for coffee at the Student Union. I dragged my plastic chair toward the table, getting ready to sit.

"And what brand of psychologist are you?"

"A clinical psychologist."

"Oh," he said, nodding his head as if understanding, "a cynical psychologist." He did not smile or hint he was making a joke. I was put off by his remark.

Over the next few months, we met for lunch several times. Mixed into our conversations, he made lighthearted critiques of psychology, always with the hint of a smile. He had variously labeled psychoanalysts "superficial navel divers," behavioral psychologists "M&M addicts," and psychotherapists "psychoboobles." I found his joking asides astute and intellectually clever even if implicitly critical. But he was helpful and thoughtful when we discussed my struggles in the department. He suggested ways to moderate the criticisms my colleagues had about meditation and tai chi. And in relation to my practice of tai chi, something he knew nothing about, he observed that my labeling what I had been doing a problem only added to the problem. Then, he said with a mischievous smile, "Fundamentally there are no problems." Overall, despite his acidic and professorial style, I liked him.

As I continue walking to my office, my agitation doesn't ease. Students jam the sidewalks. Cars and those brand-new minivans are everywhere. Traffic backs up in parking lots, not surprising at the start of a semester. Parents drop off students, students need to register for classes, and this crowd blocks my way. Can't they go somewhere else? How ironic: a moment ago I interfered with the progress of students and now they interfere with mine.

With the semester starting the day after tomorrow, I need to prepare for my classes. I have much left to do. I can now see Kramer Hall, where my office is, and pick up the pace. As I stride along the sidewalk, I remember the talk Deana and I had this morning.

CHAPTER 2

Dawn, earlier that day

The scuff of my slippers is the loudest sound as I walk along the driveway. The air is cool and moist. A breeze whispers across my cheek, and I can sense a few dangling hairs brush my forehead. I come to a stop and glance back at our house in the early morning light.

Mist blankets the fields and weaves between the trees, covering grass and scrub with an impenetrable softness. A bird call fades to silence. Tranquility draws my face into a smile. A red-orange glow bulging at the horizon hints at the inevitable unknowns to come.

I bend over to pick up the newspaper and see dew glistening on the soccer ball lying next to the driveway. Playing with my kids is fun, just plain fun. I would never have predicted I'd love playing, and them, so much.

Yesterday, Mark, my five-year-old son, and I chased each other in the front yard, kicking and tossing that ball. Ann, only a toddler, giggled as she stumbled after us and the soccer ball, without Mark's speed or coordination yet never giving up. He darted toward me, I dodged, then slipped, catching the edge of his foot, only to trip, sending us tumbling onto the grass. We burst into laughter. Then Ann came hopping to us, giggling as loud as we were laughing, and jumped on my stomach. That sent us into even greater fits of laughter. Deana peeked out the door to see what was so hilarious. She stood there, a loving smile on her face. After we quieted, Mark picked up the ball and ran away with it. I scooped Ann up and we chased him, giving him a special soccer noogie when we retrieved it. The memory evokes a grin.

As I return to the house, I pause and take a deep breath, relishing the cool, moist sensation moving into my chest. Surprised, I find I need to yawn. I stop, hold the morning paper like a baton, throw back my head, scrunch my eyes shut, and stretch upward as far as possible. Still arched backward, I scan the blue sky, streaked with pink and white—vast and entrancing yet ever changing.

When I step into the kitchen, the aroma of brewed coffee rouses me from my contemplative state. I toss the paper on the table, fill my favorite mug, a Miró-like pattern on its outside, and settle into a chair. I linger, enjoying the peace, the warmth seeping into my fingers.

The kids and Deana are asleep. As I gaze through the window at the field and woods behind the house, serenity stretches from horizon to horizon. I sigh and take my first sip of coffee.

Time to start the day. I remove the rubber band and unroll the paper. President Reagan urges stricter safety controls for our nuclear power plants after last January's Chernobyl disaster and the head livestock judge for our county fair has mysteriously disappeared. I flip the paper over and the headline below the fold surprises me. JUDGE SIGNS INJUNCTION: KICKOFF PARTY BANNED. I'm aware of my mixed and strong reactions. I am appalled that students riot for fun: burn cars, attack bystanders, destroy signs and lampposts. It is unconscionable that people celebrate with destruction. Even as a psychologist, I am dismayed by this aspect of human nature. Although I believe I should be "objective" about the way human beings are and accept and understand their behaviors as "data," this is my community; these are *my* students. Worse is the understanding, no, the realization, that violence is not unique to our students but erupts worldwide. So, from this point of view, I'm glad the court will stop the riot this year.

However, I'm struck by my contradictory and equally strong counterreaction. The court does not have the legal justification to restrict access to the streets in which the riots started last year. The injunction violates the students' freedom of assembly. No one has committed a crime. I assume that my conservative city will delight in this solution. I often feel like an outsider because of my liberal perspective.

The intensity of my conflicting feelings and opposing views amuses me: I appreciate the protection and control gained by the court order while I bristle at its violation of basic rights.

Deana's touch startles me. A moment ago, I was so peaceful, yet as she slides her fingers along my left shoulder, I jump at the sensation.

"Sorry, honey." She slips her hand across my neck to my right ear, her fingers combing into my hair, massaging my scalp as if in apology, and pulls my head to her. Her breasts yield to my cheek, reminding me of last night's lovemaking. I circle my cheek on the silky gown. She runs her nails over my scalp. Fired by these subtle movements, I glide my hand across her lower back to her hip and inch down its curve.

"Jason, the kids are getting up soon." She squeezes my hand, kisses the top of my head, and pads over to the coffee maker. A long, slow breath clears most of my excitement, and I return to the story on the injunction.

"This coffee doesn't seem as strong as usual. Did you use that new coffee?"

"Yes. Of course, I did. I was the one who bought it." I spit the words out, shocked at my sudden change in mood. "I'm not incompetent to make coffee, you know." *Why am I reacting this way?*

I pick up the paper and see Deana stop pouring her coffee to stare at me. I turn away to glance at the front page and to show I'm not affected by what just happened, but I don't resume reading. After maybe five seconds, I hear the coffee as she fills her cup.

"Jason, we've been getting along so well. Last night was wonderful. What's up? What's happened?"

"Does something have to be wrong? Does something have to happen?"

"All I did was ask whether you used the new coffee. I said it looked weak. Well, it's not. It tastes great. What's going on?"

"Nothing's going on." I shove my chair back to clear the way to the other side of the kitchen and the coffee. As I stalk to the counter, I remember getting the newspaper and the tranquility that followed. The discrepancy between my irritation and that serenity shocks me.

"I don't know what happened, Dee. Earlier I felt great, more than great. Now, I'm miffed. What I heard was your telling me I wasn't doing it right, I didn't make the coffee right, I didn't use the right coffee. I don't know why it's such a big deal, but it sure bugged me."

"I didn't mean to criticize, Jason. It looked weak at first. I only asked you a question."

"I'm amazed, Dee. I wasn't in a bad mood. But your asking about the coffee got me. I felt criticized and inadequate, as if I wasn't doing what I was 'supposed to be doing.'"

I've been staring out the window. I glance over at her. Her brown eyes twinkle. A minute before, I'd been overreacting. That has faded. She smiles and those dimples appear, her black hair framing her cheeks. I cannot resist hugging her and nuzzling her neck. I'm relieved when she hugs me back and rests her head on my shoulder, nestling into the crook of my neck.

"What have you got lined up for today, Dee?"

"I drop the kids off at daycare on the way to work. The business is starting to—" She pulls away and becomes so excited that she has to move as she talks.

CHAPTER 3

Dawn turns to morning

Deana bounces on the balls of her feet as she talks.

"We got so busy around here last night," she says, "I can't believe I forgot to tell you that Drake Chemical called. Drake Chemical! They want us to install their whole computer system, from the ground up. And, Jason, they want to use the integrated software I developed. Now floppy discs and external hard drives can hold enough data to make this workable. And even though mainframes are getting bigger and faster, so are personal computers. This is our big break. It was such a huge risk starting this business and, at last, it's paying off. These have been rough years, haven't they? The money, the time, the stress to start my own business. Drake will make it possible, Jason. This is the break we've been waiting for."

Deana is standing, weight tilted to one side, staring at a corner of the wall. With her lips parted, she looks dazed but remembers with amazement what she did to develop Integrated Business Data Incorporated, IBD Inc. She blinks, takes a deep breath, glances at me, and sits on the chair next to me.

"Ten years, Jason. We lived in Middleton; you were in graduate school and I was working on my MBA with a computer systems specialization, a new field. That's when I got the idea."

"I remember, Dee. We tried Rosita's for the first time. You ordered the quesadilla, and I got the chicken tacos. I see it like it was yesterday. Then, your mouth dropped open at your idea. You filled at least five paper napkins with notes and diagrams. You hadn't even sipped your water when I had finished my whole meal. I'm awed at the work you put into it over these years."

She nods and smiles, looking satisfied. Then she stares into my eyes and does not look away or blink.

"I can't do it without you. You know how to do the charts and tables and access the databases. I can't do that. And I remember what you are facing this semester. Will you have time?"

"That's what's been playing over and over in my mind ever since you brought it up."

"Jason." She takes my left hand. Her fingers caress the back of it.

"I know, Dee. But by now, can't you access those databases?"

"That's easy. It's the statistical manipulation. How we establish baselines and comparables. How we translate the results into useful information for a specific business. That's the problem, and where you come in. Transforming the data into usable form is a critical part of the system. Once it's up and running for a particular industry, we can sample from four or five sources to get our database. But getting there, and this time with Drake . . ."

I reflect on my responsibilities and what I'm tackling at work over the next few months. I also consider how to develop the algorithms to select the right data and the statistical procedures I might need to use. I've done this before, dry runs with small companies, so I know what's involved. It'll take a chunk of time, but with my experience, it shouldn't be unreasonable to do.

"I won't let you down. Somehow I'll do it."

"Jason, you're wonderful. Are you sure?" She asks again with her eyes. I nod. She squeezes my hand, then picks it up and kisses the back. She sighs and lowers my hand to her lap, holding it in both of hers. Her grip tightens. I glance at her.

"Jason." She grimaces. She looks at our hands. "There's something else. You remember Jack Crouque?" She darts a glance at me. I squelch my response. I remember him, and Deana knows I do.

His name is pronounced "Crook," Jacques Crouque, though Jack is what most folks call him. When I knew him he was late forties, smooth, tanned, and handsome. Jack dressed well, but from my point of view he was oily. He is now post divorce number three. I remember one awkward dinner party after he left his second wife. As he strutted across his living room, he said, "I'm in love with love and ready for love again." He stopped to look at himself in a mirror.

Jack was Deana's boss four years ago, before we moved to Terrace Hills. I suspected his motives since he kept Deana at work after hours two or three days per week. Sometimes they went to dinner, late in the evening. I discovered, with initial relief, that he was more interested in her as a professional than another romantic conquest. I could not stand him. He has been the only person to test our marriage.

As vice president of advertising, Jack needed Deana's programming skills to generate sophisticated and compelling computer graphics to integrate into presentations of their products. Retailers would then have an easy, accurate, and persuasive way to get information. Though the graphics seemed to present product information, they functioned as advertising. In the year and a half Deana worked for him, sales increased by more than fifty percent. After she left but when the company was still using her system, sales doubled.

When he found out we would be leaving Middleton, for me to take my faculty position here at Eastern State, Jack pressured Deana to stay. He offered to create a new position of assistant vice president of advertising just for her. He promised her a huge salary increase. He offered to fly her home on weekends. He said he would give her whatever she wanted if she stayed. I endured this for five months. I was furious and worried about what it meant for us. Would she consider his offers? I couldn't help but wonder if our marriage was at risk.

"It's too good to pass up," she said.

"Four years out of school and I'd be making six figures," she said.

"There aren't many women getting jobs at this level," she said.

"When will I ever get another opportunity like this," she said.

Even though Dee turned him down, Jack wouldn't give up. He wrote her the first week we were here, while we were still moving into our first house. Boxes littered the floor; a mound of crumpled newspapers blocked passage through the living room, and folding chairs provided the only available seating. The bare windows and walls were cold and unwelcoming. She read the letter, slumped onto one of the four chairs, and cried. He had upped the ante. He said the company was ready to create a new vice presidency just for her, with more than the regular perks and the extra inducement of a huge salary. It took three agonizing weeks, but, at last, she wrote him a polite refusal and asked him not to contact her again. Her decision was firm.

"Jack is my connection at Drake. He started two years ago. I didn't know until yesterday. Now I reflect on it, I guess that might be why I forgot to tell you."

Deana leaned onto her elbows and looked at me.

"It won't be like before, Jason. I don't work for him. I'm coming in as a consultant, upgrading their computer system and integrating my software into their product information system and accessing all kinds of different consumer databases. I don't want to work for Drake or for Jack. I'm my own boss now."

When she began speaking, I had pushed back against the chair, resisting the impulse to cross my arms. Now I noticed I had leaned forward but I still wanted to cross my arms.

"That makes a big difference, Dee." I shift around, trying to relax. "I so much want IBD to make it. But Jacques Croque?"

"He's not a bad person. He is good at what he does even though you don't like him."

"It's difficult to admit that, but, all right. I understand. And I'll do whatever you need. I want IBD to succeed. Big time."

She smiles and her shoulders drop. In contrast, I can still sense the tightness in my chest and face.

"So, where were we before you mentioned Drake and . . . ?" I wave my hand in the air and then dismiss it with a downward motion.

"Yeah, where were we? Oh, I remember. I was talking about work, which brought Drake Chemical to mind." Looking pensive, she takes a sip of coffee. "On the way to work, I'll drop the kids off at daycare. Oh, I said that." She tilts her head to the left as is her habit and pauses while she stares past me. The pattern is familiar and suggests she wonders how I'll react to what she has yet to say.

"Umm." She sniffs loud enough I can hear it. "Umm. As per daycare, I'm rather resenting being the one who has dropped off and picked up the kids these last few days."

Ah. So that's it.

"Well, if you're worried that pissed me off, it didn't. You are right, you have been doing that. I realized it, but, Dee, you didn't ask me to do it. You simply did it; I assumed you wanted to. Now I know, and I'm willing to do my share." I scan her face as she reflects.

"Jason, that's nice. I appreciate that, but I wish you'd offer. Don't wait for this to come from me." She's right again, and I feel a little guilt, though confused.

"I can do either one or both today. I have to prepare for the new semester, take care of odds and ends." As I imagine getting ready to go to work and going into the garage to start the moped, I'm aware of an inertia that roots me to my seat.

"And just this moment I realized that I don't want to face those odds and ends. I'm feeling guilty for not wanting to do them, even though I'm preparing for the semester earlier than usual. For once I have the time to get everything done, but I don't want to do it. And I should have completed some things weeks ago."

"Hmmm." Her tone expresses interest and understanding. She grasps her mug with both hands, purses her lips, and peers up at me. "Perhaps that's why you snapped at me, Jason."

"What do you mean?" I wait for her response, and her habitual pause before speaking irritates me.

"Look," she says as if it's obvious. "Aren't your feelings about going back to work the same ones you had to my comment about the coffee? You should be criticized for what you have not done. You aren't doing things right, and . . ."

My emotions shift. Love wells up as I feel accepted and understood. I don't want to go back to work. I should have finished most of those tasks weeks ago. In fact, the only thing I've been eager to get to, following up on my research results, I also have not done. That stimulates a different guilt. And, I realize, from yet another point of view, I've loved our time together this summer. I do not want it to end. Tears moisten my eyes, appreciating Deana, her sensitivity, and her insight.

"Thanks, sweetie."

During the brief silence, we both sip our coffee. I'm enjoying just sitting together. I realize that I should follow up on her comment about day care.

"How about if I deliver the kids to day care? Would that take pressure off you?"

"No. My meetings are late morning, so it's fine if I do it today. That will give you the chance to get done what you don't want to do. I had an idea that might help. I'll see if we can visit the Farleys at Bluewater Lake this evening. That way you'll be free to work into the evening and, get . . . it . . . all . . . done." After a pause, she adds, "And you could figure out this day care thing. Thanks for offering. I'm all right about it. But offer, okay?"

I nod.

"I'm glad, Dee. Speaking about the Farleys brings up something else I've been considering for us: minivans. When they first came out a few years ago, I read the manufacturers hadn't gotten all the glitches out. And I doubted they were as good as folks claimed. But the Farleys bought one and they love it. We might want to replace our station wagon with a minivan. That would give us more room. I wanted to mention it so we can discuss it later. And could you talk to them about theirs?"

Deana nods and says "yeah" in a distracted tone that makes the word longer than usual. She purses her lips and I hear a suppressed "Hmm." Something new is coming, something about which she is unsure. She examines the interior of her cup, turning it around and around.

"And . . ." She looks up. "Speaking of things to consider and explore later, and something you don't want to do, have you considered a third child? Ann's a month past two; Mark's five and about to start first grade. Can you believe it? First grade! We have to do this soon if we're going to do it, or I'll be pushing forty before we have another one. Well, that's a gross exaggeration, but it seems like it. The earliest we could have a third child would be when I'm thirty-four. This would be the time before my business gets busy and takes off and I—"

"Yes."

She doesn't seem to hear me and keeps talking. "With all those problems we had before, I was worried. I didn't know what to think when you weren't sure and couldn't answer me right away. I've been wondering what to . . ." She stops. She peers at me.

"What do you mean, 'Yes'?" She furrows her brow, the hint of a grin suppressed around her mouth as if it were unsure whether to smile.

"Yes. Yes, I have thought about it, and yes, let's have a third child. I think it—"

"Jason. I'm, I'm . . ." She beams as she intertwines her fingers with mine. Her face has opened with joy. She raises her eyebrows, twinkling and dimpling, and whispers, "Let's get started."

"I was ready fifteen minutes ago. Where were you?"

"Getting my delicious coffee."

"I'm excited about this," I wink, "using all the various meanings of the term."

CHAPTER 4

Morning continues

Sounds drift from the stairs at the front of the house. Mark thump-thumps down the steps. Arrhythmic bumps suggest that Ann is trying to keep up by bouncing down, step after step, on her bottom. When the carpet-muffled thuds change to sharp thumps from the entryway linoleum, they shout.

"Rabbits. Mommy, Daddy, rabbits." Mark runs into the kitchen and jumps up on the bench at the table to peer out the window. Ann comes waddling up behind and hops up on her tippy toes at the edge of the bench, straining to look.

"Wabbits! Wabbits! Wabbits!" She points upward, where she can't see, and, without moving from her chair, Deana lifts her to the bench. They crowd together, peering outside. I step to the window, lean over to look, and see the rabbits scamper off.

"Oh, go away, Daddy."

"Sorry. I didn't realize I'd scare them. If we're silent, they might come back."

"Where wabbits?"

"In the longer grass. Beyond the fence."

"Get 'em, Daddy."

With the rabbits gone, neither child is interested. They clamber from the bench and clomp to the family room. I sit where the kids had been and smile at what I am thinking of as "The wabbit scene." Out of the corner of my eye, I can see Deana gazing at me.

"Jason, I love your beard. I didn't know I'd like it." She reaches up to stroke my chin. "There's a hint of red that along with the brown brings out the subtle olive color of your skin. And your green eyes..." Her voice fades away and after a pause, in a breathless whisper, she says, "It's very sexy."

"I, I didn't realize...I'd like it. Myself." I'm surprised and flustered by her words. I don't consider myself sexy. "Here's what I have planned for the day. I intend to reach my first goal and run eight miles. I want to exercise more this semester. That way"—I leer at Deana—"I'll be ready for the special, physical work I have to do here at home. I'll take two graduate students to lunch, next go to the library, and then to the office to finish up paperwork. Lots to do. And the big event is Rick Volks returns from sabbatical. He's supposed to be in town today."

Deana slides her mug back and forth. A frown shadows her lips. I have an idea why.

"We don't have to get together, Dee." Her nonverbal reactions do not change. "Helen will not be there. You know that."

"How do you think it might go?" she asks, changing the topic. I can't tell if she's still bothered.

"I have no idea. But, based on our work before he left for sabbatical and the feedback I've gotten since, the chances look good. We should receive the answer any day now."

"Jason, I get so nervous. Tenure rests on this. And after last time, well, it would be nice to have stability."

"Yes, it would. And when Rick and I meet, we will firm up our plans for if the grant comes through."

"What's wrong? You're...you're...I don't know how to put it?"

"Well"—I struggle with my confusion—"I'm excited about seeing him, but I have this weird feeling about it. Yesterday I found a postcard in my office mail. The postmark had foreign writing on it, letters I've never seen, so I guess it was from a country in the Middle or Far East."

I step over to the back door to the garage, take my coat off its hook, and search through the pockets. "But that wasn't what I reacted to. Yes, here it is. No date. Look at this." I hand the postcard to Deana.

Jason,
Enigma and risk create opportunity. See you soon. I hope.
Rick

"Isn't that unsettling? His use of the word 'risk' and that phrase, 'I hope.' There's something ominous."

"Aren't you overreacting, Jason? He has always had an abstruse way of saying things. His cryptic manner imparted the mystique he so enjoyed at school. He's teasing you, is my guess."

"Perhaps you're right," I say, unconvinced but unable to articulate why.

"Mommee, Daddee, come here!" Ann squeals with delight from the family room next to the kitchen. From the sounds, she has been building with Legos. Deana and I share a knowing smile and start toward her, mugs in hand. I hear the click of the TV and Mr. Rogers is singing "It's a beautiful day in the neighborhood." I turn back to refill my mug—and find I'm flooded with thoughts of Rick.

Much hinges on my work with him: my publishing and my tenure. When I first met Rick he was the chairperson of the religion department and I was a new faculty member. I needed a cosponsor to support a tai chi workshop and scurried around campus to acquire what little backing there was. He was friendly and respectful when I expected the criticism and derision I had gotten elsewhere. His department would cosponsor the workshop. With a smile, he said, "Tai Chi is Taoism in action, a worthy topic for the university."

Over the next months, we got better acquainted. We met for lunch and discussed ideas: Tibetan Buddhism, Zen, yoga, tai chi, Taoism, Judeo-Christian beliefs. The lunches were invigorating and challenging. When he suggested we team teach Self-discovery: Buddhist Meditation, Yoga, and Tai Chi, I felt prized and validated.

Though at first I learned more from him, over time he told me he too profited from our lunches. He valued most my commitment to practice. "You are a catalyst for me," he said. That touched me and clarified a few anomalies, such as his smoking, a habit I cannot stand! It did not fit. How could someone involved in yoga smoke? Over the next six months, he shared other aspects of his life, even details he had told no one else. I became an important confidant, privy to his most personal concerns. Rick suggested putting our talks to paper and sending them out for publication. By the end of the year, we had written our first article, submitted a presentation for a conference, were working on several more papers, and had developed ideas for a research project that could get external funding. In spite of all our work together and our relationship, I've heard nothing from him until the enigmatic postcard.

I mailed that first paper out with significant relief. At last, I was submitting scholarly work for publication. I never told him how important that was nor how appreciative I was for his collaboration. I guess I was, and still am, too ashamed about my block to discuss it. My inability to write professional articles had interfered with an earlier university position. When I was on the faculty at Middleton College, my chairperson told me outright that if I did not publish, I would not get tenure. It did not matter how good a teacher, supervisor, or therapist I was; without scholarly activity, which meant publications, I was out. Until Rick,

I was unable submit my writing for scholarly scrutiny. I'm fine teaching a smallish class, up to fifty people. Add more students in the room and I freeze. And presenting a paper in front of professional colleagues is worse yet. I have analyzed it over and over, and it comes from the same unresolved difficulty: fear of and anticipation of public humiliation.

Our writing to date has yielded two publications, both with me as the second author. But I must be the first author on at least one to get tenure, and I will be if the grant gets funding, since it is my idea.

I've missed Rick over these many months, despite his interpersonal sharp edges. He gave me support and encouragement over the three years before his sabbatical. And with him gone, I dwelt on my inadequacies. I became more attuned to my isolation from my colleagues in the department. Few of my peers consider meditation or consciousness a worthwhile topic for psychology, let alone research. When I bring up the subject, I am met with snide remarks about chanting "Om" in the classroom or levitating in the laboratory. During his years in East Asia, Rick got training by at least three masters in using meditation for healing and pain management. A large amount of money gets spent on health care with an ever-increasing need for effective treatments. Our grant, to use meditation to speed healing and to reduce pain medication, should be a natural for funding. Rick's background and expertise are crucial for our success.

"Jason? Where are you? Are you lost in there?" I hear Deana walk toward the kitchen. I forgot what I was doing.

"Just getting more coffee. Be right there."

"That long?"

Deana greets me in the doorway, a questioning expression on her face.

"Thinking about the semester," I explain, not up to sharing my concerns. She nods, satisfied.

"Look at Ann's farm. Inside the fence, she keeps rabbits." I squat on the floor. Mark rolls over and bangs into my feet. I'm forced to reach down to balance myself on his belly and he giggles, wriggling for more. "Wabbits, Daddy." Ann picks up a huge clump of yellow blocks, which she hops around the large green Lego board. "Can I make a house in your field?" I ask, sitting down on the floor. Ann points to one corner of the board. "Let's see. What color should the house be? Red? Blue? Yellow?" She selects blue pieces and puts them into place. I choose other ones and put them alongside hers.

"I'll take my shower and get ready for my big day. Would you give the kids breakfast?" Dee reaches down, pats my head, and after getting more coffee, goes upstairs. Her words, "my big day," start me thinking about my day and about the prospect of seeing Rick.

For almost two and a half years, we met at five in the morning, three times a week to meditate and do tai chi. I've missed this since he went on sabbatical, but I liked having more time to myself on those mornings. I continued getting up early and practicing on my own.

I recall the ritual we developed. Hair disheveled, having only brushed my teeth, I would meet him at the door. He would walk in from the dark carrying his meditation pillow under his arm. I would close the door and follow him into the living room. Our verbal interaction was always cursory; our objective at this hour was to confront ourselves and to settle our minds, not to talk. He was more limber than I and, sitting on the floor, would stretch to touch his nose to his knee, folding into a full lotus. I loosened standing, rotating my body about its axis. The preliminary stretching complete, we would both settle on our cushions, beginning by attending to the breath. Around five forty-five, he would stand, holding his cushion, a relaxed smile on his face, and we would go to the front door. Depending on the time of year, it might be light. We engaged in none of the usual rituals associated with entering and leaving. There was simply coming and, then, going. That was it.

"Dad, come see my rocket ship." Mark holds a long, planelike shape made of gray blocks. It blasts off from his imaginary field and flies around the family room, landing on the couch. I turn off the TV, which has been playing, ignored, in the background.

"How about getting breakfast? Do you want to have your rabbit come to breakfast with you?"

"And my spaceship."

"Are there hungry spacemen and spacewomen? And how about those rabbits? What do they want this morning?"

Three pairs of feet, one rabbit, and one rocket ship scamper into the kitchen.

CHAPTER 5

Midafternoon

As I walk to my office in Kramer Hall, having extricated myself from the jam of students, I find myself moved by how Deana responded this morning. The decision to have a third child feels right, although I know at first it activated that old anxiety. She was elated about Drake during our phone call earlier this afternoon. Her joy was infectious.

"Honey, you would not believe what an incredible lunch I had. Jack brought the CEO with him. They want to buy the entire system from top to bottom. I must hire extra programmers to handle the workload. Of course, I need to train them and Drake's people too. It will take at least a year, maybe two or three. And they'll pay us three million dollars. And bonuses depend on how it goes. We are on our way!"

After the call, I thought about her good news—the luncheon details, what the CEO said, the three million guarantee. I realized I had been holding back being delighted for Deana and knew at once what my difficulty was: Jack "Crook." I do not trust him and am uncomfortable with Deana having any contact with him. I question his motives.

I told her my good news: our grant received funding. The letter arrived in a special delivery envelope right before lunch. Our successes came on the same day. She was thrilled for me, and, despite her ambivalence toward Rick, she urged me to call him. Rick does not bother her; it is Helen who gets under her skin. This underlying tension won't interfere with starting our research, though. I'm relieved to be at this point. And so is Deana. She does not want to move and tenure will give us the stability we need. We have come a long way in our relationship. I wish Deana reacted differently to Helen, but I can't blame her. When I first learned she was living in Terrace Hills, I was shocked too.

Rick had invited us to a party that included people from his department and a handful of friends. I was eager to meet other faculty in the university and hoped Deana would make contacts as well. I looked forward to the evening.

We walked up the steps to their porch fingers intertwined, nervous yet excited about our first party with my new colleagues. The decking was gray-painted wood, and the rest of the exterior was white. Theirs was one of the older, well-maintained houses along the tree-lined street. Through the large oval-glassed front door shone the rainbow of a Tiffany lamp. A lace curtain on the inside muted the colors and provided privacy for the house. Rick welcomed us and shook hands with Dee, saying how glad he was to meet her. He said most guests had arrived and ushered us into the living room. There we saw people scattered about, some talking in pairs or threesomes, others sitting on chairs or on several overstuffed couches. The house was high ceilinged with dark wood paneling everywhere.

Deana stopped short as she turned toward the dining room. I paid little attention and placed my palm on her lower back to urge her to move forward, only then realizing she was rooted in place. I shifted to the side and saw a woman serving punch. I recognized Helen at once. I stared in disbelief, then let out a groan. How could she be here? At this party?

She was lovelier than I remembered. Her long blond hair hung over one shoulder, a golden tie showing at the back. Her dress was fetching without being overdone and showed off her figure and legs. The material of the understated, black-and-gold-patterned dress flowed along her body and emphasized the sparkle of her necklace and bracelet. She seemed to have learned to wear less flamboyant clothes over the intervening years and now exuded a breathtaking elegance. She flashed her dazzling smile at the person for whom she was ladling punch.

Deana turned her head, her expression deadpan, and whispered, "This will be about as fun as picking cockroaches out of spaghetti and then having to eat it." She twisted away from the dining room and leaned into me.

"Did you know?" she hissed, her brow furrowed.

"This is as much a surprise for me as it is for you. I had no idea."

Deana shook her head and moved toward the drink table. Helen looked up, noticed us, looked away, looked back, and froze, ladle poised over the table. A drop of punch fell and created a red splotch on the white tablecloth.

"Well, my goodness . . . my goodness, what a surprise to see you here," Helen said to Deana. I remembered the breathy quality of her speech. She continued to hold the ladle out to the side and now waved it over the floor. A drop flew onto the rug. "And Jason. I assume you two are here," she paused, "together."

I moved forward, putting my left arm firmly about Dee's waist, as I reached out to shake Helen's hand. "We are here—."

"Ah," Rick said as he burst around the corner. "I see you have already introduced yourselves to my lovely spouse, Helen Trent. As you might well surmise, she insisted on keeping her maiden name, women's lib, you know. And this man"—he gestured toward me with his glass—"is the Jason I've been talking about." Helen gulped.

"So you are in the psychology department?"

"I am. And are you the Helen Trent who is a psychologist in town?" She nodded, now looking self-satisfied at the astonished expression I could not hide.

Rick glanced back and forth between us. "Do...do you know each other?"

Deana answered his question. "We all went to the same undergraduate college. Jason and I grew up in the same town. Jason and Helen dated," she said, emphasizing the next few words, "for a short while during our junior year when Jason and I had been having difficulties. They were both psychology majors. Right?" She looked at Helen, who nodded. "After we graduated, Jason and I got married. We haven't seen Helen since. That's been at least ten years."

"Eleven," Helen corrected.

"This is a startling turn of events." Now Rick appeared flustered. The doorbell rang, and he seemed relieved. "A new arrival. Excuse me, please, I must play host."

"I'm so glad you came," Helen said effusively. "Just make yourselves at home." She threw her arms wide open in a welcoming gesture that looked like an invitation for a hug. The action appeared forced and awkward. I tried to stop myself from cringing. "A drink?" she asked.

"Yes," Deana and I said in unison and then laughed.

That was three years ago. And now that Rick and I have the grant and will work together more, I must tell Deana about my occasional contacts with Helen.

My reverie ends as I enter the stiflingly hot office building. I realize that I am free to work without interruption. In past years, a smooth transition from summer vacation to teaching had been impossible. The kids wanted to do this, asked about that, or made noise so I got distracted and struggled to continue working. Remembering our recent activities has changed my feelings. In contrast to the strong motivation I felt a few moments ago, I don't want to work. I imagine the kids and Deana lounging on the Farleys' weathered dock, drinking iced tea, and trailing their feet in the cool water while I'm stuck in this sweltering heat on campus.

I imagine Mark yelling, "Mom! Mom! MOM! Look. Look, Mom! I threw that rock even farther. Did you see? Watch me. I'll do it again." And Ann will be right next to him doing her best to throw rocks into the water. Today neither will yell, "Dad, watch me!" I won't be there. My summer is over, and I resent it.

I think the resentment is why my teaching often gets a slow start in the fall. I imagine returning home this evening and walking into a quiet house. I hope Deana will be awake but I expect otherwise. They will be home early, and everyone will fall into bed, tired from the sun and water. The beach exhausts us, and the kids often conk out on the way home.

As I'm ambling through the airless corridor, thoughts of work have vanished. Then I remember Rick's eerie voice saying, "I sent something to your office . . ." The mailroom seems far away, though it is just at the end of the hall. I pick up my pace. At last, I turn the corner into the room and hurry to check my mailbox. A large package, over six inches thick, looms on the shelf. The address, in wide block print, reads "Dr. Jason Butler, Department of Psychology." I'm surprised at its weight. Coarse twine keeps it contained. The heavy, brown-paper wrapping is creased. A three-inch flap of torn wrapper exposes brown tape inside the package. I rest the package on the mailroom counter, force the twine aside, and rip the outer wrapping across the front of the package. The inside reveals similar brown paper, spattered with black stains across words written in Rick's unmistakable handwriting.

For safe keeping only!

DANGER! DANGER! DANGER!

DON'T open or tell anyone.

If something happens, DESTROY!!

Repeat, DESTROY! Repeat, TELL NOT ONE PERSON!
Return this to me UNOPENED.

I cover the words with my arm as I turn to check the doorway. My heart pounds. Questions flood my mind. What does this mean? What is this about? What is so dangerous? Why is Rick involved? He is a professor in the religion department. Why did he send this to me? What is in the package?

My legs feel like cement. I examine his words again. No date. The letters are different sizes and don't align well. Did he write hastily? Yet the tape crisscrosses the envelope and follows the flap precisely. That was applied with care. The twine, though pushed to the side, remains tight; I can't rip it away. Scissors.

I hurry down the hall to my office, the package under one arm and library books under the other. What do I do? What do I do? Opening the door, the heat hits first, and then I notice a picture face down on the carpet. Damn! The Escher print fell off the wall again. Is it the one with the glass frame? No. The plastic one. At least I don't have to clean up the broken glass again, but the plastic cracked when it hit the carpet. Hot summer days soften the glue and the weight of the pictures pulls the hangers from the wall. I put the cracked picture along the wall where I'm sure to see it when I leave and open both windows to get ventilation. The grounds crew cut back the bushes; they no longer block the airflow.

I drop the books and the package on top of some papers on my desk and blanch when I peer again at the words "DANGER! DANGER! DANGER!" Then I check the work scattered on my desk: three letters to write, a student's paper to read, one course outline to prepare, and several handouts to complete. An overflowing in-basket has unknowns. I notice that my hand rests on the phone. I should call. He must be at his office in Tower Hall now. If that was where he was going; the building is only a few blocks from here. I dial his number. Two rings and the secretary answers.

"No, Dr. Volks is not in his office. He was there a moment ago. He always stays until five, so I know he hasn't left the building. Why don't you call back?"

I'm put off by her lack of helpfulness. The prior secretary would have gone to find him. She must be busy with preparations for the new semester. This rationalization doesn't help; I'm still irritated. I hang up and pick up today's student newspaper. The board of trustees has voted to raise tuition $100 so that now a full year will cost $3,100. But the lead story gets my attention.

CITY COUNCIL PASSES,
JUDGE APPROVES INJUNCTION

During last year's fall kickoff party, a traditional celebration taking place the night before classes start, over 4,000 students and visitors rioted in a 10-square-block area near campus. Police from Terrace Hills and neighboring communities donned full riot gear for five hours to quell the disturbance. The event gained national attention, resulted in hundreds of arrests, scores of injuries (three serious) and one death and cost hundreds of thousands of dollars in damage. News crews televised the event on the major networks, bringing dismaying notoriety to the campus community. Mike Biggins, director of Public Broadcasting for the university, reported that most of the networks will again be on campus to televise the event. University and city officials fear an even larger gathering might occur this year, and last night the City Council passed an ordinance sealing the 10-block area, excluding nonresidents. Some students claim this violates their civil rights and intend to sue. A student representative, who wished to stay anonymous, has contacted the American Civil Liberties Union.

Last year, Dee and I drove through the streets the day after the riot. Garbage cluttered the roads. Signs and streetlight poles lay across yards and sidewalks. Charred and indistinguishable items littered the streets. Broken glass glistened in yards and on pavements and smashed windows scarred many houses. I could see the throngs of students, not more than fifty yards from here, from my office window.

If it takes place, the kickoff party will be tomorrow night.

It is now 4:25. Try again. I know his style; he answers on the first ring, the only benefit of a small office. We often joked that his office was so tiny, if you were strong enough, you could suspend yourself in the air by putting your head on one wall and your feet on the other. One ring. Two rings. Damn. He's not there. I'll call again in five minutes.

In the meantime, I'll write to an ex-student. I sit down at my desk, place a tablet of yellow paper in front of me, and discover I can't write. My heart is beating quickly. My gaze moves between the wall and the package weighing down the top surface of the desk. What could be happening? I pace. I look at the chair but can't sit. I glance at the clock. 4:31. If he resorts to his former pattern, he'll leave in less than half an hour. I'll walk over to see him.

CHAPTER 6

4:32 p.m.

Walking is a relief. I'm doing something. I'm no longer forcing myself to stay in the office. I should arrive in ten minutes.

Students scatter across the campus. Yells come from a dozen huge guys playing touch football on a field near the dorm. They must be on the team. The grass is too short for summer. Its length won't support growth in this heat. It looks dry and brittle even from this distance.

Dad would say, "Don't cut the grass too short. Longer's healthy when it's hot."

"Dad," I would argue, "grass will grow no matter how long you cut it. In fact, if it's shorter, the growth will be faster because there's less for the roots to nourish." This would always erupt into a battle.

"Listen, you young know-it-all, too-smart-for-your-britches asshole! Just 'cuz you got book learning don't mean shit. I've been a farmer my whole life. My daddy and granddaddy were farmers. And there's wisdom common folks got that books can never give." He would curl his lip as he said "books" as if the word were rotten.

Thoughts about Rick shift me away from painful memories. If I talk with him, I'll be able to solve this mystery. I lengthen my stride, eager to get there now that I see an entrance to Tower Hall.

"Dr. Butler?"

I startle to a stop. That was the second or third try this voice had made to draw my attention. As I turn, I hear the slap of her running feet. She stops a yard and a half away, breath quickened. Hmm, that look on her face. Is she reacting to my irritated expression? Debbie. Debbie Star? Starn? Stern? I can't recall her name. She had an appointment yesterday morning and didn't show. She's pleasant. Not a top student but motivated.

"Oh, Dr. Butler. I'm so glad I saw you. I just couldn't make it yesterday. I'm really, really sorry. Things came up. My new roommate moved in, and there was so much to do. And, my boyfriend, Robert, you know, well, he needed some sewing done . . ."

She forgot. She got distracted. Here I am on my way to meet Rick, thirty paces from Tower Hall, and she wants to talk this instant. No call yesterday to cancel or reschedule. My jaw gets tighter as I try to listen to her prattle. She is attempting to apologize, but it's not working.

"I don't know what classes to take. I'm a junior, so I really, really need to be sure to take the right classes for my psych major." That information is in the bulletin and in our handbook for majors. I will tolerate no more. I break into the gush of her words.

"Check the bulletin. I must get somewhere *now*."

Her surprised, hurt expression elicits satisfaction along with guilt. I need to soften this.

"You have to take statistics and then experimental psychology, in that order. English is a prerequisite for experimental." I turn away and stop. I can't resist.

"And if you make and keep another appointment, we can talk more."

She steps back half a step and tugs on the strap of her backpack. I take off toward his building. I'm satisfied with venting my irritation in that way. Our little impromptu meeting must have taken only two minutes, but it felt longer. I yank the door open. I walk past vending machines in the lobby, run up four flights of stairs, and pull open the stairwell door, panting. Turn right. His office is fifteen paces up the hall.

I never liked the new university buildings. The ground-floor walls are ugly cinder block, painted yellow, and the floors are dark gray tile. On this floor, small offices for faculty line the carpeted hallway. His office door, just ahead on the right, is ajar. He must be here.

"Rick?" I say as I push the door further open and peek in the opening. "WHA!" My stomach drops. Rick is sprawled face down on the floor, two feet from the door. His feet are near the doorway, one arm along the far wall, his face hidden. The man kneeling next to him chills me. He is small, olive-skinned, with black hair and stubble. Blotches along one thigh stain his jeans. His light blue canvas shirt hangs loose. The inside edge of his left pocket flops over, ripped from the shirt. One hand is rummaging inside Rick's briefcase. Papers, envelopes, and folders litter Rick's back and the floor. A scrap of paper slides off his body.

The strange visitor looks up, snarls, and springs toward me, jabbing at my face. He is so close I can smell garlic. Then he pulls the door open, throwing me off balance. His eyes are shiny black, wide open and bulging; his lips, pulled straight back, expose a cracked tooth. His hand stabs at me again. Falling, I notice something blue is in his hand. He tries to touch me with it. I wrench sideways to evade his hand as I continue to fall. He's trying to kill me. He used what's in his hand to kill Rick. Fear surges through me.

If I hadn't been falling, his hand would have caught me in the face or neck. Because I fall, he misses, grazing my collar. As I arch backward away from him, the sharp edge of the door cuts along my hip and thigh. He jumps over my legs, a thick, brown package pinned between his arm and his side. His dirty, mauve tennis shoe and my right arm strike the floor at the same moment. There's a piercing pain behind my right ear as I hit on my side and everything goes black.

My hand rubs behind my ear. My head aches. I hear the sound of racing footsteps. Running. A door slams. That guy! Am I hurt? Slipped and fell. He tried to kill me! Am I making that up? I've never seen the man. Why would he want to kill me? And, Rick? Rick! Where is he? He's just lying there, inches in front of me. Not moving. What happened to him? A heart attack? No. That man hurt him. Stop trembling. Get up. Check him. He's not breathing. Check again. No breath. No, he can't be dead! There's no blood. Where's the blood? There's got to be blood somewhere. Any heartbeat? Feel his wrist. Nothing. Maybe at the neck. Was he strangled? No marks. No rope. There must be a heartbeat. Press again. Where's his pulse? It's not there. Nothing. I scramble to my feet.

"HELP! HELP! Rick is dead!"

Two faculty members I recognize, one unknown, and a secretary jam in the doorway. They bend around each other to gawk, yet are afraid to cross the threshold. "My God!" A hand covers a mouth. A face disappears. Sounds of shuffling and more footsteps. Muted voices.

I dial the phone on Rick's desk and talk to the police dispatcher about the man in blue jeans. I'm so frustrated! Rick is lying there dead and all these stupid questions. *How do you know he's dead? Is he breathing? How do you know he's not breathing? Is he making sounds? Or moving? Are his eyes open? Is there blood? How was he killed? Is there a weapon in sight? How did you find him? When did this happen? What's your name? Where are you? Who killed him?* I feel foolish describing the man I assume killed Rick. It happened with no warning; I'm not sure what I saw. I can't give an exact description. I can't even answer a simple question like "Did he have a weapon?" I'm convinced he did in that hand lunging toward me, but I have no details. There is no blood from a stab wound or gunshot or any visible bruises on Rick's face or neck. I don't know. I really don't know.

"This is a nightmare," I hear myself saying into the phone. "These things don't happen. I wish it were a dream and I could wake up."

CHAPTER 7

4:45 p.m.

At last. The wail of a siren. The scream gets louder. Soon the police and the ambulance will arrive. They'll know what to do. People mill about in the hall, quiet, staring through the doorway. Occasional muted questions drift to my ears.

"What happened?"

"How did he die?"

"Who is it?"

"Are you sure?"

"Are you sure he's dead?"

I'm unable to stay still. Out in the hall, I continue walking back and forth in front of the threshold, creating a barrier, glancing at Rick's body with each pass, searching for blood, fighting the tears, looking down the corridor hoping someone, anyone, will rush from the stairs. *I should do something. Anything. What? What can I do? How long before help gets here?* A uniformed officer bursts through the door and comes running down the hallway toward the crowd outside Rick's office. I recognize him, University Public Safety. He uses his handheld radio as he runs.

"Move back, folks."

"I'm the one who called. Rick Volks..." Can't find words for ten seconds. He leans forward, peering at me. Finally, I can point into Rick's office. "Something happened to him. I'm pretty sure he's dead." I discover that my mouth is dry, and I'm shaking my head side to side as I talk.

He pushes past, ignoring me, and stops just inside the doorway for several seconds looking around the office. He stoops and takes Rick's pulse at the neck. I'm stuck in the hallway, staring at the body and the officer. A woman's voice orders the crowd to move away and make way for the EMTs. Then muffled yells.

"Where is it?"

"Down here!"

The fast footsteps of many people. Two uniformed EMTs run down the hall while a female officer keeps people back from the door. More police come in at the far entrance as I follow the EMTs into Rick's office.

"What is your name, sir?" asks a mustached policeman with a pen poised over a pad.

"Dr. Butler. Dr. Jason Butler, Psychology."

"Did you touch or move anything?"

"No. I mean, yes." I'm panicky. It is as if I'm caught doing something wrong. "I had to find the phone book to call you. I couldn't locate it, so I had to slide the papers and stuff on his desk. But that's all. Oh, and yes, I took his pulse. But I don't remember moving him." He nods, looking at his tablet as he writes. His expression does not change. He stops writing and looks up at me.

"Okay. Please exit the scene of the crime, sir. We'll handle this. And, sir, don't leave the building!"

I'm stunned. Don't they want my help? I found him! I called! I watch the floor as I shuffle out into the hallway to join the crowd kept back by the police, everyone jostling, angling, trying to get a look at what's happening. More police rush down the hall. The words spoken into a handheld radio evoke a sob.

"White, thirty-four-year-old male, deceased. Contact the coroner."

I don't want to believe he is dead. But he is. He is. He actually is.

A tall, pudgy-cheeked man with receding brown hair and a crew cut ambles out of Rick's office. I'm surprised; I didn't notice him enter. His belly hangs over his belt.

"Any of you folks here at the time of the murder?" I nod agreement, as do six others. "Stick around for questioning. Someone found him?"

I half raise my hand, looking up at him. He notices and nods. Murder. He was murdered. I freeze. Can't think. Blank.

"All right, we'll start with you." He gestures toward me. "The rest of you stay here. Anyone in charge up here? We need a space to interview witnesses."

As he talks with the chairperson of the religion department about using their meeting room at the end of the hallway, my legs tremble and then my body shivers. My jaw chatters. I want it to stop. I can't. I try to turn away, to walk away, to escape what is happening, but people block me wherever I turn.

"All right, come this way." The man inclines his head in the direction I am to follow. I have to slow my pace to control my trembling legs. They might collapse under me if I'm not careful. I need to keep my hand on the wall for support. As I pass Rick's office, I see he is lying on a stretcher belted down on green sheets. An EMT pulls a sheet over his face.

"This way, sir." The voice is insistent, urging me to move. I stare at Rick again, tears filling my eyes.

"Sir!"

I wrench away and walk toward him. His right hand is stuffed into the outside pocket of his brown, corduroy coat. His knit tie, cut flat on the end, stops too high, emphasizing his belly. The brown coat clashes with his blue tie and gray shirt.

"I'm Detective Miller, ESU Public Safety." He turns away, then as an afterthought, turns back and reaches to shake my hand. His name sounds familiar. I know who he is but can't remember.

"You are?" he asks, still holding my hand. I'm trying to control my trembling. He must sense it through my hand. I want to disappear.

"Dr. Butler. Dr. Jason Butler, Psychology. I found him."

He ushers me in, pointing to a chair, placed in the center of an open space in the room. I sit feeling vulnerable. Where do I put my hands or legs? I shift about trying to get comfortable. I want to lean on a table. Miller stands next to the door and writes on a small tablet with a stubby pencil.

"That was the psychology department?" I nod. There is an edge to his voice. "What was the first thing you witnessed when you came onto the scene?" He paces.

"This man was leaning over Rick."

"What man?"

"The murderer."

"How do you know he was the murderer?"

"I don't. I mean, I didn't watch him kill Rick, but Rick was dead when he left."

Miller stops pacing to write. He looks out the window with his back to me. He walks to my side and pauses, silent. He walks behind me and doesn't move. That is even more unnerving. As I try to answer his questions, Miller's actions throw me off kilter, distracting me -- forcing me to track his movements.

"Let's back up. What did you see?"

"Well, the door was almost closed. I—"

"Closed how much?"

"Well, maybe open an inch or two."

"Go on."

"I opened the door. I stopped when I saw him over Rick's body."

"Describe him."

"He wore a blue shirt, somewhat faded, and blue jeans. And, oh, I noticed that he had mauve tennis shoes."

"How tall was he?"

"I'm not sure. Shorter than me. Oh, maybe five-four or five-five."

"Hair color?"

This went on and on. Exactly this. Precisely that. He pestered me to unearth even more details I was not aware I had missed telling. Which knee was on the floor? How do you know it was Rick's briefcase? Oh, he had something that could kill you in his hand? What did he have? What led you to conclude it was lethal?

"You said you fell?"

"Yes, I had my hand up on the door."

"You didn't mention that earlier. When did you put your hand there?"

"Well, I'm not sure. When I first got to his office, I guess I put my right hand up, on the door, and opened the door a little so I could look in. I don't remember the precise details. No, now I remember. I put my right hand there. That is when he pulled the door all the way open, and I lost my balance and fell."

"Were there any other witnesses?"

"No. Well, I don't think so."

"So you're the only witness?"

"Yeah. I guess. My back was to the door, so I noticed no one else."

He taps the point of his pencil on the paper as he stares at the pad.

"What is your relationship to the deceased?"

"We were friends. I've known him for many years. We team-taught a course together. He got back from his sabbatical. Yesterday. And we got a grant funded." Now I choke up again. "I hadn't told him."

A sudden knock on the door makes me jump. Miller strides to the door and leaves the room. I detect conversation but can't make out the words. When it stops, I expect Miller to come back in. I listen. Only silence. Time drags. Nothing happens. Why was he questioning me that way? His approach was without sympathy, almost intimidating. As I sit and wait, wondering what is happening, my distress becomes more acute. I'm alone and exposed. Two realizations intrude with such impact that my heart pounds.

First I remember Rick's words on the package. I visualize them in my mind: reinforced block letters, vivid and clear, some larger and more emphasized than others. He must have outlined the letters several times as if to be certain each letter was unmistakable and to emphasize his message.

DANGER! DANGER! DANGER!

DON'T open or tell anyone!

Repeat, TELL NOT ONE PERSON!

Rick is dead, and I received a package from him warning me of danger. The danger must be real.

I recall him walking toward me, just hours ago, looking haggard and exhausted. The way he was searching all around him now makes sense. He was afraid of someone. "I sent something to your office . . . If something happens." Something did happen. He was murdered. And his last words: "Tell not one person." I tremble, feeling more alone and defenseless than ever. The package, the package I have in my office, must link to his death. His only words, written and spoken, are to tell no one. But I can tell the police. Certainly I can tell Miller.

Miller! The second realization. I now remember how I know his name. Two and a half years ago, a woman and her three children were referred to me for therapy. She had separated from her husband, was considering divorce, and was struggling with that decision. She also wanted help to deal with her children. Her husband was a detective. That was the problem: he was always in detective mode. He would track down inconsistencies in what his wife and kids said or did. He was severe and exacting with consequences. Nothing slipped by him. His family felt under siege. But to his mind, the facts exonerated him. If his suspicions proved wrong, then he said he did not have the correct facts before and, now that he knew them, the situation was settled. It might have been resolved for him, but it was not for the rest of his family. That he was suspicious, that he interrogated family members, that he questioned intentions undermined his relationships with everyone.

His wife had tried to talk with him. From his point of view, his questioning was not personal. He focused on the facts; that was all. When he stopped, he was finished. There was no carryover for him, and he acted as if his interrogations never happened. He couldn't understand why anyone would be upset.

When his children entered elementary school, his questioning increased and became intolerable. I learned that Miller was a man who lived his job, a man who was exacting, careful, and always did what was right, regardless of the consequences. Once he decided, he stood by it. When pushed, he could get angry, though he hit no one nor broke anything. He would yell and slam his fist down and make threats.

After five therapy sessions, she told him of her decision to divorce. He was furious. During his diatribe, she told me between sobs, he yelled at her that she did not understand, that her coming to therapy created the problem, that he hated psychologists, and me. He was a driven man, committed to his job, and did not know how to be like a regular guy with other people. His only role was being a detective. I could hear his caring and his concern for his family, but it was not enough for her.

Footsteps from the hall warn me that someone is coming. Despite my expectation that someone would enter, I startle when he barges into the room at full stride holding a white, letter-size envelope in front of him. He takes three fast steps and stops two feet away, forcing me to look up at what he is holding. I read my name and office address written on the outside of the envelope in Rick's unmistakable scrawl. With white-gloved hands he slips a piece of paper out of the envelope and examines it. Then, he scrutinizes me. He shifts his eyes back to the paper and reads, emphasizing each word separately.

"Contact with you is dangerous. Not one word more, ever. Stop trying to contact me."

Moving nothing but his eyes, he raises them to examine me and my reaction. I can feel the sweat, and I can hear my heart pounding. I'm forced to swallow several times. He continues to stare at me. . . . I get uncomfortable and want to squirm to escape his eyes. I try to sit as if the words have no meaning.

To my dismay, the words penetrate, reactivating the alarm and the confusion I experienced this afternoon after opening the package. "DANGER!" he wrote. "TELL NOT ONE PERSON!" he wrote. "If something happens . . . ," he said. Now he is dead, murdered.

Miller disrupts my swirling struggle by reading the words again. I hear the words afresh. This time I hear Rick; this time I hear Rick warning me; this time I hear Rick saying, literally, tell nobody anything. Across the chasm between death and life, Rick speaks directly to me through this note. I realize I am deciding, a momentous decision, a decision driven by fear. I will not tell Miller. Not yet, anyway.

After the second reading, he slides the paper back into the envelope and places it in a plastic bag, which he seals. He does not take his eyes off me. He tosses the bag on a table where it slides, almost falling to the floor. As he takes off the gloves, he walks behind me.

"Why were you here?"

He fires the question; I flinch. I'm put off but not surprised at his tone. But I'm startled by my sadness. The police should help and side with the innocent. Now I realize I'm a suspect. I pause. I'm alarmed. What does his question mean? He examines me from my right side, not looking down at his pad. I've delayed answering this question longer than any other.

"I came over to talk. I was worried."

The decision I made not a few minutes ago seems less solid. I'm swamped by conflict about what to do and how to protect myself. I realize that from Miller's point of view, I could be creating a story to defend myself. He knows none of the facts. He might suspect I murdered Rick. Will the package make it worse? Will it make it better? Rick's warnings flash to mind again. "Danger! Tell not one person!"

"I saw him leaving the Student Union today. He looked terrible, so I got worried about him. I tried to call him several times during the afternoon but never reached him. I walked over to connect with him in person."

"What time did you call him?"

"Gosh. Let me figure that out. It was before I got here. Between four fifteen and four thirty."

"How often did you call?"

"Three times, I think. I reached the secretary once."

"Hmm-mm. Did you ask her to leave a message?"

"No."

"Why not?"

"Well, I didn't need to."

"I thought you wanted to talk with him. Didn't you say you were worried?"

"Yes. I wanted to talk to him on the phone. Not leave a message."

"Why didn't you keep calling?"

"I wanted to look at him, face to face . . . and, I was concerned that he would leave by five."

"How long a walk is it?"

"Oh, ten to fifteen minutes."

"Do you usually walk over to talk to someone when you can't reach him by phone? Don't you usually leave a message?"

"Well, no. I mean, yes, I leave a message usually. But, Rick was a special friend. I had looked forward to seeing him. I wanted to tell him we got our grant. And, I was worried. I kept thinking about him."

"Dr. Butler"—Miller shakes his head in disbelief—"why did he write this note to you? You claim you wanted to see him, and he is telling you not to have any contact with him."

"Detective Miller, I do not understand that note. I have had no contact with him since he returned from his sabbatical. In fact, I've not talked to him since last January when he left. Well, as I mentioned, I saw him earlier today at the Student Union. We said hi as we passed each other, but nothing more. The only time I tried to contact him was this afternoon, and I never reached him. I can't make sense of that note. Since we haven't even talked, it makes little sense to stop it. Are you certain the note was for me? I saw my name on the outside, but he might have intended to readdress it to someone else."

He nods. There is no change in expression. How do I decode that? Does that mollify him? Does he still suspect me? Did he suspect me from the start or am I being alarmist?

"Then why was your name and address on that envelope? Why was it in a stack of outgoing mail?"

Miller continues to pierce me with his unblinking eyes. At last, he looks away and takes something from his wallet and writes on it.

"Here's my card and phone number. Contact me if you think of any more information. I must get a formal statement from you tomorrow at 2:30. You must come down to the department to do that. Call that number if you can't keep the appointment. But stick around in case I have any more questions."

He walks out without another word. What am I supposed to do? Do I stay in the room or leave? Once again, Miller is yanking me about and keeping me confused and off balance.

CHAPTER 8

5:32 p.m.

At last, I'm out and in the hallway. I seal the door to what I call "the interrogation room" and peer at his card. I tap it on my open palm, debating, and then I return to ask Miller a question. I cringe as I step back into the room. He does not glance up. I continue to stand and say nothing. Did he notice me enter? He must have. The door makes rubbing sounds as it passes over the carpet. But he doesn't acknowledge my presence and continues jotting notes. I'm uncomfortable. I'll leave. He stares at me.

"What about his wife?" I blurt.

"The officer in charge will go to the house and tell her face to face." His eyes lose focus as he drifts off thinking. He snaps back, grimaces, takes a deep breath and looks at me. His expression says, "What next?"

"I'll, I'll get out of your way."

I'm heavy-hearted as I walk toward the main hallway. I can't stop imagining Helen's pain. My relationship with her is conflict-filled, but I can still empathize with her intense reactions. I visualize the officer, standing at their entrance, looking at his feet. As I envision her opening the door, sobs come. I cry at my grief and my loss. I don't care if people find out. Where's the tissue? I crammed a bunch in my pocket. The crying doesn't stop for a long time. I want to talk to Deana, but how to do it surrounded by all these people? I yearn to be at home with my family. I can't. I have to wait for more questioning. And even if I could leave, I realize, they would not be home. They're at the lake.

A short while later, Miller returns to the hallway and asks the crowd if anyone else saw what happened. No one. I'm the only witness. I'm the last person known to be with Rick.

"Did someone observe any individual enter Dr. Volks's office?"

The two people who were in the hallway as I walked toward Rick's office raise their hands. My stomach sinks. Witnesses saw me go into his office and the next thing anyone knows, Rick is dead. I didn't kill him, but what does Miller think?

"You." Miller points to one person. "Come with me." They start the walk to the conference room he has used to interview witnesses. "I'll meet you in there," Miller says and points to the door. He turns around and walks back to where I'm standing. "Dr. Butler, I need you to stay here to answer questions." In response to my overt irritation, he adds, "You don't want me coming by your house at all hours, do you? Much better to get this done now." It might be better, but I still loathe the process. And, sure enough, after the second witness walks out from questioning, he comes for me.

"Dr. Butler, we need to learn more about your relationship with Dr. Volks. Any conflicts with him?"

"Detective Miller, as I've told you, he was traveling, out of the country, for over six months! How could I be in conflict?"

"Before he left, were there any fights, conflicts, differences of opinion?"

"Well, the most telling difference was with the focus of our research if we got the grant. As a professor of religion, he was interested in the spiritual aspect of the meditation we will use, while I was interested in its utility to speed healing and to manage pain. The latter was what we wrote in the grant, but he kept pushing to test the spiritual. We debated this for weeks and had a way to do it consistent with the grant. I felt we were fudging. It was ironic that the person interested in the spiritual would bend the rules. That was it."

"Will you profit from his murder?"

"Well," I pause, gathering my composure, "we are both PIs, primary investigators, on the grant. His death will make me the sole PI. I'm not sure that is an advantage."

"Does that mean the results will be yours alone?"

"Yes."

Miller furrows his brow and stares at his small tablet for a long time.

"And what about his family?"

"Excuse me? What are you driving at?"

"What about his wife? What is your relationship with his wife?"

"We, that's my wife and me, avoid getting together with them. I, we don't have a relationship with her."

"I'm puzzled, Dr. Butler. If you have this relationship with Volks, why wouldn't you get together?"

"Is this necessary, Detective Miller? Why dig up problematic history." His expression makes it clear I cannot avoid this.

"Her name is Helen Trent. When she married Rick, she didn't change her name. I did not understand who she was, since, when I knew her before, she was Helen Jones. My wife, Helen, and I attended the same college. There was a time when Deana— that's my wife—and I had been having difficulties. It was our junior year. Helen and I dated. Deana and I got back together and married after we graduated. Helen enrolled in graduate school on the East Coast and got her doctorate in clinical psychology, marrying and divorcing along the way, and then married Rick. Trent was her married name—from her first marriage, I mean. We avoid socializing with them because of this history."

"Did you have a sexual relationship with her?"

I shake my head in disbelief at being dragged into this; yet I now realize, after my time with Miller, that I will need to answer this question. "Yes, Detective Miller. Yes, I had a sexual relationship with her. That was ten years ago when we were in college. And the number of times? Three. Do you want positions and activities as well?"

"No, Dr. Butler. That is enough. And that is all I need right now." He gestures for me to leave and walks to the door, which he opens. As I near the threshold, he shuts the door. I stop, facing the closed door. Miller's hand is on the doorknob; his arm blocks my exit. We are standing inches from each other.

"There is one last question." During the pause, I groan. "Do you have a sexual relationship with Helen Trent now?"

"This borders on the absurd," I mumble as I step away from him. "No. No, I do not have a sexual relationship with Helen. And, no, I have not had one since I joined the faculty. Detective Miller, I love my wife, and I am committed to her. I am monogamous. You don't understand my marriage and the effort that's gone into developing what we have now. Can I leave? Or do you have other indignities?"

Stone-faced and silent, he pushes the door open. I'm surprised to find the hallway dark. It is after "quitting time" and the lights have been turned to dim to conserve power. I walk away dirtied and incensed. Unsure where to go, I stop, leaning against the cinder block, and peer down the hallway where two police officers are putting yellow tape across Rick's door. Miller walks by me and down the corridor. He says something muffled to the officers and all three walk to the far end of the hall where they push through the door that opens into the stairwell. It slams shut. The clock halfway along the hallway shows it's 7:20. It can't be that late. I check my watch. Why am I standing here? Why aren't I escaping now the police have left?

The answer pops into mind: I need to be alone to cope with Rick's murder. The memories freeze like still photographs: Rick's body covered by green sheets, the stretcher in the hallway, Rick sprawled facedown across the office floor, the sound of the zipper shutting the black body bag. They haunt me. Then terror plunges through me again as I recall the murderer striking out toward my face and I fall. I fall. And I fall again.

I slide my hand along the rough cinder block as I drift toward the stairwell door. Three hours ago, I pushed open this door and walked to Rick's office. I pause, peer back at the yellow tape, drop my hand from the door, and hang my head. This has been horrible. I'm not sure how long I stand this way. At last, I decide to escape Tower Hall and push open the door to the landing, ready to leave the murder scene. My shoulders are lighter as I make my escape. My legs carry me down the steps, and my mind clears. Several deep breaths help. Soon I'll be back at my office, and I can go home. I plan what I'll take. The letter from my student. Those handouts. The outlines. The cracked picture frame. Shit. The package! It is sitting out in the open on my desk. Anyone entering my office will see it.

Then I'm stunned by a new realization. I am struck with such force I sit on a stair. I discover that I'm holding my head in my hands and words are coming out of my mouth: "Oh my God. Oh my God." How would Miller twist this?

The scene is clear in my mind. I see Helen sitting across from me in the dark bar, and I can't breathe from the cigarette smoke. The small table forces us to sit close, knees almost touching. Her hand brushes mine when she picks up her drink. She appears unaware, and I wonder what the action means since nothing else suggests other motives. Just in case, I shift my chair away and pull my hands to the table's edge.

"My life is fine," she states as a fact, though her tone implies complaint. "Helen Trent. You didn't figure out that was me?"

"Nope," I say as I slowly move my head side to side.

"Of course not. You couldn't know after you, after we, grad-uated, I met that jackass BuhBuh Trent. That's," she imitates a deep-voiced guy, "Bob to you if you don't follow football. I was hot to make my mark and to get my man and, by God, I did. What a disaster."

She takes another sip of Merlot and stares at the tabletop. She slides her glass back and forth, back and forth.

"We divorced after six months, and I kept his last name. My maiden name was so damn ordinary, I hated it." It took effort, but I remembered, what it was: Jones. "Then, after a break, I went to graduate school in clinical. The money from the divorce helped. Late in my program, I got into therapy, toned down, and met Rick, who was a college professor. He was a kind, sensitive guy but sort of intellectualized. You've seen that. So we married and moved here. I'm glad you're here too. I can refer clients to you, and it'll be nice to get together."

"Helen," I say, "after what happened, I couldn't do that. I'm guilt ridden having a drink with you at this conference. Deana would have a lot of trouble with it."

"Nothing will happen, Jason. Not now." Helen looks at her wine, rotating the glass on its base so it swirls around.

"That doesn't matter." I'm aware I sound firm, almost annoyed. "I love Deana and love our life together, and I'll do nothing to undermine it." I take a swig of Guinness. I notice the country music in the background and the hubbub from the crowd.

"You're married; I'm married. Can't we forget the past, Jason? Can't we be friends? If not friends, then acquaintances?" She smiles, lowers her head and glances up.

"Well, we're here and we're talking. We might as well catch up on old news. But I won't ever meet you back at home. Deana would feel too threatened. There is no point in it." After a pause,

I add, "And meeting this way feels like a betrayal." Helen shrugs. And so we talk about our jobs, about the conference, about our families.

That was how our strange and distant association started. If Helen and I were at a conference, we met for lunch or dinner and talked about our clients or professional issues. This happened five times. I relaxed more each time. Growing older, therapy, and marriage had changed Helen. Our discussions became more open. The memory of one particular meeting, the last, is vivid and disturbing.

I loathed the smoke in the bar, and the music was too loud. My eyes stung. The sessions ended at 9:30, and after talking for quite a while with other psychologists who had been at the conference, I drifted by the lobby toward my room. That's when I ran into Helen. We stood in the hallway and rehashed the meeting until 10:30 when we agreed to get a drink. Doing so at that hour broke the pattern we had established, but both of us were tired and agreed to make it brief. In the past, we each had a single drink. This time, after two, she had a third.

As we sat there, I had been reflecting on how I could apply in therapy ideas presented earlier in the day. Then I realized that Helen had said something. I jerked back and noticed her puzzled expression. In the dim light, she looked beautiful. Her hair fell over one shoulder, and her left earring sparkled. Her lips reflected light, seemed moist and parted; her open eyes showed a mixture of eagerness and restraint. Suppressed excitement flushed her cheeks.

"Do you tune out now? Like that?" she asked.

"Yes. The product of having kids. I find that I have to to keep my sanity. There is so much distraction that, if I don't, I can't function."

"You've learned little about us," she said after a short silence. "Despite your relationship with Rick." She paused again. I waited. She swallowed. "We can't have kids." Helen plunged on as if driven. "We tried. Then we had tests. Rick doesn't have a high sperm count."

Her face sagged and her head drooped. I let the silence continue because I was uncertain what to say. She slumped back in her seat, looking morose. I thought I saw the start of tears in her eyes. Then Helen continued speaking.

"You were right, at that first conference, about our not talking. I wish we never did this. It makes it more difficult. I'm older and wiser. I've learned things since we were dating. If I'd known then what I know now, I wouldn't have let you get away. I would have married you. If I weren't married, I'm not sure what I'd do." She paused and examined her wine. "I'd try to take you away from Deana."

My mouth went dry. I was light-headed. I noticed that my mouth had popped open and stayed that way. I snapped it shut, hoping she hadn't seen. I looked to the sides of the table, away from Helen. To stall, I took a large drink of my Chardonnay. I held it near my lips for thirty seconds while I considered taking another swallow and then put it back. I needed a clear mind. The long silence became awkward and then uncomfortable. Filled with misgivings, I talked.

"You remember, don't you? I wanted to marry you. But you wanted nothing to do with someone as uncool as me." I heard the bitterness in my voice and that surprised me. Helen bobbed her head. "And I felt unloved and unlovable because of what had been happening with my breakup. I was a mess. It was long ago and both of us were different. It might not have worked out. But if you had said yes, I never would have gone back to Deana."

"Then why didn't you return my calls or respond to my cards?" Her words were sharp and staccato. When I glanced up at her, though, her eyes and lips drooped.

"It was too late, Helen. Dee and I were back together." I had to contain the emotions welling up. "Every time you tried to contact me, Deana found out, and we had huge fights. You undercut my efforts to show her I cared, that I had a commitment to her, that I was trustworthy. You kept on for months. I was furious with you. I will not do this to her again."

"Nobody had ever left me before; I always left them. Right now I can say I'm sorry. But then, I hoped it was messing up your relationship."

"If I'd come back, you would have left me."

"Not anymore," Helen mumbled. Her words were just loud enough to unscramble from the noise. She continued staring into her glass of wine. She held it with both hands and didn't look up. My heart was pounding and I could not get a full breath. My face was hot. She wanted me to reach out for her. I could not move. I couldn't find words. A single tear, glistening since it caught the dim light, traveled downward along her right cheek.

I shake my head to dispel this disquieting memory. More distressing is imagining how Miller could twist this human and delicate situation into a sordid murder plot. I force myself up, onto my feet, holding the railing, pause, and then start down the stairs. I smile at how the intangible ambiguities of relationships can be exaggerated, misunderstood, and used as weapons. *Ever the psychologist!* Then I laugh at the irony. The laughter is nice, a relief from the inner darkness. And I laugh again; it echoes in the stairwell.

Though many routes lead out of Tower Hall, I'm retracing my earlier course into the building. In my mind, I see the package on my desk. What are those stains? Is that grease? I thought they were coffee at first, yet they looked like oil. The murderer ran out holding a similar package. I had forgotten that, even during all the questioning. I wonder if I have what he wants. He must have killed Rick to get it. I'll bet the murderer broke into Rick's office to get the package that is in my office, and when he opens what he took, he will find nothing. What is so important that he killed to get it? I again see the word DANGER reinforced again and again. Whatever is in that package is lethal. And, according to Rick, I must be silent. I must tell no one.

These thoughts leave me weak-kneed even though I've tried to ignore it. I get to the ground floor and am near the doors to the outside. In these newer buildings, a three-yard vestibule separates the main lobby from the outside. I push through the first set of doors and stop six inches from the outside door. I have to pause and think before I leave the building. I lean my back against the wall next to the main exit doors. And that note from Rick. Miller considered it evidence I am the murderer. I'm frantic. Threatened. I need to focus my jumbled thinking. The assassin seemed surprised that I showed up. The events took place rapidly; I wonder if he got a good look at me. Would he recognize me? Will he come looking for me? I take three deep breaths and relax my shoulders, which are tight and hunched.

I'm a little better and move toward the main doors. As I place my palm on the frame, I glance through the glass. Fear slams into my gut like a fist. The murderer is walking along the sidewalk toward this door. Had I continued, I would have been in view. He seems to have come from an adjoining building and walks with no overt concern about being in the open. There is a jaunty quality to his gait.

Adrenaline pumps as I run away along the ground floor. Classroom doors whiz by on both sides. The slap of my footsteps on the gray tile echoes off the walls of the long, empty corridor. A pair of doors with glass panels from top to bottom affords entrance to a foyer at the other end. A courtesy phone hangs from the wall to the right of those doors. Thank goodness I remember the number of Public Safety. Try to catch my breath before I call. After dialing I peek through the glass, down the hall to the main doors.

"Detective," I have to inhale, "Detective Miller, please! It's an emergency! This is Dr. Butler calling. He was here, in Tower Hall, a short while ago, about a murder. It's that murder."

"I'm sorry," says a monotone voice, "Detective Miller isn't in right now."

"Get him on the radio or something! My life is in danger." I can't get my words out. "The man who killed Rick Volks is right outside Tower Hall and he's coming for me. Shit, he's in the hall and walking toward me. Tell Miller!"

I yank away from the glass, hang up the phone, and slide to the floor, as if that will hide me. I'm sure he didn't see me. I'm thirty-five yards away with these closed doors between us. The narrow windows in the center of each door will expose me if I move across that doorway, even if I crawl. But that is the direction I want to go, since my office is several hundred yards to my left. I want to go straight there. With nowhere to hide, I press my back into the west wall of the foyer, trying to disappear. I must get away. I must get to my office where I'll be safe.

My eyes dart around the large, open foyer, exploring, probing, and hoping for escape. The door to the hallway, the hall he walks along, is only a foot to my left. The phone is above me. Bulletin boards are on the wall across from me. Next to the bulletin boards are doors leading further into the building. To my left and across the foyer is a short vestibule leading to a pair of exit doors. To my right, another set of exit doors. That's the way to go! How did I miss it? I'll slip out through those doors, going south, circle around the back of the building, and then run north to my office.

I take a deep breath, then roll along the wall to stay low and inconspicuous, and slide through the first set of doors onto the side vestibule floor. Now stand up. A large step to the exit doors. Shove through the doors. Run.

My neck is taut, wanting to check behind, wanting to know if he is there, but not daring to pause. Ears strain for the smallest sound that betrays the doors opening. I hear nothing and I keep running. At the first corner, I peek back. Check, listen again; I must be positive. No sound. No movement. Nothing.

CHAPTER 9

7:45 p.m.

Kramer Hall is in sight. The prospect of being in my office comforts me. I hope people aren't in the building; no one should be since it's evening. I don't want to small-talk and act normal.

After entering the south doors, I walk five paces, stop, and look to my left down the hall to the main office, thirty yards away. Empty. Silent. My office is two-thirds of the distance, on the left. Closer still, ten yards away, an exit doorway is on the right. Overhead, a red glowing sign with the word EXIT casts light on the floor. I step into the hallway, expecting the relief that will come from shutting my office door behind me. I envision leaning my back against its surface, now able to relax.

A tall, stooped figure shambles into the hall from the exit doorway. He turns in my direction and stops. My elder colleague, Henry Asgood, blocks my progress. He is gaunt with raised cheekbones that highlight the underlying hollows. His thinning hair is steel gray and brushed straight back. His black-framed glasses emphasize his bushy eyebrows, and his brown eyes stare without blinking. Other than raising his eyebrows, his face seldom changes expression. Though the day has been hot, he wears his tweed jacket with leather elbow patches. The stem of a pipe sticks out of the breast pocket. He does not wear a tie, which I assume is a concession to the weather. I consider him the stereotype of a professor. And he is influential.

I recall our last department meeting. Twenty faculty sat around tables arranged into a large rectangle. "New business," which included plans for the coming year, was the topic under discussion. To plan for the department's teaching needs, the chair asked how many had applied for grants, what the funding decision dates were, and whether the grants entailed reduced time for instruction. After three other colleagues spoke, I mentioned, with hesitancy and embarrassment, that I too had submitted a grant. Henry turned his stare on me, and after a brief silence delivered a statement that has troubled me over the summer months.

"I hope," he said, "that the grant does not involve that meditation foolishness."

"Well," I said, stalling, struggling to organize my thoughts, "well . . . it does involve that foolishness, a foolishness that millions of people practice . . . in other cultures. Rick Volks and I plan to show its effectiveness in pain management and self-healing. There's a significant body of literature on meditation."

"And who is the primary investigator?" he asked, emphasizing *who'* and sitting even more upright. I recognized the agenda behind the question. The PI gets first authorship on articles that result from the project, and I needed to be first author on a paper to get tenure.

"We share that honor," I said, attempting to hold my head high. I wished someone else might speak. The ensuing silence implied endorsement for Henry's position. My stomach sank. No one responded to support me, and then to my relief, the chair spoke and elicited nods from many of those sitting around the table.

"We need to keep in mind that funded research has been evaluated by professional colleagues, and in academia, we enjoy the freedom if not the implicit charge to examine what is at the edges of knowledge. As a department we should support the growth and development of our fellow faculty. It behooves us all."

I snap back from my memories and continue down the hallway to my office. My steps take me toward Henry. He does not move to let me pass.

"Hello, Jason. Welcome back. Did you and your family enjoy your break?"

"Hi, Henry," I mumble, continuing to move forward, expecting he will shift aside. I can't fault him for friendliness but I notice my body shrinking away from him.

"Yes. Yes, we had a good vacation, although we never left town. Very relaxing." I'm forced to stop.

"Any word on your grant?"

"Earlier today, we received notification it got funding." Henry's eyebrows flick upward. "We should start soon." He stands unmoving, looking at me. I don't have the slightest idea what he might be thinking.

"Well . . . I guess that's good." His tone of voice suggests otherwise.

I take a half step, invading his personal space. He shifts to the side, a quizzical expression on his face.

"Wish I could talk more," I lie, "but I'm in a rush. Something's come up." After I'm past him, I rummage in my pocket for the key. Glancing back, I say, "Something pressing." Henry has swung partway round and his eyes track me. As I unlock the door, he turns and strolls away.

In my office. Lock it. Even though it's warm, I'll close the windows and the blinds. Check for anyone outside the building before twisting the blinds closed. I can't see anybody. Are there more assassins? That awful thought stops me in midaction. What was I going to do? I remember—contact the police.

"Is Detective Miller there? This is Dr. Butler, and, yes, it's urgent. It's an emergency. My life is in danger! At least, I fear it is."

"No, sir, Detective Miller isn't here," the dispatcher says. "After your last call, we reached him, and he said he'd check Tower Hall as soon as possible. He might be there. I'll leave another message for him if you'd like."

"Please, yes. Yes. I'm at my office. He should phone me here. He has my number. It's extension 4276. Will you ask him to phone right away? It's urgent."

I feel secure now. I'm convinced the murderer can't know who or where I am. He saw me briefly as he ran out of Rick's office. I only need to keep out of sight until the police catch him. I sigh with relief, and my mind drifts back to what happened in Tower Hall.

Despite looking at his body, I can't believe Rick is dead. How will I write that publication now that Rick is gone? His understanding of how meditation affects fear and pain is vital for the success of our research. I don't have his skills. I can't teach others how to meditate. I've always had trouble dealing with these two states, states that link to my problems with embarrassment and public humiliation.

I'm disheartened. The future now seems bleak. I begin examining the package on my desk. What's in it? Why kill for it? In particular, Rick! He is a scholar. Should I wait for Miller to respond? It's reasonable to await his call, but I need answers.

What about my family? The murderer can't learn where I live. Will my name be in the newspaper? It will. Of course, it will! There was a reporter interviewing people in Tower Hall. Although I refused to talk to him, he spoke to everyone he could find. No question. My name will be in the paper; then the killer can find me. Without that, he couldn't know who I am. Damn.

Without noticing, I have been slowly edging the package closer and sliding a finger under one flap. Now I yank my finger away and clutch it as if it were injured. I can't plunge into this without considering the risks. Rick wrote "Danger" and told me to destroy it if anything happened to him. He realized his life was at risk … and that risk relates to this bundle. He never mentioned opening it, but urged its destruction. I guess he expected his killers would not realize I had it. Now the killer knows. No! I'm being ridiculous. He can't know I have it. But, I can identify the murderer, and I can describe him. The police had left the building for at least twenty minutes when I got to the exit, a reasonable interval for him to assume it was safe to come back. He probably was trying to find the package, not me. In my panicky state, I assumed the assassin had returned to Tower Hall to look for me. When he can't find the parcel in Rick's office, will he guess I have it? No. He has no reason to consider me. Even if he does not suspect me now, when he finds out who I am from the newspaper story, he will realize my close relationship with Rick and might guess I have the package. I must thoroughly weigh this. The situation has changed from when Rick wrote that warning. He assumed I'd stay unknown and thus destroying it would keep me protected.

As I imagine opening the packet, my jaw tightens and my body tenses like a spring. I thrust myself from the chair and back away from the desk. I continue staring at the package as if it might explode . . . or offer solutions. I'm shifting my weight from one foot to the other, fists clenching. I inhibit the impulse to smash it to pieces. I take a deep breath, hold it, and let go.

This is incomprehensible. The explanation must be in that parcel; and only by opening it will I solve these mysteries. Should I? I'm terrified, yet I realize I will open it. I'm holding back, delaying this inevitable action whose consequences I can't foresee. But secrets feed my worst fantasies. With information I can choose: to act or to wait. Or to inform Miller.

CHAPTER 10

7:56 p.m.

The package weighs more than I remember. Twine still keeps the outer covering in place. I hesitate, as I sense the pressure of the cord on the scissor blades. A tingle floods my arms. I pause, then I cut through it. More tape seals the inside wrapping. I see again the reinforced words DANGER! DANGER! DANGER! Words that so far have kept me immobilized. Should I do this? I set the parcel on my lap and close my eyes. Whether or not I open it, that guy will come after me. Opening it cannot change what he does. But after seeing it, I might learn how to find safety for me and my family.

As I tear away the wrapping, I notice a musty smell. Underneath is yet another layer of brown paper, taped with care and exactitude. Words, written with strokes of thick red ink, jump off the surface.

FOR SAFEKEEPING ONLY. GIVE ONLY TO ME!
JASON. DO NOT, I REPEAT, DO NOT OPEN. DESTROY
THIS IF SOMETHING HAPPENS TO ME.

No signature. My tongue sticks to my mouth. I swallow. This is a turning point. I stare at the brown wrapping, hesitating, hand rubbing the rough and uneven texture of the surface. The paper comes from a distant and unknown land. The internal debate again tumbles through my awareness. My arguments convinced me I need to, I must, open it—but I'm afraid. I'm terrified to discover the hidden secrets. I delay by crumpling the outside wrapper into a large ball and tossing it in the wastebasket. When I turn back, my lungs burn from holding my breath. After I exhale, I say it aloud to affirm my decision.

"OK. I'll open it. I'm ready to find out."

I push my fingernail under the tape. The wrapping and tape are tougher than I expect and do not tear. I wiggle the point of the scissors into the small opening left where the flap seals, rip the paper, and cut across the top.

With the shades drawn and the sun setting, the light has dimmed. My eyes strain to pick out details. Darkness deepens, and I can't read. I stand up and step to the light switch and freeze, arm poised in the air. If I turn on the lights, the assassin could see it! I shake my head at my own suspicious thinking: he cannot know who I am, so worrying is pointless. But I cannot escape this fear. A solution pops to mind. Because of frequent power failures, I always keep a flashlight available. With the blinds shut and the streetlights shining, the glow will be undetectable.

The flashlight creates a bright circle on the package. Inside are two thick sheaves of papers, difficult to see since plastic bags, sealed with more tape, protect them. A set of stapled pages are folded askew so the edges mismatch. Faint traces of blue show through the paper. Closer inspection shows handwriting. Heart thumping, hands sweating, I pop the pages apart and read.

My dear Jason,

I write this note with tablet on lap at the airport -- thus my indirect apology for my handwriting. As you are aware, waiting area seating is seldom comfortable and hardly conducive to fine penmanship. I have many hours to wait pre-flight so I have ample time to write.

If you are reading this, you chose not to heed my warnings. I was going to seal the envelope and expect you to destroy it. But as I considered your personality, it was feasible you might open it, regardless. Beware! You do not comprehend the threat of what you have opened. You still possess the choice not to go ahead.

Many years ago, my researches led me to a sect that has taken the ascetic vows of the Shra'kufans to the extreme. They are not averse to killing either themselves or others when it furthers what they consider spiritual growth. On this particular trip, I chanced upon a collection of their manuscripts in an out-of-the-way pawn shop in a bazaar. From other sources, I determined that this "store" was a special and secret place where Shra'kufans exchanged information. To my horror, I discovered that they murdered my informant after I procured the texts. I am positive the sales clerk will see his own demise. I don't think the diminutive fellow understood what he was selling me. He bumbled through the various and obvious components of self-enterprise (the most conspicuous being his confusion over the hand-operated cash register). Thus, I concluded he was but a part-time or even temporary employee. I surmise that the owner was holding it for someone else to buy. I got there first, to the owner's eventual chagrin. When I looked at the manuscripts closely, I discovered they are spectacular—and originals. I've attached a synopsis I wrote several weeks ago summarizing the "facts" I learned regarding this group during my most current four months here as well as gleaned over many previous years. Gathering this recent evidence has been amongst the most difficult tasks of my career. Furthermore, I have translated (in diverse stages of completeness, as will be clear) sections of the documents themselves.

These manuscripts are sacred in the extreme; consider that they themselves are worshiped by this sect. Only the holiest may gaze upon them. Were I, "impure and defiled," merely to look at them, I profane them forever. If they learn I possess them, they will stop at nothing to recapture them. Their personal safety and survival is irrelevant in the face of having these secrets exposed. Anyone who knows these texts exist will be killed once the Shra'kufans gain that information, since that person is a threat to their religion as conceived and promulgated by their tradition.

My itinerary will take me far so that despite the snail's pace of mail in this part of the world, this might reach you by the time I return to the university. I will mail this from the airport. An inconspicuous act as I bought the stamps yesterday and a proper letter box is nearby. No one, I hope, will know I have them let alone mailed them.

The Shra'kufans are a mysterious group. On the one hand, they are unknown to the point of invisibility. Ask questions, and from journalists and police alike one gets a genuine blank look. Yet amongst the most elite intelligence communities in this part of the world, they have the reputation as deadly and skilled saboteurs as well as spies. I questioned my informants concerning this paradox to no avail. To my dismay, and now undoubtedly your own, they are ignored by the police in every country in which they live. This, in part, is obviously why they stay hidden. I shall elaborate more on this later.

They have, as one might expect, an uncanny knack for self-preservation and for obtaining information. By the time I reach Terrace Hills, I should have clues if they've found me out. I have niggling concerns since some of my possessions are missing, yet I am still alive. Their assassins are relentless I've heard. If one assassin gets killed in the line of duty, they send another—or several—until the job is done. So beware the poison called the "Blue Sky." (In their language "Samatma.") It works quickly and painfully (I have heard)—numb, immobile and then unconscious. These people seem to have developed an immunity to its effects.

If you are stupid enough not to destroy the package after reading this letter, at least secrete it in a safe deposit box. NO ONE CAN KNOW YOU HAVE THIS!! I've told nobody, not even Helen. As you will undoubtedly understand, I do not want her endangered. She will possibly be in danger if I am discovered. Possessing the manuscripts is a death warrant. DO NOT UNDER ANY CIRCUMSTANCES LET ANYONE KNOW. If someone slips up, and the word gets out, you are dead! And so are they! These are very dangerous people. I urge you again: demolish these documents and forget. If you can't do so, and I expect that possibility, I repeat, lock this in a safe deposit box and leave it there permanently. Keep this whole thing a secret since they will kill anyone who knows they exist, and they will be even more relentless trying to retrieve these papers and texts.

I am cognizant of the complete unbelievability (to coin a word) of what I am attesting. What I describe might be the outrageous fulminations of a crazy fanatic. Such were the impressions I myself had when I began to formulate my understanding of the Shra'kufans. How is it possible that law enforcement, the government, the newspapers acknowledge nothing concerning them? This must be nonsense. Such, I confess, was my own opinion. Then, after talking to specific individuals, primarily police detectives, intelligence officers, and security experts, my informants independently corroborated what I had concluded. These particular people were highly specialized in their jobs. They had "proof." Even though I had come to this deduction individually, the confirmation warped my mind. My conclusion smacked of the delusional: their secretiveness, their hiddenness, their lethality, their unknownness was true and real. I was thrown into a twisted reality that I did not recognize, an unbelievable yet terrifying world. Thus, I share the following which I experienced personally.

I've got to take a break. Reading this is like being sucked into a different world. I set the letter aside and, when I stand, expecting to walk, find I'm immobile with my mouth half open. I'm dumbfounded. Rick stumbled into a pit abuzz with dangers and now so have I. Hoping this will make a difference, I lift my arms as far up as I can and stretch. I turn and start walking back and forth--and can't stop thinking I should return to the letter. I become aware I avoid looking at the desk. Damn, damn, damn. No matter what I do, that letter looms in my mind—and I can't continue to avoid it.

I heard stories involving collectors who purchased their religious artifacts, supposedly in secret, only to have them stolen and then afterward been murdered. I obtained personal knowledge of such an event before my own acquisition. (Foolish of me, I recognize, to buy these texts when I knew this. Ah, the hubris of fame.) An acquaintance, a collector of religious memorabilia who had been of help to me, confessed, distraught, over lunch that the prior evening his illicit purchase, for his investment group, of a Shra'kufan amulet had been stolen. His distress was piqued since he believed no one could know of his procurement. Furthermore, he had been asleep in his house, protected by alarms, a fence, dogs and a groundskeeper. That very night, after our meal, his automobile rolled down an embankment, killing him and doing much damage to a hillside flower garden. The metaphor of death defacing the beautiful was not lost on me; a weird juxtaposition I must tell you. Curious about the event, I at once examined the police report on both the burglary and the accident. He had suffered a massive heart attack and brain hemorrhage that apparently caused him to lose control of his auto. The theft was extraordinary in its cleanliness. The massive safe in which the amulet was secreted was resealed and the automatic alarm never triggered. Only careful detective work showed that wires were cut and reconnected at one window, and the paint on the frame of the window was barely scratched by an entry tool. I returned a week later to follow up on these reports. They were gone! No one at the police station could find them. What motivated my follow-up was the demise of every member of his investment group. Every one of them died via massive vascular rupture, either in the brain or heart. I knew them all since we had interests in common. My acquaintance told me (the day he expired) that he had discussed with his group the hazards of purchasing the amulet. The purchase, he claimed emphatically, was totally secret and via third, untraceable parties. Both they and their new possession were protected, he thought. Obviously, he was wrong. For several weeks following my lunch with him, I lived in fear for my life as I had knowledge of the amulet.

This alarming loss of information by the police but, more persuasively, their complete indifference to its extirpation as well as the crime itself proved insidious. Since this happens regularly (so I am told), it becomes obvious to me why law enforcement might be unaware of Shra'kufan activities and possibly be reluctant to pursue investigations. Furthermore, my discreet and high-level contacts emphasized that the Shra'kufans mostly live in remote regions (such as deserts and mountains) and are most circumspect whenever they act. Their ostensible invisibility, they asserted to me, was carefully maintained by the sect and totally within reason given the infrequency with which they come into contact with police and journalists.

I'm guessing, my psychological friend, you are asking, Why? Why did you do this? Why did you buy these manuscripts? Why did you put yourself in jeopardy? My answer is this: Because, in the context of the recent rash of terrorism, and this group's in particular, my knowledge might, in the long run, save lives and clarify their underlying beliefs. This, however, was not my original aim. At first, I was researching ascetic sects, one of which was the Shra'kufans. Then, as I continued, I found a few obscure yet crucial references to these Shra'kufan terrorists. This stimulated my interest since they are active and unknown. Then, on a fluke, I bought these texts. (Though it was, as one might surmise, not a complete accident.) Over the course of my researches, I've learned about various shops and the merchandise potentially available. This store was amongst that group, although never, in the context of my prior interests, worthy of an extensive examination. Nonetheless, I had before bought material from this same shop. It specializes in arcane documents and demands a high price, too, thus my less than enthusiastic opinion.

When, after I had them in hand, I considered the enormity of the threat I faced, I entertained burning them. My dismay escalated when I recalled I had signed the receipt, a necessity for my grant expenses, although I had used only an account name at ESU. At the time, the likelihood of someone tracing me back to Eastern appeared remote, though I now question my wisdom in drawing that conclusion. As well, I remembered the chaotic mess of paperwork in the store which, in my judgment, afforded a protection in its own right. Later, I adjudged the texts a stroke of "good fortune" and decided it was worth the risk. No one has been following me. Nothing untoward has happened except for the loss of some items. I am taking this precaution to separate myself from these papers.

Why, you might ask, did I not keep them? As I contemplated the possibility of my discovery, it appeared that my best protection was not having them in my possession. It is entirely reasonable to suppose that I will stay protected until they find the texts. That happened with the amulet and, I should add, with other deaths I researched extensively. I considered returning them, but, according to my informants, my life would still be at risk (after all, I had seen them!) and I would also be sans manuscripts. Once owned, keeping them proved the best solution. Furthermore, I studied Shra'kufan retaliatory methods and so far none of the small precursors have appeared. I hope I am completely safe. I believe I can escape and, most importantly, Shra'kufans have never killed outside this region.

With you, my friend, I must be honest. There are many more personal motivations as well. I always longed for fame and to be regarded as THE EXPERT in a unique domain of scholarship. I am surprised that I'm only slightly embarrassed by my selfishness and scholarly greed. In part, I believe that is because I truly could become the foremost expert on the Shra'kufan religion. If you read the accompanying material, it will be plain why this group has remained so hidden from mainstream religious research.

Separate from the religious perspective, the discovery of these texts is momentous in linguistic circles too. The texts are either an undiscovered Indo-European language or a startling and significant modification of known grammatical structure or BOTH. The language in these manuscripts is the find of a lifetime.

Why you? Why did I mail this to you? To you, I told secrets never shared with another. As well, I know this from personal experience, you not once shared them with anyone, not even your wife! You are trustworthy! Moreover, despite our scholarly work together, you are not a close friend in a public sense. Now don't get hurt. I mean that no one else—other than my dear wife—knows about our friendship. It is not of the usual poker-till-3 a.m. or beer-Fridays-after-work relationship. Sending this to you should keep you safe if they assume I have the texts and are pursuing me.

I apologize for dragging you into this. Do note, it was your choice to open the package and not mine. I attempted to dissuade you. And, I must again emphasize—nay, urge you—to destroy these documents so no one can discover you have them. But, if you are reading this, you will possibly get involved. Even now, despite my earlier reassurances, I have nagging doubts concerning this for myself, let alone for you.

My best to Deana and the kids. Take care, my friend.

Fondly and fare-thee-well,

Rick

CHAPTER 11

8:00 p.m.

My stunned, blank state of mind continues ... Then one thought, another, and another ... and I am back.

I look in front of me, staring at the wall behind the desk, feeling helpless, and then want to ... need to ... do something. Anything. But what? What can I do? I'm trapped in my office. I swivel the chair a turn and a half and stop facing away from the desk. I explore the blinds, outlined in twilight blue, as if they hide an answer.

I know more now. I have answers to a few questions and understand why Rick looked as he did. Although his letter is mild and considered, he was haggard and furtive when I saw him this afternoon. He must have suspected the Shra'kufans were stalking him. Will he hunt me and try to kill me? Is this reasonable? Am I creating an imaginary threat? No. Based on what I read, the risk is real. I believe he attempted to murder me in Rick's office. Why do they want to eliminate anyone who knows they exist?

That stack on my desk might hold the answer. I close my eyes, aware of feeling anxious about discovering what is in those papers. I inch the chair closer. I never jiggle my legs, but that is what I'm doing as I stare at that pile. Leaning forward, I pick the topmost document. Though typed and double-spaced, lines cross out words and sentences, corrections litter the margins, and arrows show where to move passages.

SHRA'KUFAN TERRORISM:
A SOCIOCULTURAL PERSPECTIVE

The Shra'kufans are an obscure sect of ascetics, unknown in the Middle and Far East and, as a natural consequence, the rest of the globe. They remain more enigmatic than any other cult. Their beliefs differ from the major religions of Islam, Hinduism, Buddhism, Christianity, or Judaism. In contrast to some religious traditions, men and women have equal roles. My sources are not typical for scholarly research: arcane texts discovered in out-of-the-way libraries and shops, scattered news reports over the past century from numerous countries, and informants whom I befriended over the preceding two decades. I met them when I researched here, and they are representatives of the academic, political, and intelligence communities. I have known a wide spectrum of individuals over this period and few had heard the name, Shra'kufan. I myself, an expert on religion in this part of the world, had also never seen the name until fifteen years ago. To my surprise, even my interviewees who knew scant information talked, hushed and cautious, and with anxiety if not noticeable fear.

The early conclusions I formed about the Shra'kufans were difficult to accept. I found it hard to believe the interpretations that followed from what I learned. What I had figured out fit with data from a lunatic fringe. However, a coherence and consistency developed from disparate disciplines and countries. These pages condense and summarize the commonalities that, to my surprise, coalesced into a remarkable yet distressing overview. To assert the obvious and to toot my professional horn, none of what I write is available in any organized and published form nor, based on my understanding, from any individual but myself.

In 1652 the sultan of the region outlawed Shra'kufan practices. So heinous were their acts that anybody caught engaging in their religious ceremonies was executed. Despite official and social sanctions against them, the religion persisted, albeit secretly and sparsely, in remote, mountainous regions and in small enclaves hidden near poor foothill villages bordering the desert. For reasons that will become clear, Shra'kufans thrive in economically, socially, and geographically destitute localities.

The Shra'kufan religious system proclaims that the human body is the root of all evil* and, as a consequence, prevents the spirit-principle from soaring to its destiny.

On the back of the page, Rick wrote a footnote for *evil*: "I translate this word as 'evil,' in the context of most religions. I could translate it as 'problems' and 'pain' comingled together. It does not encompass the moral connotation found in other religions." I returned to the text:

The flesh must be subdued! Devotees go to hideous extremes to suppress the body. These are not the "transcendental" or altered states associated with fire-walking, in which the feet seem protected since they are unscathed, not even blistered, after treading on hot coals, nor with the miraculous self-healing that occurs after mystics plunge hooks through their tissue and with which they drag heavy objects. This sect does not seek to dull or transcend the pain with altered states. Believers go to excess to inflict suffering, torturing themselves and others. They torture themselves without mercy on walks across scorching deserts with soles bleeding and cracked. On returning, they refuse drink, food, and medical treatment to prove mastery over the body and the pain it produces. These are the beliefs and actions of the most conservative and traditional Shra'kufans.

The terrorist sect, the Ballag'cha, makes the traditional Shra'kufans appear ordinary. They are the guardians of the

One Eternal Truth Beyond All Other Truths. According to their views, the acts of the Ballag'cha are inspired. (The textual words are: "Their actions arise like the sun, emerging from Beyond the Beyond, piercing the dark with light.") Their current practices elaborate bodily mortification and subjugation to extremes. Death, from the viewpoint of the most conservative Shra'kufans, frees the spirit, now unhindered by the physical body, to soar into the blue heaven and unite with the Eternal. From the perspective of the Ballag'cha, torture aids the torturer, and the tortured to merge with "God*."

Rick made another annotation, also on the back, written in small letters along the edge of the page. Hard to read. *"God* here differs from the Judeo-Christian concept. A literal translation would be 'Beyond the Eternal Beyond.' In future passages, therefore, I will translate this as 'Eternal' or 'Eternal Beyond' rather than *God*."

Rick's writings explain, in the context of their history, why the Shra'kufans are dangerous. I had at first thought they were a recent, extremist sect, but they go back over a millennia. Given their secretiveness, I wonder how Rick obtained his information. To my dismay, what I have read so far only increases my sense of dread. I wish it didn't. Deep breath. Time to get back to reading.

Taking this logic to an extreme, the terrorist sect believes that when a guardian of the Ballag'cha kills, that death is a spiritual favor for both. To kill anyone with a different religious belief enhances the virtue of the killer*.

Flip the page over. Another comment. "As much as this is consistent with their views, it logically extends to killing as many people as possible. If killing is a spiritual favor for both, why not kill as many as one can and collect the maximum religious benefit? My conclusion, because of this analysis, is that this practice started as a way to kill individuals who are a threat to the religion. This fits with Ballag'cha history."

Their daily rituals and training help them confront a grizzly ceremony where, once a year on a holy day, a randomly chosen member is tortured to death. To die an agonizing death without overt reaction is the highest spiritual attainment. Based on their beliefs, such a death creates a link between the believers still "caught in" the Earth (e.g., the torturers) and the Eternal Beyond. I will spare the reader an exposition of the details. Whatever one might imagine does not approach the horror of these rites.

I must clarify the social and historical context for what appears barbaric. Consider, for example, that death, painful and unexpected, was a frequent event in pre- and early Shra'kufan society. These beliefs and practices played the sociological role of making such unpredictable and uncontrollable events endurable to the survivors. In addition, the religion prepared them for survival by training them to tolerate the extreme circumstances they would confront in daily life.

A thousand years ago the religion served a sociological function. Present time, the terrorist sect has been, from my outside point of view, channeled toward violence. ("Terrorist" is my word assignation, while "protective zealots" captures their function from an inside perspective.) The few who have any knowledge of the Ballag'cha, like my informants, regard them with dread. Nothing seems to deter the sect from achieving their ends.

One terrorist brought a bomb into a legislative assembly amid deliberations about curtailing religious extremism, in particular terrorists. He and fifteen legislators died. The leaders of the political movement attempting to stop all extremist groups, with the Shra'kufans included, were amongst the dead. No one has proposed further legislation. Explosives are an unusual form of assassination for the Shra'kufans. They must have been imperiled to resort to such an "irreligious" method. Most of the time they kill with the "Blue Sky" (Samatma) since, according to the religious beliefs, it helps the victim soar to the Eternal.

I cannot corroborate the accuracy of this account, but one of my informants reported a similar assassination of legislators in an adjoining country, also a home to Shra'kufans. On live television, several Shra'kufans (they were not so designated in any news report, according to my informant who is a member of the intelligence community) used the "Blue Sky" to murder nine elected representatives in full view of the rest of the governmental assembly. The police shot the assassins, but not before the attackers murdered their targets. As mentioned, I cannot ascertain the veracity of this information.

CHAPTER 12

8:13 p.m.

I do not want to believe what I read; yet I've drawn the same conclusion I fight accepting. It seems indisputable. Rick tried to warn me. I dismissed it since I did not have the information. But the result seems inconceivable.

If I tell anybody about them, about the Shra'kufans, about this secret, a secret I don't even know, about their existence or the texts, then I put that person's life in danger . . . and my own. It's a crazy conclusion, but it seems true. I can't share this with Deana. Or my friends. Or my colleagues. Or Detective Miller. I can't depend on the police . . . unless they catch him.

I pick up the next set of pages from the pile and then push away, rolling several feet. I glance down at the papers resting in my lap and fling them back at the desk. They scatter across the floor. Displeased with myself, I roll closer, gather them up with a sigh, and return to reading.

THE ORIGINS OF SHRA'KUFAN TERRORISM

The Shra'kufans are an anomaly in the Middle and Far East. Isolated and protected in the foothills of the Taurus Mountains from 200 to 600 A.D., pre-Shra'kufan enclaves maintained separation and distance from the profound cultural changes taking place around them in urban areas and agricultural lowlands. (Note: The Taurus Mountains connect to the Himalayas. The foothills, in which the Shra'kufans lived, extend from Turkey, through Iran, Afghanistan, Pakistan, and India, to Tibet and Nepal. I can't specify their actual origin let alone current home.) By 700 A.D., centuries of marginal living in an inhospitable climate that bridged desert and mountain developed a rigid but life-sustaining set of social and religious traditions. Life was meager. Climatic extremes, isolation, starvation, and drought had meaning as religious challenges designed by the One Who Watches Over (a pre-Shra'kufan conception of "God") to prove fortitude and faith. These beliefs served a sociocultural function that helped the group survive and reinterpreted suffering as tolerable and enhancing. Only when they had suffered, asserted their doctrines, being pure despite severe depredations, would the One Who Watches Over allow them to join him in the Blue Sky above: constant, peaceful, pure, absent all suffering.

During the eighth century, decades of drought followed by an invasion prepared this subculture for Baya Z'r, the Shra'kufan prophet.

The phone.

If it is Miller, what do I tell him? I let it ring several times, trying to sort out my feelings and thoughts. Each ring shatters my concentration. I lift the handset.

"Dr. Butler please," says a nasal voice I recognize. My decision not to tell Miller about the texts springs to mind.

"Yes, Detective Miller, I called." I flash back to my interrogation, the word "danger" popping into my mind. The stack of papers on my desk serves as a vivid and immediate warning. And Rick's words, "Tell not one person." And the note from Rick that Miller read. I notice I've been silent.

"Excuse me. I'll return in a moment," I say to give me time.

Without giving him a chance to respond, I clunk the phone down on the desk, stand up, and scrape my feet to create the illusion I am doing something. I need to think. Why wouldn't I tell him? That might put him at risk. Why do I care? To the extent I know police procedure, they would dismiss what I consider a genuine threat. But the texts and the terrorists could never stay secret with Miller. All would become public, possibly soon. The facts would require documentation and discussion. Since the Shra'kufans are foreign, the CIA would get involved. In my mind's eye, I see the information rippling out from the middle of Iowa to both coasts. More than that, my name, my identity, would be included every time. I cannot remain unknown to the Shra'kufans. In fact, they would learn about my possession of the texts. No. I can't tell Miller. Perhaps I'll inform him later.

"I thought I had more information . . . but I was wrong. I'm terrified. I think the murderer is after me since I'm the only witness. He was there at Tower Hall when I was leaving, and he followed me down the hallway. Well, I don't know if he followed me specifically, but he walked right down the hallway after I did. It seemed as if he was following me."

"I didn't catch him," says Miller, "and no one in the building has seen him. I got there not ten minutes after you called. I found no evidence that a person had been on that floor. That was the west door, wasn't it?

"Yes."

"Unless he dropped something distinctive on the ground, we would have no evidence anyone was there. We found none."

"His showing up like that scared me. Do you have any suggestions?"

"Keep out of sight until we catch him."

"I'm not sure I can, what with the semester starting in two days. I'll hide until then but after that I have to teach. Could you keep my name out of any news releases? If he finds out who I am, I'm worried about my safety and my family's."

"I'll try, but it might be too late. A reporter was there, and I can't control the press. There is no clear evidence, Dr. Butler, that your life is in danger despite your worry."

"Well, it was an idea. Just the notion of my name in the paper scares me. I don't know what to do. If anything else comes up, I'll call you. Please advise me of any developments. I'm petrified not only for myself but also my family."

"I can understand that, Dr. Butler." A silence. I wonder if I should say something, and Miller talks again. "Back to Tower Hall. Were there other people around who might have seen this man entering the building?"

"No."

"Was there anyone in the hallway who would have seen him?"

"No. I could see no one else there."

"Why were you in the building?" My heart thumps. This is a sharp question that implies I am a suspect.

"I'm distraught about his death and watching a murder. I have never in my life experienced something like this, and I'm rattled. I needed, I still need, time to cope with the emotions kicked off by this, so I lingered, struggling to come to terms with what happened. Can't you understand this?"

"Did you do anything?"

"Do anything? Like what?"

"Like do anything."

"I don't know what you mean. All I did was stand around trying to sort out my emotions."

"Couldn't you have sorted out your emotions somewhere else, Dr. Butler?"

"Well, yes, I could."

"Why didn't you?"

"It didn't cross my mind." At first, the silence is awkward; then it becomes a nonverbal battle—accusation opposed by denial. I wait him out.

"Dr. Butler, one more question while I have you on the phone. Which direction was Volks's head pointing when you walked into the room?"

"He was facedown, turned to the right. To his right." I'm at first irritated by his query, and then I get worried that there is something else I don't know about that could be a problem for me. We went through this several times during the face-to-face interrogation.

"Did you move him once you entered the room?"

"Just in minor ways when I was trying to find his pulse." I try to force away the sensation of Rick's lifeless body as I felt his wrist.

"Did you ever have any disagreements or conflicts with Dr. Volks?"

His question wrenches me away from the awful memory. "We got along well. The most we disagreed on was how to proceed in teaching our class, but we resolved that. And also the focus of the grant."

"Did you ever share investment opportunities?...Or women?" I'm offended. I'm convinced I shouldn't but I will say it.

"That is insulting. Detective Miller, I've told you we were friends and team-taught a course. You wrenched the information about Helen from me, history I consider irrelevant and did not want to share. That's it. Why should there be more?"

"All right. Sorry if I upset you, but I needed to ask." Another silent pause. What now? "Though I found nothing on the ground floor, I discovered something on the fourth."

My heart sinks. For some unknown reason I feel even more threatened.

"You claim—" He clears his throat. "You claim you did nothing while you waited. Is that right?"

"I told you that. Yes. I waited around."

"Then, Dr. Butler, how can you explain that someone broke into Dr. Volks's office? The seal we put on the door had been broken. Objects moved."

"Detective Miller, it's obvious." My heart is pounding. "That man went upstairs after I saw him and broke into the office."

"Dr. Butler, we have no evidence he was there. No one observed him. We have evidence you were there. And, I would emphasize, this is the second time something happened and you were the only person there. What conclusion would you draw?" He pauses and clears his throat again.

"But another man could have been there. Just because you know I was there doesn't exclude another person from being there, someone you don't have evidence about."

After a protracted silence, he adds, "We'll check for fingerprints." He is silent again. I don't know what to say. "Does that change what you want to say?" he asks. Neither of us talk. The awkward silence drags on.

"My conclusion," Miller says, "is that whoever broke in was looking for evidence we might have missed, evidence that might incriminate him." Miller is silent. I hear his accusation: I was the one who broke in to get rid of damning evidence.

"Nothing to say, Dr. Butler? Just as well. That's all the questions I have . . . for now. But I'll be back in touch. You can be sure of that. Good-bye, Dr. Butler."

"Detective Miller? Please don't hang up."

"Yes, Dr. Butler, what is it?" He sounds disinterested.

"I am afraid that this man is coming after me. I fear for my life. I am hoping you will keep looking for him."

"Dr. Butler, we will do our job. I hope you understand our situation. You claim this man, a man no one other than you has seen, a man that no one else can describe, is coming after you. When we look at any of the evidence in Dr. Volks's office, we only find your fingerprints. We will do our job and be on the lookout for someone like the person you described. We will find whoever killed Dr. Volks . . . have no fears we won't. Is that all, Dr. Butler?"

"Yes," I say, feeling defeated and even more afraid. Miller, the police, are not a resource. He suspects me. He doesn't believe the assassin is real. He doesn't believe my life is in danger.

"Good-bye then."

I hang up the phone by holding it between two fingers and letting it drop onto its cradle. I am a suspect. He disbelieves whatever I say. Will he help me if I need it?

My only hope is myself and the manuscript on my desk. I turn back to it.

CHAPTER 13

Sunset

After four decades of drought, scraping a marginal living off the land by herding goats and by farming small plots of arable soil provided the pre-Shra'kufans marginally sustainable conditions. Circumstances worsened. Livestock died and plants withered. The young, the sick, and the elderly perished from lack of food and water. This readied the region for a most impactful change: invaders smashed the social structure. This subculture, stable over hundreds of years, changed virtually overnight. Some intruders remained in the villages and became despotic leaders. Although the nonmilitant and already frightened townspeople cowered and complied, clandestine rites maintained their religious beliefs and carried on their traditions. The drought and the invasion were additional trials, affirming their religion, to endure for the One Who Cares and Watches Over.

According to legend, Baya Z'r, the originator of the Shra'kufan religion, was born in a remote and mountainous place. The invasion occurred during his childhood. The malevolent invaders who assumed governance of his region maintained control by intimidation and torture. As punishment for his parents' "crime" of hiding grain, Baya Z'r, while still a boy, was forced to burn off their fingers, one at a time, and then to disembowel them, punishments linked to their crime of taking grain. Afterwards he himself suffered abuse, losing three fingers and developing a permanent limp. Three years later, Baya Z'r embarked on the traditional mountain quest required to pass into adulthood. Every adolescent male needed to survive for at least five days, having taken no food or water with them, accepting "whatever the One Who Cares" provided.

Baya Z'r returned after twenty-five days—gaunt, bruised, bleeding, near death. Later religious texts extol his virtue and his closeness to the One Who Cares and to That Which Is Beyond, describing his slow and erect hobble into the village, leaving a trail of red footprints. Despite his cut and bloody feet, he showed no pain. He smiled, and his lips were so dry they cracked and blood flowed down his chin, trailing red dots on the ground between his footprints. But, say the texts, his smile was undimmed. (Some texts make much of the symbolism of his blood, the embodiment of pain and humanness, flowing back to the Earth.) He said, "Though I have walked the earth, I am of the sky. This body keeps me no longer from the Eternal Beyond the Sky. Release yourselves from agony and join that which is Beyond the Eternal Beyond the Sky."

At first villagers and later the elders followed Baya Z'r's revelations and prophecies. The momentum of this new religion increased. From this author's point of view, at this historical moment, these people needed a leader, and Baya Z'r fulfilled that need. His impassioned speeches, his religious dogma and his prophetic statements spread through this deprived and subjugated region.

Oppressive social and physical conditions and previous beliefs and attitudes coalesced in Baya Z'r's new religion. He appeared at a time of volatile change, widespread fear, social oppression, starvation and drought. Baya Z'r's religion elaborated the preexisting beliefs in helplessness and in the value of suffering by interpreting oppression as the will of the Eternal Beyond the Beyond. The invaders who now ruled them tried to eradicate it; but this fueled Shra'kufan fervor and validated the new doctrines. After a few years, they realized that the new religion expedited their oppression, and they then supported it. In less than a decade, the Shra'kufan religion, although small, was established.

The religion persisted without substantial modification over the next thousand years. The industrial innovations of the 1800s infiltrated these remote regions and started minor, yet in the long run, critical shifts not only in belief but also action. These alterations led to the terrorism which characterizes one of their sects today.

The Ballag'cha, the Protectors or Guardians, first developed around 1000 A.D. The sect believed torture brings one closer to the Eternal, a conviction originally connected to the Shra'kufans and, with this sect, generalized to any other person. Thereafter, in the name of the Eternal Beyond, a fervent believer would torture or kill an unsuspecting and innocent traveler as a religious favor. This small sect remained peripheral until industrial advances invaded their area. They then became more active and obtained support by mainstream Shra'kufans. However, in 1843, the only nephew of the sultan, a pasha or governor of a territory, returned from an ordeal without a hand, one eye, half his right calf, and a large section of his abdomen hollowed and blistered by glowing coals. He also could not speak correctly, due both to brain damage and injury to his tongue, lips, and larynx.

Following this outrage, the sultan started a campaign to exterminate the Shra'kufans. Because they lived in remote areas in the mountains or foothills and had maintained their isolation, finding them was impossible. In addition, Shra'kufans had no territorial boundaries. As soon as threat to their safety became clear, the vulnerable moved. In reaction to the sultan's attempt to destroy them, Shra'kufans became even more secretive and made the Ballag'cha a clandestine sect, intended to act as police and protection. Killing or torturing individuals who were not a threat, as had happened with the sultan's nephew, now became taboo, since it exposed Shra'kufans to retaliation. Membership in this sect involved only the most devout and trustworthy. Potential members proved themselves by enduring the most grisly of tortures. This terrorist sect persists to the present day.

After the sultan's decree in 1843, being a known Shra'kufan became a death sentence. The Ballag'cha killed anyone suspected of informing outsiders about the religion, and as a logical progression, slaughtered those who knew about the Shra'kufans since that knowledge put them all at risk. Murder matched their belief system as it released the victim from the earth and allowed him to merge with "the Eternal." The more torturous the bloodshed, the greater the cleansing. Only the most "pure," however, could engage in the honor of religious sacrifice.

The changes due to industrialization, coming from Western influences, threatened the Shra'kufan way of life. Manufactured products lured the body away from the Eternal, bringing it into the world again. The Shra'kufan elders asserted that industrialization would undermine the most basic patterns of nature. In opposition to modernization, Shra'kufan beliefs and practices became more rigid and contact with outsiders was, whenever and wherever possible, eliminated. The attempt to stop the infiltration of industrial advances failed. The desperate Shra'kufan solution was to halt the inevitable changes by destroying them as they invaded their territory. Telegraph lines, for example, were destroyed. Railroad tracks were undercut so that the bed gave way from the weight of trains. Roads were sabotaged. Two examples: passage blocked by boulders or the foundation weakened so that traffic would break the road. The sustained threat of modernization galvanized the sect into becoming more militant and self-protective.

Based on the most up-to-date information, the present-day Ballag'cha are uncompromising in their duty. Mercy is nonexistent. They track down every lead and err on the side of caution by killing any person who is a threat and destroying any suspected evidence.

My skin prickles. I rub my eyes, trying to lessen the ache that has crept in. My mouth is so dry it feels filled with cotton. A sip of water will help. I move to the closet where I keep a jug. The offices in Kramer used to be dormitory rooms, and the closets are large. I step into the closet and reach up to take a jug from the lower shelf. The swig refreshes me. I wander around the office and discover that I'm pacing like a trapped animal. I stop, stare at the closed blinds and then at the door. My behavior is reflexive, automatic. Looking for an escape? I smile at the accuracy of my insight and look down at the desk. The unread stack looks ominous. I force my eyes away, a lump developing in my throat. I wish someone, anyone, were here to share this. I long to be with Deana.

She is sensitive to my emotional state, and based on how I have been reacting, I won't be able to hide it from her. I need to concoct an excuse for arriving home after they are all asleep. If Deana is awake, I'll talk and my distress will be unmistakable. What do I do? It is now around 8:40. I better call and explain, but what can I say? I lift the phone and pause, considering my words. Holding the handset off the cradle, I can hear the dial tone. The right words finally come. I dial. Three rings and the answering machine picks up.

"You have called," says a young voice that then giggles, "You have called . . . What do I say next? Oh, you have called the Butlers. We sure would like you to leave a message." I smile as I hang up. They're not home yet. What do I do now?

I pace again. Thoughts about what I've been reading come to mind. Are the Shra'kufans dissociative? Their exposure to pain must lead to the psychological mechanisms designed to reduce it or make it tolerable. Since I know about dissociation, it would seem, based on the literature and my clinical experience, that most of them are dissociative. I know about remarkable "feats" that patients with dissociative disorders perform. The bookshelves lining my office include many books addressing these issues.

Dissociation and severe abuse have also provoked public and professional disbelief. Serious doubt about the frequency and severity of child abuse preceded its acceptance as true, whether by professionals, the media, or the public. Similar questions have been associated with multiple personality disorder. Even professionals—psychologists and psychiatrists—will say "I don't believe in it" despite its official recognition in the American Psychiatric Association's diagnostic classification scheme.

Given the Shra'kufans' low profile and (according to Rick) the almost nonexistent newspaper reports, they would be unknown in their own countries. Only a few, rather specialized and intelligence-linked individuals would even know about them. I understand why they would frighten the few people who have information about them and yet be unrecognized in their homeland. As I think about this, my chest and jaw tighten up. I'll try calling home again; that should help. An answer.

"Hello, hon? It's me."

"Hi, sweetie. Missed you today."

My thoughts are in a jumble. I want to blurt out that a terrorist murdered Rick, that I'm terrified of his killer, that we all might be at risk. But I'm worried about telling her, that in doing so I'm putting her and the kids in danger. I can't. I can't do something that might create problems.

"Jason?"

"Sorry. I got distracted." I have to get a hold of myself. "Yeah, I missed you too. You must have just gotten home. You didn't answer a short while ago."

"We stayed a little too long."

"I was envious of your time at the lake. I wanted to be there with you and the kids. But I have to stay here longer. I got an emergency call from the client who was in crisis last week. He's coming over soon. I'll work till he gets here. He's in rough shape, so I might work late. The way things have been going, I'll get home after eleven, after you're all asleep." I cringe inside. I lied to my wife, something I have a rigid commitment to never do.

"Just don't wake me; I'm bushed. I guess we'll start on that other project another evening. OK, lover?"

"I did not know until our marriage how exciting such projects are. How are things at home?"

"Since we got here five minutes ago . . ." Deana's voice gets fuzzy and muted.

"Mark, please stop pouring juice and get ready for bed!" I hear a scratching noise as she brings the phone closer. I can't figure out what it is.

"Ann fell asleep in the car. She stayed asleep when I carried her in and is zonked out on the couch in the family room. But Mark is still excited and, after he drank part of a glass of juice, decided he'd pour it back and forth from glass to glass. Mark, stop it! We had a great time. Ann swam today, Jason. I wish you had been there to see it. Maybe we have a swimmer on our hands."

"My daughter the athlete! I wish I had been there too. Sounds like you had fun. Did you have dinner at the Inn?"

"No. Hot dogs from the grill, chips, potato salad, and pickles. No mustard! You wouldn't have liked it, Jason. Popsicles from the local store for dessert. We all walked down to buy our own. It was a quick and easy meal. Mark, get off the counter. Jason, I've got to get him. See you later; I mean, in the morning."

"Love you. I really love you, Deana. I mean it."

"Jason, is something wrong?" I can hear her distraction. She wants to respond to Mark but knows there was something discrepant in what I said.

"I realize, being away all day, how much I miss you and love you—you and the kids. That's all. Bye, love."

"Bye, Jason." I can hear a question in her voice. "Mark! Bye."

That was emotional. Wait and let the feelings settle. My throat and chest remain tight. A few more slow, deep breaths and I should be able to think again. I hate lying to her, even for her protection. Secrets within secrets! The connections are fascinating: Secrecy because of the Shra'kufans has translated into secrecy for Rick and now secrecy with me. What secrets are they hiding from themselves? What secrets am I hiding from myself?

Talking with Deana is out of the way for now, though I'll confront it again tomorrow. What if she calls back? She won't because she thinks I'm working. But when I imagine answering the phone, I realize that someone in the hall could hear me talking. I would be more protected if I put my telephone on call forwarding. That way the calls will go to voicemail after first ringing in to my secretary. I'm surprised at my paranoid thinking. But this will give me the time I need to think, and I can now figure out what to do.

The ominous stack of papers on the desk repels me. I feel the tension in my body, pulling away. I stand and turn aside yet continue to crane my neck to look back at the stack. I rotate to face away and hang my head, knowing soon I'll confront it. I do. I rub my face and end up with both hands over my mouth staring at the pile.

"Danger," Rick had written. "Do not open," Rick had written. He was right. Damn him, he was right. I never should have opened this. Maybe I should have given it to Miller and let him assume the risk. I have to force myself to take a step closer. My legs feel heavy and immobile. I close my eyes and reach out to touch the back of the chair. My body shudders when I open my eyes and see the heap. I drop to the chair and close my eyes again. My heart is pounding, stomach nauseous. Eyes still closed, I slide a reluctant hand along the desk. A swallow and a deep breath. I feel tears form just before I open my eyes.

The Ballag'cha uses a specific poison as its primary method to kill. "Samatma," the name of the poison, means "sky fruit" and also "blue sky." They distill it from a red evergreen berry that only grows on the upper slopes of mountains in this area. When distilled, the color is a vivid blue, not unlike the sky, and according to Shra'kufan beliefs, it allows the victim to join with the Eternal Beyond the Beyond in the heavens. Religious dogma and ritual pervade the distilling process that entails mixing other roots, leaves, and berries. These details are guesswork. Shra'kufan religious texts assert that the process of making Samatma, the experience of taking Samatma, and the outcome of becoming one with the Eternal Beyond the Beyond are three spiritual equivalents. Ascent to Heaven, symbolized by the blue of the Samatma, releases earth and pain, symbolized by the red of blood, which, in the ascent, is transmuted into the purity of freedom and the Beyond. Traditional Shra'kufans use Samatma only during their religious ceremonies. It is an integral part of their highest rituals where, unsubstantiated stories tell, the aspirant ingests the drug yet lives, thus proving religious progress and readiness to assume a significant role. If the person dies, he was not ready to lead and rejoins the Eternal.

For the Ballag'cha, however, Samatma is the prescribed method to assassinate, since this drug establishes a direct connection to the Eternal Beyond the Beyond. Killing nonbelievers with Samatma is a religious act which is quick, yet painful. The Ballag'cha violate their vows if they kill any other way, since different murderous acts (use of guns, knives, or strangling, for example) use the sinful body or earth-derived products as instruments. Despite these restrictions, in the modern social and political context, the Ballag'cha in fact resort to other methods. This might represent a shift in their views.

I can't read any more. I must digest what I've been learning.

I have in my possession some secret, sacred texts belonging to these deadly Shra'kufan terrorists, the Ballag'cha. They will kill to get them and will kill whoever knows of their existence. Besides my being the only witness, the assassin now has two more reasons to kill me: I know the terrorists exist and I have the texts. I don't know if he knows this; but when or if he does, he has reason to kill me. As I reflect on this, what I have asserted seems bizarre and improbable. Had I read these materials earlier I wouldn't have believed it. After what I have experienced, I believe every word. "Believe" is the wrong word; "know to be true" fits better.

What can I do? How will I keep myself alive? The situation is so preposterous that I doubt anyone would believe me! I can't tell anyone because of the risks, yet that seems to be the only way to get help in what is an impossible situation. I can't deal with this on my own. I'm only a college professor. I know nothing about protecting myself from terrorists, let alone physical self-defense.

I want to stay alive and want to protect my family. How can I do that? Will I die like Rick? If not, will I spend the rest of my life running from assassins? Constantly looking over my shoulder? Continually wondering when disaster might strike? Is my family doomed? Would the Shra'kufans kill them too? The prospect of their killing my family is chilling. My temples start to throb and my jaw aches.

I must develop a plan. First, I will leave after dark so he cannot recognize me. Do I return to work tomorrow or stay home? Do I leave town and hide? Shit, I'm exhausted. I find no solutions, only more questions, more uncertainty and more problems. I can't stop pacing. Back and forth, back and forth. If I could only talk to him, to them, whoever "he" and "they" are. I don't know if the assassin can speak English. I assume he does; otherwise he wouldn't have been sent to this country. If he does, would he wait long enough to listen before he killed me? If I wanted to contact their leaders before he finds me, I wouldn't know how. I don't even know their names.

Any communication, any communication at all, makes plain I know something, that they exist as a religious group. I would die as soon as I made my appeal. I can't even contact them, let alone negotiate.

Why so damn secret? Why death to anyone who knows? Yes, I know what I've read but I have difficulty accepting it and it makes little sense right now. It doesn't fit the way the world works, at least the way my world works.

CHAPTER 14

8:55 p.m.

If only I were a Vietnam veteran who had learned to kill, to defend himself. I'd use a gun or a knife or piano wire to decimate this asshole. Who am I kidding? Given my personality, I couldn't do that. And killing one or two assassins would not protect me. Others would still track and kill me.

I'm pacing again. I'm baffled to discover myself pacing with no memory of standing. Pacing, pacing while all these books watch from their shelves, silent. I've read most of them, but I always collect more books than I have time to read. Fascinating books flood to awareness. I take the Greens' book, *Beyond Biofeedback*, from the shelf. Flipping through the pages, I recall images from their film *Biofeedback: Yoga of the West* and the extraordinary feats performed by yogis and other "normal" human beings.

Footage in the biofeedback film shows Jack Schwarz pushing a sail needle all the way through his biceps. The needle is rusty, dirty, and germ covered. The wound does not bleed, heals instantly, and never gets infected. Another part of the film shows a yogi who lowered his metabolism and was then sealed in a Plexiglas box. Despite the lack of air, he survived for a long time. I don't recall the exact time. In their book, the Greens report on Swami Rama, who "stopped" his heart and performed other amazing physiological feats. At a conference, I talked with the psychiatrist who took Swami Rama to the Greens the first time. Smiling, bemused if not amazed, I recall how he described his first meeting with the Swami.

"Bring the doctor here!" the Swami ordered. This psychiatrist was the only doctor in the vicinity, so they brought him to the Swami, not knowing if he was the intended "doctor." He found one of the Swami's legs empty of blood. It looked dead. Then the Swami filled it again so it was normal. The Swami also created and dissolved, in only a few minutes, cysts the size of golf balls.

Astonishing, but from a different point of view, hypnotized people can stop sensory input. If a light flashes at a specific speed, researchers know how the brain responds. When these hypnotized subjects hallucinated a box, the brainwave showed that nothing was getting through to the brain even though the retina was being stimulated by light. Light was going into the eye but not getting to the brain. Somehow these hypnotized people were using their minds—or should I say, an altered state of mind—to stop sensory input.

And multiple personalities. Their astonishing feats also push the limits of human functioning. I had not even heard of Multiple Personality Disorder in my graduate course work. During my internship year, one of my supervisors was knowledgeable about this new field. In the first month, she taught me about dissociation and its relationship to trauma. I was polite though skeptical. A single body couldn't contain two different identities, let alone the eight to thirteen that she claimed was the average.

While still a novice intern, I worked with three clients diagnosed as MPD. The first one was inadvertent. This client had been accused of shoplifting, but all he claimed to remember was the plainclothes detective stopping him in the parking lot. The evidence was inside his underwear, under an armpit, and in both shoes. His pockets bulged with chocolate bars. Store security stopped him at the door. Ironically, he had the money to buy the stolen merchandise. From my point of view, he was diagnosable as an antisocial personality and lied to save himself from the consequences. I had training to use direct and clear confrontation, almost aggressive, with these kinds of clients, since they lied to get out of difficulties. This was the way to break through their automatic denial.

"Bullshit!" I confronted him. "You aren't taking responsibility for your actions. You're trying to wiggle out of the fact you screwed up and got caught. You are lying. Lying to save your ass."

"Listen, you GODDAMNSONOFABITCH, nobody's going to talk to *me* that way! He *deserved* to get caught. We do all we can to take care of that weak-kneed slob and he wouldn't buy us that candy. JUST ONE FUCKING CANDY BAR!"

My mouth went dry as this frightened, confused, and diminutive man transformed into a volatile streetfighter. It wasn't his words that rattled my composure. This was a different person. He looked big and imposing. His face and body were different. I stared in disbelief, trying to figure out what was happening to my eyes, what was taking place in front of me. It made little sense. I was plunged into a twisted reality in which people were not as they appeared. I was in a waking dream.

I tried to appear professional. I controlled my anxiety, established a relationship, met this new alter personality, and ended the session. Then I ran to my supervisor for support and help. My work with individuals with multiple identities made a compelling introduction. I earned a reputation as the intern who worked with MPDs, and within a week, I got two more referrals. By the end of my internship year, I had worked with eight MPD patients, gotten exclusive training from a leader in the field, and attended a conference devoted to dissociation.

A paper session at that conference reported that MPD individuals could influence their brains at the cellular level. They could influence single cells. Amazing. I remember the incredulous expression on the presenter's face, a pharmacologist. "The injection should have knocked this person unconscious, yet he was sitting upright on the examination table, carrying on a normal conversation. He acted as if no drug was in his system. And then, when he shifted personalities, he dropped to the table like a rock.

"The implications for human functioning are staggering," continued the pharmacologist. "He must have been influencing the metabolism of single cells in his brain."

I heard another presentation that showed MPD individuals could influence their immune systems. One alter personality was deathly allergic to oranges while another was not. If the nonallergic personality ate an orange and, before it was metabolized, the allergic personality came out, the body had a lethal allergic reaction. Yet, if the nonallergic alter remained in control, no reaction followed. What are the implications of this for us "normals" if the mind is able to turn an allergic reaction on and off?

I'm looking at books again. So many are relevant and interesting. But are they useful in my current predicament? A passage from Tarthang Tulku's book *Knowledge of Freedom* comes to mind:

> The sensation we now call fear can be a gateway to inner awakening. Whenever we taste fear, we can suspect that we are close to knowledge we have hidden from ourselves. Whenever we approach the boundaries of our experience and begin to perceive something new, fear will arise like a shadow, concealing whatever we most need to know.

How does this help? What does confronting fear accomplish if I will die? How can this be useful when a thief points a gun at me in a dark alley? The outcome is obvious. Death. Anyone would be scared. In another book, he writes about transforming all sensations into positive and enhancing states. How can my current situation be positive? Survival, staying alive, is the issue. I toss the book on the desk.

I again didn't notice my pacing. And now, in my mind, with my jaw clenched, I hear my tai chi teacher quoting the *Tao Te Ching*. I take the book from the bookshelf and open it to the passage: "Learn water wisdom. Yield and be preserved whole. Lose the battle, win the war. Yield and be preserved whole. Lose the battle, win the war. Yield and be preserved whole!"

I shake my head, trying to clear it. How can I do this? I see no way. I know for a fact that the Shra'kufan assassins will kill anyone who knows about them or has the texts. I can only yield by allowing him to kill me. How can I win then? By dying, he wins and I lose! If I lose the battle, I lose the war and everything else too! I notice that my body is in a strange position. I'm leaning forward, right arm locked straight with the hand flat on the closet door, left arm dangling, so that my body angles forward and I am looking down at the dark floor. I'm puzzled by what I'm doing. Now, I hear my teacher saying another of his favorites: "When you are stuck, turn. When you are stuck, change. Change is the only truth that is unchangeable."

CHAPTER 15

Dusk, 9:33 p.m.

The wonders of a digital clock . . . when set accurately. I might as well get ready to leave. I don't want to stay here. I don't want to read or to think any more; I want to escape.

What do I need to take? I turn in a circle, scanning the office. My gaze stops at the stack of papers on my desk. Do I take it? As I consider straightening the stack, I take a step away. I don't want to touch it. I envision locking the pages in my desk, the only good hiding place. Then a realization hits me: I can't leave them in the office. If he breaks in, he will find them. Then he will know I know, and he will definitely try to kill me. Despite my aversion, I must keep them with me.

I will take them home but I can't let Deana or the kids know about them. I can't let them know. Or see the texts. Given that possibility, should I change my mind and leave them here? As I consider again leaving them in my office, I'm convinced he could open the desk. They are safer with me. I must take them and keep them hidden.

I move toward the desk realizing to my consternation I need to handle that stack of papers to pack them up. I place them back into their envelopes and then into my backpack. Might as well take the course outlines, the unfinished letter, and a tablet of paper. I have pens at home. What else? I scan my office, looking for cues that can help me decide what else to take.

The room looks so ordinary. The contrast with my internal state exacerbates my anxiety. I want to do something . . . anything.

A solution comes to mind. Since it is time to leave, I can actually do something. I'll give in to my paranoia and peek through the blinds to check the front of the building. Pull the edge of the blind back to glimpse outside. The glow created by the streetlights reveals a person wearing blue jeans entering the south door, the one I entered earlier this evening, the one that stays unlocked, the one that opens to the hallway outside my office. I hear the door rattle as it closes. I visualize the hallway stretching thirty yards from my office to the lobby where that door just closed. I wait, listening. The sound of footsteps drift down the hall. I hold my breath. He could go up the stairs. No. Now too far. He's past that place. He's coming down here. Stopped in front of my door? Yes. Right outside. I hear rustling and shuffling. What's the person doing? Is he looking at my door or at my neighbor's across the hall? Did I remember to lock the door? Think, think. I remember locking the door but was that earlier today or this evening?

Knock, knock, knock.

I will not answer it. My heart is pounding and I don't know what to do. Do I wait? Do I block the door? How long do I stay in here?

Knock! Knock, knock.

Silence.

Knock!

I jump.

The door handle jiggles.

Locked! I let the air out of my tired lungs. I didn't know I was holding my breath. I feel relief and I can breathe.

"That Butler is *never* in his office. I should know better than to come over in the evening."

More relief floods me. It is John, a student who wants last semester's paper. He left several messages earlier in the week. Since he is there, I assume the assassin shouldn't be, and I turn on the light. With the shades closed, if the assassin's there, he probably couldn't see into the office from outside. Open the door.

"Hi, John," I say to his back. He is already several paces down the hall.

"Gahh," he blurts, twisting around, eyes wide.

"Sorry. Didn't want to come to the door since I was working on something. When I heard your voice, I knew what you wanted."

"Oh. Yeah! OK!" He takes a deep breath and swallows. "Well, I know you aren't here much at night. Just took a chance. Do you have my paper?"

"I have it right here," I say, handing it to him. "I set it aside for you when I got your note."

"Thanks, Dr. Butler. See ya."

"Bye, John."

Feeling incredible relief, I watch him walk down the hallway and turn the corner into the lobby. I hear quick, rubber-squeak steps as he leaves. I lean against the doorjamb, enjoying the calm. The squeaky steps stop. I glance up and see the assassin standing at the far end of the hall, in the lobby. He stares, unmoving, down the long corridor between us.

I yank myself back into my office, heart pounding, eyes and ears straining to pick up clues. Stay or run? Better not close the door and give myself away with the creaks. I zip my hand to the wall and click off the lights. Did he recognize me? He was a long distance from me, and the lighting is poor. Holding my breath and being still is a childish response, as if he wouldn't know I'm here, as if he would forget he saw me. But I do it anyway.

Footsteps! Which way are they going? Closer. Still closer. Slow and deliberate. Now stopped. What do I do? If I don't close the door soon, he'll see the open office and know where I am. Maybe he can see it now. Better do it. A groan and then a creak accompanies the slow closing of the door. Was it loud enough to hear above the other random noises in the building? At least I know I locked the door.

How can he be here? How did he find me? It is eerie—it is perplexing to have him right down the hall.

Now be silent. The outline of the door glows, the bottom edge highlighted by a bright strip of light. I can kneel on the floor to look as he goes by. I can hear his steps, slow and steady, the unmistakable squeak of rubber soles. They are near now. He is right in front of the door. I can see his shoes—dirty mauve gym shoes. I'm thrown back into the memory of seeing them land in front of my face as I fell against Rick's office door. My fear and confusion tumble back over me.

He has stopped. His feet shift a little as his toes readjust. Holding my breath, I wait. I hear a faint rattle of the doorknob. I swallow so loudly he must have heard. Sweat pops out on my neck and back.

The toes of his shoes rise and turn toward the door. I see a knee come down on the floor. He will look under the door. It is dark in here, so he can't see anything, but I scoot back anyway, eyes fixed on the glowing strip of light at the bottom of the door. I am breathing quickly. Must quiet down. His dark shadow blocks the light as he looks under the door. He shifts back and forth. After an agonizing time, he stands. I relax. I can feel my chest loosen and my shoulders drop.

The shadow does not move for what feels like several minutes. What could he be doing? What is he waiting for? If he breaks into my office, then I'm dead for sure. What could I use to protect myself? What? Think. Think. Scissors! I have a pair of large scissors. I make my way to the desk, careful not to make noise as I get the scissors. I sense this is wrong, yet I feel stronger and safer holding a weapon. At any other time, I wouldn't handle a confrontation with violence, but this is different. Fury surges up in me. If that guy comes at me, I will stab him! I will kill him! I can see my arm slamming the scissors into his chest again and again and again. I scream at him in my mind. THIS IS FOR RICK! THIS IS FOR ALL THE OTHERS! THIS IS FOR ME! YOU'LL NEVER DO IT AGAIN! NEVER!

I return to the door, legs quivering. There are no shadows under the door. While I was getting the scissors, he left. Where is he? I listen, holding my breath. A scraping noise travels along the vertical edge of the door. I should have known the assassin wouldn't stop. He is sliding something between the door and the frame to push back the latch bolt.

I smile, feeling smug. Several years ago, when I locked my keys in the office, I could break in with a credit card. That's what he seems to be trying to do now. The administration finally admitted that the offices were not secure and installed plates over the latch bolts so thieves could not break in.

A thought jars my self-assurance: He is not a typical thief. This is the assassin the Shra'kufans sent to the United States to get the texts. He must be one of their best at sleuthing and breaking in. The scraping continues near the latch. I stand immobilized, to the side of the door, staring, mouth open. I imagine putting my shoulder to the door to stop him from opening it. Then I consider his strength versus mine and give up. I clutch the scissors in my fist. The noises slide down the door to the latch plate, continue, and then disappear. He pulled the device out of the door. It worked! The plate kept him from opening the door.

I stare at the dim outline of the door, trying to catch any hint of what he might be doing on the other side. He must be skilled at breaking in. It will not be long before he opens the door. Now he knows I am here. Well, perhaps not me but someone, someone in this office with my name on the door.

Dark shadows of two feet appear in the light on the floor at the handle side of the door. Diffuse rubbing sounds emanate from the door's edges. Is he sliding his hands around its contour? Is he trying to find other ways to get in? The door rattles in its frame. He must be putting his shoulder to it, trying to find out how solid it is. I'm surprised by how soon the rattling stops. The shadows of his feet seem to leap away. Then I hear soft, running steps back down the hallway.

CHAPTER 16

Dark

What is going on? Why did he leave? Did he give up? I want to believe he left but I know he wouldn't do that. A door to my right slams, followed by a clunk. New noises come from the direction he ran, the foyer I walked through entering the building. The sounds are familiar but I can't place them. At first it is an indistinct undertone that transforms into whistling, getting louder as it enters the foyer. The custodian! He starts work at ten o'clock. It must be ten. And he is down there locking the doors. I'm locked in. No. Not correct. Other people are locked out. I can leave any time, through any door.

Is he gone? I stare at the door as if it will answer. How long do I wait? What do I do? Again no answer.

The layout of the building, a remodeled dorm, is peculiar. It houses faculty offices, a counseling center, the graduate school offices, and, on this floor, in a weird juxtaposition, a series of hospital rooms. If I exited my office and turned left, after five paces I would walk down two steps and, presto, I'd be in the office. Its entryway is open, with no door. Ironically, there is an actual door on the opposite wall of the main office, which the staff lock at five. No one has come in or out of the main office or I would have heard that door bang shut. It is now locked, so only someone with a key can enter. The hallway to my left and main office are safe. So, I can exit my office, turn left, and run into the main office in seven steps without meeting the murderer, since he went the other way. Once I get through the main office door, I have four options: left out a main entrance door, right out the side door, down the stairs to the basement, or up the stairs to the second and third floors. With those options I might escape.

Making this plan confronts me with its risks. I'll be vulnerable. If this guy gets me tonight, I will never see Deana and Mark and Ann again. Shit! That is the worst fear. The pressure builds in my throat and behind my eyes, then gets stronger and bursts out first as a sob and then uncontrollable tears. I try to control it, to make it as quiet as I can. Painful. Hurts my chest. The ache in my throat and tension in my face mirror my anguish. No goodbye. No "I love you, all of you, so much." No "I'm sorry I had to leave you all this way. I didn't know. I didn't choose it." "It's not fair." "I'm sorry. I'm sorry!" I have done nothing to deserve this. I pound my fist on the wall. I want to destroy something. There's a pile of tissue in my wastebasket. I have no awareness of using so much. I do not want to die. I will not die.

The custodian opens the stairwell door between my office and the foyer to the right. His whistling softens after the door bangs shut. I can hear the jingle of his keys.

Think this through. I parked the moped behind Kramer Hall, off the sidewalk and next to the exterior door he locked. The most direct route to that door is back toward the foyer. It's good I didn't drive the car. I would have had no choice but to walk through the open parking lot. It didn't start that easily the past few mornings when it sputtered and then finally caught after several tries.

How long has it been since he was here? Ten, five minutes? How long do I wait? I know he went back down the hall. But how far? Where? Did he go outside? Should I leave now while the custodian is nearby?

I peek around the blinds. It seems dark enough that, if I get outside, I can hide.

The custodian's keys jingle as he whistles past my office. I hear the flick on and then off of the main office lights, the muted slam of the main office door, and then the familiar rattle of the outside door as he locks it. He has one more exterior door to lock on the ground floor before he goes up to the third floor to empty trash and clean bathrooms.

Get ready to leave. My briefcase stays here for once. It would hinder me too much. I'm glad I keep a backpack in the closet. I slip the texts inside. Anything else to put in the backpack? No. Zip the backpack closed, put on my coat. Check the pockets. Yep, my keys and wallet are there. Slip the backpack on. I'm ready. I take a deep breath when I reach for the doorknob. My hand stops. Wait. Listen. Continue listening. How long do I wait? Another breath.

Something down the hall. My mouth goes dry. The sounds remind me of his footsteps. Are they? Turning my ear to the door, I listen. I can't distinguish the sounds. Then, I hear it; the squeak of rubber gym shoes. He was down the hall. He was waiting. As soon as the custodian started up the stairs to the third floor, he came back to my office. In my imagination, I cower across the room, watching as the door smashes open, crashes against the wall, and the assassin rushes at me.

A memory pops up. During a regular workday, student workers sometimes get the master key to let themselves into my office and drop off tests. That way the booklets don't lay out in the open, available to passersby. When I'm working with a client, I sometimes ignore the knock. One session I had been helping a traumatized client access the pain of having been violated physically, despite his attempts to protect himself. The knock terrified him. On impulse, I grabbed my hefty straight-backed wooden chair and jammed the back under the door handle and the legs deep into the carpet. The door would not budge. My client and

I listened to the student's confusion and effort at trying to open the unlocked door. It relieved and delighted my client.

That's it. That's the solution. He knows I'm here, so I need not be quiet anymore. I snatch the same chair from the wall and bang it into place. I jam it down and then force it against the door as solidly as I can, shoving the back tight against the doorknob, legs deep into the carpet. Scratching sounds along the doorframe now evoke interest and not fear. What is he trying to do? The sounds are sharp and metallic. They move into the lock mechanism. Within fifteen seconds, I hear the lock retract. My stomach drops. I shove down on the upward-facing edge of the chair. Through the chair, I can feel him pressing on the door. Sit on the seat to add counter pressure. The edge cuts into my legs. First the handle turns and then a smashing vibration thuds through the door and the chair. He must have rammed his shoulder into it but the door did not move even a millimeter. This will work. I have a little time. I have to keep my weight on the chair; otherwise I would call the police. No. No. I can't afford to do that given everything that has happened.

I still need to escape. With him in the hallway, I am trapped. He smashes into the door. I hear a sharp crack as the door pops out a short distance and then crashes back. Will he try again? I look across the office at the curtained windows as if they had an answer. I hear the doorknob turn, and after a much longer delay, he delivers a powerful blow that rocks the door further. I hear the wood crack again. Nothing happens. I wait. Still searching the closed blinds for solutions, I realize that as he tries to smash through the door, I could escape through the windows. Why hasn't he done anything? I leap off the chair, worried he might at any moment hit the door. I check the strip of light under the door for shadows. Nothing. Where is he? I will take the chance. When I hear scraping or movement, I'll come back to reinforce the chair.

I'll peek through the gap between the blinds and the wall to see if he is lurking outside. Clear. Examine the small bushes and shadows for indications he might lurk there. Nothing out of the ordinary. Now, holding the bottom of the blind, slowly edge three slats away so there are no sudden movements visible from the outside. Holding the slats back, I move next to the wall to reach into the space and unlock the window.

Headlights swing toward Kramer. I yank my hand back, let the slats go, slink next to the wall, and, through the small gap, watch the car approach. I scan the blinds for telltale signs of movement. None. A second car follows. As the leading one passes under a streetlight, the rooftop lights of a police car spring into view.

My reactions confuse me. I want to open the window and yell for help; I want to hide because I'm sure Miller considers me his prime suspect. To my surprise, first the police car and then the second car turn onto the sidewalk that leads up to Kramer Hall. One stops ten feet away, in front of my office. Through my closed window, I hear the squawk of a police radio, and then out in the hallway, the unmistakable sounds of running toward the open foyer. I move away from the window and smile. The assassin must also have heard them arrive. I'm safe! Gingerly pulling the corner of the blinds away, I glance again. Miller ambles toward the entry, talking with a uniformed officer. I drop the blinds. It ripples, broadcasting my presence to an astute observer.

What do I do? I stare at the door. I am certain Miller suspects me.

Though I'm now shielded from the assassin, I can't tell Miller about him. He wouldn't believe me. In addition, all of Rick's writings make it clear it would be dangerous to tell anyone. That would place Miller and me at risk. Given the way our legal system works, my name would get out and then my whole family would be at risk too.

My attention snaps back to the room. I realize that I've just now been rehashing my arguments about not telling Miller because I want to, because I am terrified, because I need help. Yet the texts have spooked me, and I'm terrified about telling anyone. The entry doors down in the foyer rattle as they open. I startle. Of course, police can get into all the buildings; they have master keys. I slide the chair down and away from the door; then place it back against the wall. I hear their footsteps and muted voices. A handheld radio chatters. My eyes dart about the darkened room. The closet! There is plenty of room. I open the door and shut it behind me. I am now in total darkness.

I hear their voices outside my office door though I can't understand a word. A key rattles in the lock and the door opens. The switch clicks, and a glow seeps around the edges of the closet door. Both enter.

"Nothing out of place. He's not here." I don't recognize the voice. Footsteps move around the floor. Will they look in the closet? Is anything out of place?

"Nope." It is Miller.

"Miller, look at this broken picture. What do you make of it?"

"No foul play, placed against the wall like that and cracked. Over there on the wall, you can see where the hanger was by the glue marks. Must have fallen off the wall."

Silence lingers. No scraping feet, no grunts. Holding my breath, so my ears can hear the softest of sounds. Staring through the closet wall, I try to see what they are doing.

"This is strange. Nothing is out of place or looks suspicious." It was Miller again. "Let's look for him. Better have him picked up and brought in. Let's go."

Their heels click on the tile. A click and the glow along the edge of the closet door fades, plunging me back into the dark. The office door creaks as it closes. Miller's voice gets muffled as he moves into the hallway, and I hear static as his radio goes on.

"Radio, go to scramble. All other units, let's look for Butler and find . . ."

The door shuts. His voice becomes unintelligible and blurs with the sound of their footsteps.

I'm all right for now, but I am correct about being a suspect. I rehash Miller's words, "Better have him picked up and brought in." He wants to arrest me. I'm not just a suspect. I hear them wandering down the hall. I let myself out of the closet and creep to the door. As soon as they're gone from the area, the assassin will return. That was the mistake I made when the janitor was on this floor. As soon as Miller exits the building, I'll leave the office.

Why does Miller stay down in the foyer? I press my ear against the door but can't make out what they are saying. Frustrated, I move away from the door. They continue talking. Without warning, I hear the sharp rap of the bar as someone pushes open the exterior door, followed by the clatter of office doors as the air pressure changes. I move to my office door and put my hand on the knob. I'll wait for the rattle when the exit door closes. There it is.

I turn the knob quietly. Now, slowly open the door. Peek around the corner. I'm afraid to do it. I do not want to look. Heart is pounding. Here goes. To my relief, the dim hallway is empty. No one there. Into the hall and close the door. The door groans. Turn left and run down the hall, in view, to the main office where it is dark. I know of no other departmental office connected to the hallway without a door. Given this, I never understood why they bothered to lock the main door. Oh, well . . .

When I jump down the two steps into the office, the protective dark covers me. The window in the door on the other side of the office will give me a clear view into the hallway. I slip over to the window. I want to be careful while I check details.

Freeze! Back down the hallway, the stairwell door opens. Listen! I turn to look back at the dim opening to the hallway, straining my eyes to catch shadows or movement. One set of steps, and then whistling, whistling that travels away from me. He drifts off down the hall. I breathe again.

It now takes almost nothing to trigger the prickly sensation that courses through my body. Much too gradually, my body calms down. I glance back at the lighted opening to the hallway, which throws its light along the carpeted floor of the otherwise dark office. I breathe thanks to the carpet that muffles any of my noise.

A shade covers the window in the door. I can peek around the edge and see a stretch of wall on the opposite side. No one is there, and nothing is out of the ordinary. This is my best option. I have to take it. Might as well go to my right. There are more options going that direction since I can go up, down, or out. I hope this building is as confusing to him as it is to most newcomers. I visualize my actions before doing them. I open the door of the department office. In the hallway, exterior doors to the front of Kramer are ten yards to my left. In my mind, I turn the other way, where, one step to my right, there is a stairwell door. In the stairwell, stairs go up two floors. Two paces farther and stairs go down to the basement. One pace more leads to an exterior door. Down three outside steps and I have broken free.

Wait a moment. If I go back and exit through the stairwell halfway down the hall, where the custodian was just a little while ago, the moped will be next to the exterior door on the grass. But I can't afford to go back that way. He is back there somewhere. That's the direction he ran. No. Going that way is too risky. My original plan is better. I'll go out the exterior door near the main office, go toward town, and then circle back to the side of Kramer where the moped is. I should be able to stay hidden.

I feel elated by an idea and weight seems to lift from my shoulders. I can use the doorstop here in the department office to jam the stairwell door in case he is there and follows me. I hope he is not lurking in the stairwell. I would run right into him. I have the doorstop in hand and the backpack secured. Here goes.

I inch the knob around as silently as possible. Pull the door a smidgen. Wrap my hand around the edge. To open the door wide, I need to shove to counteract its strong spring. I'm ready. Scared but ready.

Now!

CHAPTER 17

Into the night

I shove the door open and lunge one step to my right. I glance back and fear flashes through me. Not ten yards away, peering out the double main entrance doors, stands the assassin. I never expected him here! His head pivots in my direction, and his body twists like a spring. I plunge through the door to the stairwell and slam the door shut with my shoulder. I drop the doorstop and ram it under the bottom of the door with my shoe.

If I go up the stairs, he will see me, hear me halfway to the second floor when he comes through the door. That will not work. I take two steps toward the next choice point: the stairs going down. My thoughts run fast and clear. He will hear me going down, just as he would have detected me going up. Either way, I would be trapped.

My only option is the exit door. I burst through it. I hear a crash behind me, then explosive yelling, sharp words in an alien language. I leap down the steps and out of the light, into the protective night. A second crash. Pushing into the welcoming dark, I hear a third. My heart pounds louder.

I bolt deeper into the dark, legs driving into the ground. I veer toward the vague silhouette of a short pine tree, hoping for safety. One stride. Two strides. The outer door smashes open, followed by the smack of quick running steps that stop. I stop too. I let my body drop flat to the ground. As I fall, I wait for the sound I'll make hitting the ground. I hit chest first, lose my breath, jar my head. My right cheek smacks the ground. The backpack jolts my spine. My heartbeat overwhelms my hearing. I want to groan but force it down. Did he hear me? He must be listening, searching. My hearing clears. Night sounds fill the air: a car speeds up; the marching band's bass drum thumps across the quad. A car drives by, windows open, and I can hear Madonna singing her newest hit, *Papa Don't Preach.*

I take deep, silent breaths. I see I landed a few feet from a large maple, the pine shielding me from behind. As stealthily as I can, I edge toward the tree. I keep the small pine between me and the door so I stay in its shadow. I slither toward the black trunk. It seems distant, impossible to reach. Slowly. Quietly. Does he see me? Hear me? I stop to check. Nothing. But I don't trust my safety. I listen as I crawl forward and at last, find safety behind the trunk.

Keeping my back against the tree, I inch up and then peek around its trunk. Light through the glass door throws a bright rectangle away from the building. If he is standing next to the door, I couldn't see him. I am forced to wait. But for how long? I imagine slipping away from the tree and my legs weaken with fear. A lump rises in my throat. I would love a drink of water. I settle down onto the ground to make my body as inconspicuous as possible, my back against the rough trunk. The bark snags my clothes, pulling them up. I scrunch my body down even more so he can't see me. I wait. Alert to any strange sound, my ears strain to catch the slightest hint of danger.

If we didn't live five miles out in the country, I wouldn't need to ride the moped. I could walk. If we had a bus system here or even a cab, I could take one home. I could call a friend to give me a ride. No. No. On second thought, I couldn't. I could never explain why I needed help to get home. Once I got home, how would I explain it?

I close my eyes and tune in to every sound, scanning for anything unusual. I slow my breathing so it doesn't interfere with my hearing. At first, my eyes dart toward every sound. Then I begin to relax my taut body and limbs . . . and my mind begins to quiet its frantic jumping around and panicky reaction to anything new. Surprisingly, I drift into a semi-alert, drowsy state of mind, occasionally snapping to alertness to check on a strange sound.

Suddenly, I pop back to being fully aware it is dark and I'm sitting on the ground back against the tree, hiding from a killer. I shift forward and stretch. How long has it been?

CHAPTER 18

10:08 p.m.

It has been more than half an hour. How much longer should I hide? My skin itches from sitting in the grass. The ground is hard and lumpy. My legs ache, and my neck and back are sore from keeping myself immobile. I peek again at the entryway. This time I see a slight movement beside the door, and the side of his face pops into view, only to disappear a half second later.

The assassin has been standing flat against the wall, hidden by the shadows alongside the door. The single exterior light shines downward from above the door onto the steps and sidewalk. It casts a V-shaped cone of light that misses the wall. As he leans forward, the light angles across his face while his body stays in the shadows. I can now detect his shadow sneaking along the wall, toward the front of the building. I'll leave once he has rounded the corner. It will be better not to go right to the moped. I'll walk toward town and then circle back to get it.

I sneak along the sidewalk, staying in the shadows, and then, as I increase the pace, can feel the backpack jostle against me. Dash across the first street. I guess I'm safe. Check to be sure. Slip behind some bushes and look back toward Kramer. I can see the side door and a section of the building's front. Nothing moves. I wait, scanning the terrain. Nothing. I look behind me, in the direction I want to escape, and notice that the sidewalk is in shadows. Staying behind the bushes, I walk backward, keeping my eyes on the open space between me and Kramer, and slide onto the shadowed sidewalk. I turn and run. Faster and faster.

Damn, I want to escape from Kramer. I'm pushing as fast as I can. Have I gone far enough yet? Stop and check. Slip behind a tree and listen. Check the street and then the sidewalk. Nobody. I can relax! The tension in my shoulders and back loosens. I realize how tense my abdomen is, how tight my breathing. I continue to notice unusual sounds and examine my escape route. Though I do not see or hear him, I don't feel comfortable. I must be cautious.

Two blocks away, the glow of headlights brings an intersection into shadowed relief. The car crosses and disappears. With a start, I realize it could have been a police car. I must watch for police cars and the assassin. I imagine being stopped and searched. The texts in my backpack will be evidence, my motive for killing Rick! Oh my God! I've been trying to keep them secret to protect myself, and Miller might accuse me of killing him to get these "priceless" texts. Am I being irrational? I have no way to test my reasoning. I unroll my imaginative scenario further. If I'm jailed, I would be even more frightened for my safety since I would be trapped. And—I'm certain about this—information would get to the press and . . .

I'm filled with dread. Envisioning my death revives that old pain of agonizing loneliness. I now feel loved and have a family. I'm living a rewarding and satisfying life. But our early relationship was littered with problems. I lost count of our conflicts, outright fights, and breakups. Deana and I have been through much work, pain, and growth over many years. I despair losing everything when it's so good.

As I walk block after block, hidden in darkness, hiding from cars, listening for threatening sounds, the feeling reminds me of the dark rainy nights when I felt desperate. I stop in the shadow of a large tree. I'm exhausted. I am fighting the anguish. I cross my arms and press my lips straight and tight. Memories surface and come into focus. Unthinking, I step forward onto the sidewalk and into the memories.

Dad believed his job in town would free him from the farm, and Mom would see him as more worthwhile and be happier with him. He never talked about this, or about anything else, but that was my impression. Despite his silence, he seemed more energetic after he worked in town. What helped financially was the discovery of oil beneath our fields, not as plentiful as Oklahoma but still lucrative. Tension at home dropped for a time. But, when she died, his motivation died with her.

After that, life worsened each year. My brothers and sister left. One brother moved to the east coast and worked in finance. The other brother moved to the west coast and worked in aerospace. And my sister married a rich executive manufacturing electrical devices for cars. Worries about money, despite the oil wells, forced Dad to rent our unworked fields to the neighbors, though we still planted ten acres and kept some of the animals. He advertised to sell some of his substantial acreage, though none that was oil producing. Dad gradually increased how much he worked as a mechanic; he began working two days a week, then three and finally five.

One night when Dad was drunk, he threw things at me. Then he came at me with a baseball bat. I ran out of the house. It was still light as I slogged along the gravel road, kicking stones in big showers. A neighbor gave me a ride to town. As I had nowhere to go, on a whim, I asked him to drop me off at the end of Deana's street. I paced back and forth in front of the house gathering the courage to knock. When Deana's mom opened the door, my composure broke and I sniveled, struggling to keep back a sob.

"Jason, what's wrong?" she asked as she put her arm around my shoulder. I cried as I tried to tell her. Convulsing with tears, unable to say another word, I felt a comforting hand on my shoulder, glanced up to discover it was Deana's, and lost all restraint.

By spring Deana and I were inseparable. Every day after school I was at her house, talking to her. No one had listened before. She pulled me out of my shell. I remember asking her what she saw in me. I worried it would end, and I asked for reassurance but believed none she gave. I kept my crush a secret for two years, acting like we were just friends. The embarrassment at telling her would have been crippling.

A car rumbles by and I find myself back in the present. I discover I am now two hundred yards from the moped, which stands next to the back door of Kramer Hall. I have, without paying attention to my route, gone north, then east, then south, then west, and now approach the moped from the east. The sidewalk snakes around until it goes straight for about forty yards to the door. I can see the moped on the grass next to the door. It is illuminated by the light over the door, and lampposts light the sidewalk every ten yards. To get there unseen, I'll stay on the grass, in the dark. But over the last twenty yards, I'll be visible. Exposed.

CHAPTER 19

10:28 p.m.

Am I being irrational? Who would believe this? I can't believe it myself. I imagine how my good friend and colleague Jim Rowen would react. Clearing his throat and pursing his lips, he would squeeze out his words with careful deliberation.

"Well, Jason," he would say, lengthening the *a*, "have you considered the possibility that perhaps there are other factors operating in...this...um, case?" A long pause would emphasize his concerned, piercing stare. I wouldn't miss the implication that "I" am the "case" in question and am not being rational.

The handlebars of the moped shine from the lights and the redbrick wall and exterior door are as clear as if in daylight. The lights along the sidewalk are bright enough to make visible individual blades of grass. I restrain my impulse to run. Too noisy. Walk briskly. And only on the grass that remains in the dark. Like a barrier blocking my escape, fifteen yards of sidewalk, exposed and lit, stretch toward Kramer. Get the key in my hand. Quicken the pace. Ten more yards. Time to sprint across the well-lit walk. I check all around to be sure.

There he is, just coming around the corner of Kramer. Only fifty yards separate us. How could he get there? Run! The backpack slaps my back and interferes with my stride. He also is running. Faster! How did he find me? Did he circle back and see me leave or watch from the other side of Kramer and see me approach from the east? I have to start the moped and get out of here. If it has those problems starting, what will I do? I picture him crashing into me, the moped smashing to the ground trapping my left knee, leaving my throat exposed to his poisonous hands. Key in. He's closer. Set choke to max. Closer. Push on the starting pedal. It doesn't start. Again, harder. Yes. It starts! Push off the kickstand and escape!

The pounding of his feet gets louder. High gear, full throttle. I'm away, gathering speed, but he's still close behind. It's not a powerful engine. His panting and the scuff of his clothes gets louder with each stride. The sidewalk is smooth and will allow the bike to gather speed. I bump onto the parking lot, turn left, speeding up. At last, he is losing ground. When I hit the street, I'll turn toward town. He might see me for blocks, so I'll confuse him by weaving in and out of various streets. Keep it full throttle. Don't pause for the stop sign. In the mirror, I see from his silhouette he is bending over, with his hands on his knees. I've escaped. I've escaped again. I'm safe . . . for now.

• • •

I zigzag several times, taking alternate blocks and routes. I feel comfort in knowing he cannot follow me to our house. Though, since he found my office, I bet he could discover where we live. My heart sinks again. He knows my name. He can find our address in the phone book. It even provides him a map if he doesn't know where our street is.

How did he find me? It is eerie. He not only found my office but almost caught me when I got the moped. How could he do that? And why, if he did those other two things, didn't he find me outside while I was hiding? Could he have an accomplice?

I let up on the gas and coast to a stop in a stretch of dark sidewalk. Hidden by large bushes, I hop off the bike and inspect the street. Nothing suspicious. Time to start home.

Back on the moped. Starting it takes a great deal of effort after it has warmed up. At least six times, I put all my weight onto the starting pedal and push down as hard as I can. I have to stop to catch my breath. I am wrung out! My eyelids burn from being overtired and stressed. I wait to regain my composure and to let the gas drain out of the carburetor. At last, the damn thing starts. I long to be home with my family. I want to feel the firm floor of my home where I am safe, and to see, to touch, and to hold Deana in my arms.

The edges of large, black houses outline the dusky opening of the street. My dim headlight opens a small patch of the darkness, and as I gather speed, the coarse pavement blurs. Bumps and holes in the road appear and jar the bike. A four-way stop looms. A car's lights are approaching from the left four or five blocks away. Shocking realization. I've been so intent on getting home I've been heedless of the police. I must cross rapidly before the headlights expose me. I gun the motor, continue down the street, sneak down an alley, and turn off the headlight. Think. Think this through. Riding without lights is foolish; riding with lights is risky. Be sensible. Avoid traffic and take side streets. Once out of town, stay on dirt roads. Then take the one that goes through the woods and lets out less than fifty yards from our house. When I get close, I can pedal or push to keep the engine silent. I set off again to put my plan into action.

I'm glad to be going home at this hour when I can stay hidden. And I'm relieved that the kids and Deana will be asleep. I couldn't hide this turmoil. Deana would notice and then what would I do? Tell her, and I guarantee her death. It seems I believe what Rick wrote. Or is she in more jeopardy if I don't tell her? I don't want to upset her or to put her in danger. But would she be better off knowing despite Rick's warnings?

Not one squad car appeared while I was in town, and so far not even a distant headlight has appeared on the county roads. I'm reassured. The trees are so dense they block the starlight. At other times, they part and I have a clear view of the stars. In front of me, the dirt road goes uphill, rising out of this dark, low section of the woods. The top of the hill is about thirty yards from the main paved road. Go left on that road, walk twenty-five yards, and there's our house. I press on the handlebars to push the moped up the incline. My shoes make a scrunching noise when I step on the gravel. The moped's wheels tick softly as they rotate. The crickets' song pulses loud and fills the night. As the grade gets steeper, I lean into the bike's weight and sweat moistens my back and arms. My breathing deepens. The front wheel wobbles when it strikes small rocks and then, a moment later, pulls to the side as it follows a hidden rut. I detect the crest by the shadow it cuts across the horizon above me. I've drifted to the right edge of the road and have stopped at the top next to the trees. I need to rest and gather my thoughts before continuing to the main road.

Of the many back roads crisscrossing the county, this is the closest to our house. Deana and I have walked along it countless times in the evening and on weekends. We've lost ourselves in its blaze of yellow and red in the fall and in its stark brown and white in the winter. And on vacation, we love exploring: walking down city streets, walking along a river, walking through woods and fields.

The night is quiet and peaceful, but something got my attention. A moment later, off to my right, I hear the throbbing of a car's engine in the distance. Our country roads form a rectilinear grid, each road one mile apart from the other. This car must be driving down the paved road that runs in front of our house. I wait until it passes. Even thirty yards back in the woods, I can detect the glow of the headlights through the trees as the car approaches. I peer down the dirt road to watch it pass. As the headlights brighten the pavement where the dirt road intersects the paved one, I see the dark shape of a car parked against the right-hand side of the dirt road. The car is back from the intersection, giving it a clear view of our house to the left. And, through the rear window, I see the unmistakable silhouettes of two heads that track the car as it passes through the intersection. Plunged into darkness, my eyes throb and shapes I could detect a moment ago are gone. That must be a police car! A police stakeout. I slide the moped closer to the trees at the side of the road, dismayed at the sounds I made.

Did they see me? Did they hear me? My heart pounds, and I crouch behind the moped as if it would hide me. Why would a car be on this dirt road at midnight? Two teenagers must be parked so they can make out. No. I know this is wrong. First, the two people were not sitting close together. Second, as the car passed, the two heads tracked its movement. Third, the car is closer to the main road than I first thought. If they were lovers, they would park further back. That car is parked where the occupants can observe the driveway and the front of our house. Had I ridden the moped up the hill, they would have heard and seen me. They would have nabbed me for sure.

CHAPTER 20

10:50 p.m.

I stay close to the trees bordering the road and swivel the moped around to start back down the hill. After a few steps I stop and stand motionless, listening for the sounds of a starting engine. The crickets are loud, and I have to strain to pick out any extraneous noises. As I push the moped downhill, I plan what to do. Another side road leads to a foot trail, passing a hundred yards behind the house. I'll ride down that trail, leave the moped in the woods, approach the house from the rear, and enter through the side door of the garage. Bushes grow along that side of the house so the door is invisible to the stakeout. Once inside, I'll keep the lights off, and they'll never discover I'm there.

At the bottom of the hill, the road runs straight and flat for a half a mile where it intersects another dirt road. That's the one I plan to take. Ride to the right for three-quarters of a mile and turn right again. Much too far to push. I know, given my distance from the stakeout and the intervening hill, that they won't catch me starting the moped. But my anxiety gets the better of me, and I continue pushing an additional fifty yards. Heart pounding with dread, I start it but do not get on. I hitch the backpack off my upper arms and onto my shoulders. Then I move two steps away to listen for the scrunch of tires on gravel. I scan the top of the hill for the glow of headlights, coiled in readiness to spring onto the bike, hit the kill switch, and run it amongst the trees along the side. I wait well over a minute. The engine sputters and, by the time I return, has died.

I sit on the moped and it takes four tries to start it again. Less anxious now, I begin my circuitous ride to the house. As I scan the trees along the road and keep my ears alert for any threat, memories of tai chi classes surface. I once again hear my teacher saying, "When you are stuck, turn."

We were doing Repulse Monkey, a movement similar to the crawl in swimming, only stepping backward. One hand out in front, the other hand has circled down from the ear to the chest. Next, with the palm, I pushed the monkey off the front arm. I was in the back row. Out of the corner of my eye, I saw the wall getting closer with each backward step I took. I wasn't sure what to do. Two more movements and I would collide with it. And then one.

"Turn," he said before we ran into the wall. "Have the wisdom to turn, to reverse your direction, to change your position. When you are stuck, turn. And be prepared to turn again."

After the turn, I was at the front of the class even though we continued moving backward. "Thousands of times," Mr. Shen said. When the backmost row got near the wall, we turned and then turned again, and again. I was unable do it, gave up, and, without trying, succeeded. To my surprise, no longer struggling had let me join the flow of the movement, and it came together. The effort, the attention, the wish to do it "right" had interfered with allowing it to happen naturally.

"Very good. Try again later." He looked around the room and sniffed through his nostrils. "I tell you, tai chi is a growing art. Very challenging. Challenge your ego. The less ego, the more energy. Very nice. Learn to yield. In tai chi we use non-doing, wu wei, or non-interference. Do you know wu wei?" He looked from student to student, waiting for an answer. Someone nodded. "Very good. Do not get in the way of what is natural. In tai chi we teach unlearning, not learning. We teach yielding, not force.

We do not hit force head on. We yield. This is the art of conserving energy."

Back in the present, the main road looms a hundred yards away. I turn off the headlight, slow down, and creep toward the intersection. When I arrive, I peer down the dark road in both directions. Nothing out of the ordinary. No cars coming. I continue across, knowing I'm almost home.

I remember the first time I met my teacher. It was a glorious day in early fall. The sky was an iridescent blue, the trees still green and the air cool. There was no need for a jacket. I was a college freshman taking a study break, ambling through downtown. On a whim I took a cross street and passed a store whose window advertised ta chi, qigong and Taoist meditation. People of all ages milled about inside. A doorway sign advertised a free introductory class about to start. As I walked up three wooden steps, the voice of someone talking with a heavy Chinese accent drifted out the open door. I was curious but decided not to take part.

"Take off your shoes and leave them by the entrance. Very good. Now sit down in a circle. In tai chi we like circle. No beginning, no end. In tai chi all movements are like circles or arcs, no sharp corners. In nature, no sharp corners."

I lingered at the entry to observe from a distance. Twenty people were on the floor in various positions, some in lotus position, others hugging their knees, and yet others lying on their sides. I had never heard of this. I didn't want to get involved and hovered near the entryway. The instructor did not look like an Asian master. He was short, with brown hair brushed straight back. His bushy eyebrows emphasized his black horn-rimmed glasses. He had removed a brown tweed sport coat, which now hung on the back of a chair, and a pair of brown wing-tipped shoes rested on the floor, centered beneath the lower rung. He wore brown slacks and a beige polo shirt. What jarred me most were his legs. As I walked up the last step, I saw him put rubber bands around the cuffs of his pants, to keep them snug against his leg. The appearance was similar to riding pants, bulging out at the sides. His brown argyle socks had a crisscrossed pattern of red, green, and yellow lines. His joyous good humor bubbled over as he bounced around in front of the seated group.

"I tell you, tai chi is the challenge of challenge. We use water wisdom. Water yields to all things, nourishes all things, but can be very strong. Learn the power of yielding." He pointed at a girl sitting at the front and gestured for her to stand. She did so, taking a step back and crossing her arms.

"Push," he ordered, holding up the back of his wrist. She grimaced while she examined his position and then stepped forward, pressing with both of her hands on his wrists. I could see the look of surprise on her face as she tumbled forward and rolled along the floor past him.

"There's nothing there!" she exclaimed. From her sprawled position, she stared at him open-mouthed.

"Very good," he said. "First lesson."

I found this difficult to believe. I shook my head. It had to be a setup. Not for me. I drifted down the foyer toward the door.

"You. Your turn."

I looked out the window in the door, preparing to leave. When I glanced back, I realized he was talking to me. I pointed at myself, asking, "Do you mean me?"

"Your turn," he repeated.

I took a step onto the floor.

"Shoes," he said. "No shoes. This is a sign of respect, a sign of yielding to the larger situation."

I slipped them off and walked to the front of the room where he waited. He raised his arm into the same position. As I got nearer to him, a deep silence seemed to emanate from him. He was standing. That was all. I already sensed a marked difference between us. I was agitated. Thoughts, plans, emotions, self-judg-ment, and analysis buzzed about like insects on a hot summer day. He was quiet. Settled. Just there.

I mimicked his position, stepped forward with my right foot, and raised my right arm to touch him with the back of my wrist. I shifted, and he moved with me. It was as if he was attached to my wrist, but delicately; I could barely discern it. I drew my wrist back a little, and he moved with me, matching me exactly. It was a weird sensation. I thought of what that girl said. "Nothing there." It was like pushing nothing. I pushed toward him perhaps six inches and then retreated. There was no resistance on his side. His wrist and mine remained connected. How can he defend himself? He was open and responsive! So, on impulse, I lunged forward, trying to knock him over. The experience was like fall-ing off a cliff and being flung by a magnetic field. All my force went into emptiness, and then out of nowhere, I felt my feet lift off the floor and I was sailing past him. My face had the same expression of surprise and wonder I had seen on the first student. After he pushed hands with anyone who was interested, he again invited us to sit on the floor.

"In the *Tao Te Ching*, it says, 'He who conquers others has force; he who conquers himself is truly strong.' In tai chi, ego is our true opponent. Learn to yield your ego. Learn to be weak; learn the strength of weakness. When you do tai chi, relax. No tension. Then your energy can flow to your whole body and mind and spirit, and you can direct your energy with your will."

I shift my attention to the present and guide the moped off the dirt road onto the trail that winds through the woods toward our house. I stop in an area that is flat and dry. I push the moped onto its stand, turn off the engine, and lock it. Among these trees, no one can see it from the dirt road. I thread my way under the branches and walk toward our backyard. Even though it is dark, I know the path. I can see the shadows of roots, large rocks, and dips in the ground, which I avoid. A break in the foliage allows me to view the back of the house, the kitchen and adjacent dining area. The warm glow of night-lights delineates the wooden door of the pantry, the white refrigerator, and the shadowed entrance to the family room. I'm encouraged and relieved to be so close. I quicken my pace.

Approaching the house, I reflect on my recollections from tai chi, those first and then ongoing lessons about yielding. I don't understand how to use these lessons. If I don't use force, how can I survive? Won't I be killed? I cannot imagine how to survive and not use violence. I can't envision a solution other than violence even though I'm committed to nonviolence. When I consider what I've learned about the Shra'kufans, if I kill this assassin, they will send others until I'm killed. Because of their actions, I am forced to respond in the same way.

I remember Mr. Shen saying, as he looked around the group of students, "I know you and I know your end. Because you are violent, you will have a violent death." Violence breeds violence. I smile remembering how he pronounced it. "Violence bleeds violence." And to meet violence with violence produces more violence.

I fish for a jumble of keys in my coat pocket, finger the surfaces, peering at them in the dark as if I saw them, stumbling on the right one, which I slide into the lock. The key to the side door of the garage turns with force and a jiggle. I have to pull the handle up to lift the door's bottom from the sill, but it grinds anyway. Don't make noise! Don't wake them up. I yank and push. The door pops loose and then scrapes. Listen for any reaction to the sounds. No response reaches my ears. Leave the garage light off. Retrieve the key from the outside lock, close the door, and lock it from the inside. I'm home. Pleasure and relief evoke a spontaneous, ear-to-ear smile.

CHAPTER 21

11:11 p.m.

Careful. Knock nothing over in the pitch-black garage. I make my way around the front of the car toward the steps leading to the door of the house. On impulse I lean against the hood for comfort and discover it is still warm. All are here under the same roof. I envision them in bed, sleeping. There is palpable comfort in knowing they are here.

I open the door into the back foyer near the kitchen. Safe. The backpack feels uncomfortable as I lean back on the closed door to the garage. Despite the lump at my back, warm comfort suffuses me. I close my eyes. Am I shutting out what might get in? Lock the door. That's absurd, since the automatic opener seals the garage door shut and I locked the outside door, the only other entry to the garage. Nevertheless, locking it is reassuring and hanging my coat on my hook next to the back door welcomes me home.

As I walk into the kitchen, my legs quiver. The night-light throws a diffuse glow over the stove, toaster, and microwave. Envelopes and magazines, today's mail, are scattered across the counter. Try to ignore the shaking. Anything interesting? I have to squint and angle them into the light—bills and advertisements. I'm trembling more. Stop it! I can't. I can't stop shaking! Damn, damn, damn! I'm terrified. My body won't stop. My teeth are chattering, and my stomach muscles are convulsing.

This is why people drink. Better not. I must keep my mind clear. I've got to rest or I won't survive tomorrow. Sit at the kitchen table until this runs itself out. Elbows on the table, head in my hands, I take a few deep breaths. Massage the back of my neck. My body, my mind settles. I envision Deana upstairs, asleep, and want to run up the stairs, wake her, and tell the whole story. No. I can't. I can't put her at risk.

Drink a glass of water and find something to eat. I'm starved. I forgot; I ate no dinner. Open the cabinet and fold my fingers around a glass. Don't clink it. Trickle the water so it's quiet. I let it run over my index finger to find out when it gets cold. The backyard is dark. No moon. I can't even see the trees I skulked through ten minutes ago. I recall seeing the refrigerator and pantry door outlined in the soft glow of the night-light. My god, the windows! The curtains aren't down. Even in this dim light, someone could observe everything through these windows. I'm in full view standing here at the sink. I have to lower the shades. I turn off the water, put down the glass, and grab the edge of the shade over the sink. As I pull it down, I envision the position of the stakeout. Is the assassin out there too? What if a downstairs window is unlocked? The assassin would only have to slit the screen and slide the window open. I must pull down all the shades. We latch the windows in summer because of the air conditioning. They are okay.

Done.

Check the answering machine after I get that water. We always unplug the upstairs phone so it doesn't wake us while downstairs the answering machine takes the messages. Three messages. Let's see. First, set the playback volume to low. I push play, the mini-tape rewinds, and a mechanical, computer-generated voice speaks.

"You have three new messages."

Pause.

"Dr. Butler, this is Miller. Please call me as soon as possible. Tuesday, 10:30 p.m."

Pause.

"Dr. Butler, this is Detective Miller. Call me, will you? It's important. Tuesday, 10:48 p.m."

Pause.

"Butler, this is Miller again. Where are you? I'm giving up for now, but call me! This is very important. Call me as soon as you get in! Tuesday, 11:05 p.m."

Miller last called only a short while ago.

What is he calling for? Does he have more evidence? I'm innocent, yet he believes I'm guilty and has a stakeout down the road ready to pick me up. And I'm suspicious about why he sounds friendly when he intends to arrest me. He is setting me up. He gets me to call, and the cops down the street arrest me. What do I do? Nothing. Wait; think again. Before I dismiss this, should I reconsider talking to him? That might be wise. However, as I think about the situation, what can I tell him? If I talk with him, I must tell the whole story. I'd better not start, or I'll create a problem by giving him only part of it. I am convinced he would ask questions that would expose my secrets. To say nothing works better than trying to lie. When I'm clear about what to do, I might, just might, talk to Miller.

The night-lights spread a soft blanket of twilight that allows me to walk around the house. A table lamp on my desk in the study will let me read and keep me invisible from the outside. I'm hungry. What's quick and quiet? Peanut butter and jelly. The refrigerator light illuminates the kitchen. Store-bought peanut butter is okay but what we made on the farm was better. Our homemade jelly was great too, and the raspberry was my favorite. Mom's bread was the best...when she was baking. Ann calls this "puhbuhjay." This sandwich is a welcome treat. A sudden longing for Deana comes up. I'm lonely and want her here, with me, for comfort. I long to share what has happened. I want to be near her. I'm surprised by my sudden change in state. Three bites ago, I was famished and now I'm stuffed; three bites ago, I delighted in the pleasure of eating, and now I'm sad and alone. I try to recapture my earlier state by picking up the sandwich, but I stop midway. I'm full, even though I've only eaten a quarter of the sandwich. I lower it to the plate, holding onto its edge for a minute before I let it go.

My wife, my wife. I want you in my arms so I can kiss you and tell you how much I love you. Our lives have had their difficulties, but being married has been the fullest part of my life. I've told you this so many times. But I want to tell you now. Will I ever tell you again? Damn right I'll tell you . . . if I get out of this. I can leave you a note. Yeah . . . a getting murdered note. "Just want you to know how important you are, how much I love you, so, good-bye, I'm getting murdered." Although stupid, this yanks at my feelings anyway. I have to distract myself to control my tears. Why? Why me? Damn, damn, and damn! Why now? *Now* of all times. Damn. I itch to destroy something, anything. No. Not anything, I realize. I'm trapped and terrified. I want to break free.

I don't even own a gun. I wasn't interested in hunting like most guys where I grew up. I won't buy a gun, but I need a weapon. I need something for protection, but what? Ah, a solution . . . the brass-handled shillelagh would be perfect. Tiptoe to the front hallway and open the closet door. My hand slides along the wall and grips the thick, oak cane, smooth and solid, with a heavy brass knob. As I lift the shillelagh, I sense its weight and notice palpable relief. I start back to the study and imagine hitting him. I swing with all my strength at his head . . . no, at his arm, at that damn arm reaching toward me. I smash his hand until it looks like pink putty and turn to smash him in the face and head. Each new blow crushes more bone in his skull until he lies dead at my feet. I'm safe. Yet the consequences are unavoidable. What would the police do? What would the courts do?

"Your Honor, the prosecution finds groundless the assertion by the defense that Dr. Butler killed this poor man in self-defense. He was unarmed and helpless. Whatever Dr. Butler's claims in relation to Dr. Volks, one cannot kill people even to vindicate the death of a friend. The prosecution contends that Dr. Butler killed him to avenge his friend's murder."

My name and picture would be in the papers, and the Shra'kufans would send someone else to kill me. Either way I'm doomed. And I do not believe violence resolves problems. The solution to violence cannot be violence; but I'm so damned scared. I'm terrified and grope for solutions that slip out of reach.

Years ago, I lived this lesson, although I didn't learn it till later. That isn't accurate. I still haven't learned it. I've heard about it and believe it and have even done it. That differs from integrating it as a lived belief. I was a white social-group worker in the inner city. I was immortal like every adolescent, though I was in my twenties. One hot summer evening, I closed the community center at midnight. I was alone turning off all the lights in the rooms where older teenagers came to play pool and cards and where we held our afternoon groups with younger kids. It was balmy. Spotlights illuminated the asphalt and cast crisscrossing shadows of basketball backboards. There was a lightness in my step as I went to lock the gate of the high, chain-link fence. A circle of fifteen shadowed figures surrounded the exit and my car. I recognized older toughs from the area. Many played pool or hung out at the community center. I don't remember fear. I don't even remember experiencing threat. I turned my back and locked the gate. Glancing at the one who stood closer than the rest, I nodded and walked past him. I looked at none of the group, got in the car, started it, and drove away. They moved apart as I started forward. Afterward, I gave it no thought. I was neither afraid nor bothered. I don't recall telling the director of the center. Only months later did it hit me I might have been in danger and that different actions might have provoked violence. Nonresponse to the implicit violence defused it.

After years of my therapy, after years of doing therapy and now training others to do therapy, I realize that violence is not a solution to conflict. Violence-as-solution only applies to the stronger or scarier or better armed. Violence ignores the other party, denies his or her needs, and undermines the effort to reach a common solution. Often, working with families in which there is physical violence in the home, I've seen a father or mother alter their tone of voice or get red-faced or without a change in facial expression clench a fist, and at that moment, open and honest interchanges between family members stop. The father or mother, perhaps for self-protection, can't afford to let others express certain feelings or make honest observations and, driven by fear, react with anger to stop it, and, if that fails, violence. Violence, even the threat of violence, can be a powerful control. As I reflect further, desperation can also trigger violence. Violence works for the perpetrator but not the victim. With violence, there is only one winner.

My tai chi teacher often said, "Yield." I can hear his voice in my mind and remember what happened in one of our classes. As usual, after we had been practicing the solo exercise, he did corrections with every one of the nineteen students, our legs and arms getting taxed while holding the position. The wait seemed interminable. He stood back, arms crossed, and scanned me. He had me loosen my hips, so I sank lower, my rear leg lengthened and I could feel a tremendous stretch while my forward leg took more weight. My eyes widened at the effort. Next he adjusted my body position so it was more vertical. My legs ached at the additional burden. I wanted him to move on to someone else so I could move, so I could stop the discomfort.

"Better," he muttered. After a pause during which he continued to look at me, he repositioned my arms. Hands parallel, shoulders down, elbows down, a little further away, all of which increased the support needed by my already screaming torso muscles. I thought he had finished, except I had shifted my torso while he adjusted the arms. One hand on my lower back and the other on my upper chest, he again made me vertical and a little lower. My already exhausted legs quivered. God, this is awful. Why am I doing this?

"Very good," he announced as he moved away. In what sounded like an afterthought he said loud enough for everyone to hear, "Learn to love the thing you hate! Learn to develop your will. Do lower, hold longer. Then you will take root and bear fruit."

His words caught me as I was about to move, so I held the position longer, my legs trembling more. As he had taught us to do earlier, I tried to relax into the discomfort; I tried to sink my energy; I tried to relax my belly and use the energy to support my body. I slowed my breathing, relaxing my lips, cheeks, and throat. The trembling traveled from my legs to my lower belly. Surprised, I tightened, and the trembling stopped. I relaxed again and the trembling resumed. As I relaxed my body more, a continuous ripple traveled from my legs up my body to the top of my head. I felt as if I were shaken all over from deep inside. In the distance, he told the class they could move. I continued to hold the position a while longer, exploring this incredible new experience.

"Sit down," he said gesturing in a large semicircle. "Learn to take break." People folded onto the floor, many sitting cross-legged but others lying down. A few folks groaned about our most recent "correction." I stayed at the back, my legs still trembling, wanting to move.

"Lose the battle and win the war. Learn to yield. Yield your ego." He looked around at the class, stopping at me. "Anger and anger produces more anger and conflict. Yield. Yield your ego.

When you resist"—he mimicked this by pushing on his arm with the other hand—"your arm's ego must yield." At this he let his arm drop, and his hand pressed space. "No problem! No conflict. When things are in harmony, things grow; things get better and better."

He asked a student to stand, putting the back of their wrists together.

"Push," he ordered. "Harder."

The student got red in the face, stopped, dropped his arm, and rubbed the wrist.

"If both pushing, both yang, more conflict, and pain." He picked up the same wrist, putting it against his own again.

"If one yields, plays yin, the other plays yang, pushes, no conflict. My turn to play yang, to push, your turn to play yin and yield. Exact matching the push." They moved backward and forward, the wrists making a circle. A cycling backward and forward developed, one pushing and the other yielding, alternating and balancing. Instead of escalating conflict, a harmonious dance began.

"When things are in harmony, they grow. Love grows. Friendship grows. Have sound sleep and healthy appetite. Very nice!"

I smile remembering my teacher's words and discover that I'm leaning against the outer edge of my desk, arms and legs crossed, staring at the large blind that covers the sliding door. I glance around the dim room and imagine moving through the house. The warm glow of night-lights bathes most of the downstairs. A few places are dark—the living room and front entryway. There are no night-lights along the upstairs hallway that connects our bedrooms. I can imagine Deana, Mark, and Ann sleeping in their beds, unaware of the internal struggle going on downstairs. I can't walk into our bedroom and risk waking Deana, but I can look in on the kids. I can give them good-bye hugs and kisses, ruffle their hair, gaze at them as long as I wish since they will stay asleep. That I might be hurt or killed compels me to see them, to touch them one last time. They endow me, my life, with purpose and meaning.

CHAPTER 22

11:25 p.m.

I wander back into the kitchen and see the blank whiteness of the closed shade above the dinette table. In my mind, Deana and the kids find the shades closed tomorrow at breakfast. Cereal boxes litter the table. Spoons and bowls clank and then the kids run from room to room discovering every curtained window. I must remember to open them before I go to sleep. I want to leave nothing suspicious; the unusual might lead to questions. Tension has increased around my shoulders, eyes, and jaw.

As I return to my desk, my heart races and sadness tightens my throat. Standing next to the desk, I realize the fingers of my right hand are drumming on the desktop. Stop it! The fingers stop, rigid, pressed together. Why? Why stop? There is no need to stop. I try to drum my fingers again but they won't work. I can't do it. I'm battling inside. With clenched jaw and fists, I shake my head and stomp around the desk, throwing myself into the chair. Damn! I hate this. With these reactions, I'll never be able to hide my emotions. I'll be apprehensive, teary, and agitated. I want my feelings to go away but they don't. I want to run upstairs and tell Deana the whole thing. Whenever we talk, she is helpful. I can count on excellent, perceptive suggestions. Oh, how I long to do that. I have to fight getting up from the chair.

The countless mishaps in our relationship make its survival a wonder. It died only to revive again. That happened from the start. Taking a deep breath, I reflect on the operations of my mind. Like taking a deep drink of refreshing water, I realize that I am assessing, coming to terms with, and putting into perspective my total relationship with Deana. I guess its depth and significance comes from our chaotic history and the role she played for me. And, in the light of Rick's murder, there is another twist.

CHAPTER 23

11:28 p.m.

During our junior year at college, we had another one of our separations, the separation that eventually solidified our relationship. As with all of our other breakups, conflicts, fights, misunderstandings, I found it excruciating.

The weather had turned colder even though spring was approaching. I had given up on my relationship with Deana. Despite my deep longing, despite my commitment to it, the relationship was not working out. Our current separation seemed more terminal than any other. I talked about it with friends. I even discussed it with her parents. They were nice and supportive but stood by their daughter. She had to sort out her relationship with me, and they were reluctant to get involved. They knew how much she mattered to me. I went back and saw my therapist. He said I could not make her love me or want me. That got my attention. I gave up. And this enabled me to transition to other relationships.

After classes one Friday afternoon, some of my classmates and I were hanging out on a grassy lawn in the center of campus, and one of them said they were having a get-together at their apartment. Would I like to come?

"Sure," I said. What did I have to lose?

When I arrived that night, there were too many people in the apartment. People were trying to dance but it was so crowded, they kept bumping into each other. There was a keg of beer in the kitchen alongside a large steel tub filled with ice and beer cans. People sat on the floor talking and an occasional couple ignored the group, exploring each other. Even though two of my classmates welcomed me, I felt alienated and alone and a little on edge. I poured myself a beer and made my way to a corner where I could watch the crowd of people. I closed my eyes and let the noise fill me. It was chaotic, discordant, jarring. I finished the beer and then headed back to my place. It was hot and uncomfortable. It was a mistake to come.

I headed for the front door and felt some slim fingers slip around my arm, in a familiar, almost inviting way. Now what? When I turned I saw a stunning blond woman with big blue eyes and full lips. Her figure was voluptuous. She kept her hand on my arm, but in marked contrast to the contact, spoke objectively.

"You're in Robbin's experimental psychology class. Right?"

"Yeah?" I was uncertain how I wanted to respond or whether I even wanted to talk to anyone.

"I'm in there too."

"You are?" I squinted at her, trying to match her with my memory of the other students.

"Yes," she responded with a slight nod. "I always sit in back near the door and you sit on the side in the second row."

"Oh," I said. "Ohhh," I said again as I placed her. In class, she usually had her hair tied back in a ponytail. Since I always sat in the back row, I saw her from the side. Now, up close, face to face, her hair down, I hadn't recognized her.

She was the beautiful woman who I assumed would never even look at me. I felt so intimidated, so inadequate around such people I became tongue-tied. All I could do was take another swig of beer. She had still not removed her hand from my arm. I perspired even more and wiped my forehead. Then, in what was both a strange and intimate gesture, she reached out with her other hand—I noticed she was holding a tissue—and wiped my brow, just below the hairline, from temple to temple. She came back across my forehead, just above my eyebrows and, instead of continuing all the way back, wiped down to the tip of my nose. Her hand was so close I had to close my eyes, and I could smell her perfume. My eyes popped open, and I stared at her open-mouthed. I didn't know what to say.

"Uh . . . thanks." I knew I looked and acted like a dope, an awareness that led me to feel even worse.

She smirked. That pissed me off.

"Want to dance?"

"No. It's too crowded, and I was on my way out."

"But it's early." Still touching my arm with one hand, she reached up with the other to finger her hair, rolling a few strands between her fingers. "I don't think I've ever seen you at one of these parties."

"Well," I said with more edge to my voice than I expected, "I'm not the partying type."

Besides being beautiful, she had poise and self-confidence. The more we talked, the more inept I felt. But now she tilted her head to one side and pursed her lips into a small "O" while her brows furrowed. She stayed in that position for fifteen seconds while she peered at me.

"Would you like to go for a walk?" She squeezed my arm to punctuate her question.

"Okay, I guess." I sighed. "I was on my way to do that anyway."

"Then let's go." She took a step into the mass of people, heading toward the door, pulling my arm behind her. I was all turned around, so she had to stop and then let go of my arm, an action that to my surprise, felt disappointing yet also a relief. When I stepped toward the exit, I didn't see her. Now my feelings crashed, and I felt terrible. What is going one? Is she toying with me? Trying to squelch my dismay, I pushed through the folks blocking the doorway and stepped out onto the second-floor balcony. The air was cool and clean. I took a deep and grateful breath. I glanced in the window, feeling alone and unlikeable, and started toward the stairs.

"Where are you going?" she asked from behind me. I turned to discover she was striding toward me. "I thought we were going for a walk. I got each of us a new beer. Here, catch!" she said as she tossed me a can of beer.

I flinched when the droplets of water hit me in the face, a few getting in my left eye.

"Good catch. Sorry about the water." By now she was next to me. She peered at my face and with her finger wiped the moisture from my eyebrows and cheek. Again I closed my eyes, her finger was so close. And then, she brushed the area she had wiped off with her lips.

"There. All better," she said and stood back to look at her handiwork.

I was so surprised, so off balance that I stared at her, my mouth agape again. Why me? Why would she want to spend time with me? I looked more at her expression, and she seemed to scrutinize me. As I thought about what to do, I got anxious about saying or doing anything. I failed to find my voice. Feeling even worse, I turned away and walked to the head of the stairs leading down to the ground. I could see her at my side, keeping up.

"Do you know my name?"

I swallowed, hoping I could talk. The word stuck in my throat so I shook my head. At last I could say, "No. No, I don't."

"I know your name. It's Jason Butler, the top student in psychology."

"I am?" I stopped several steps from the bottom and looked up at her, where she had stopped two steps higher.

"Yes. Everybody knows it. Don't act humble."

"You don't understand. I don't see myself that way. I'm just interested in learning and figuring stuff out. I'm not competing with anyone. I think no one has ever said that about me and ..."
I turned and strode onto the walkway at the bottom, trying to get away from her. She kept pace.

"You weren't just being humble, were you? You really don't see yourself that way."

I increased my speed, hoping to distance myself from her. But she kept up without a lot of effort.

"Hmmmm ... you are an interesting, but sort of difficult guy."

I kept my fast pace up for a little time longer and then stopped to face her.

"What are you doing?" I asked. The beer had loosened my restraint, and I was now speaking more freely.

She took a step back, startled. "I'd like to get to know you."

"Why? Why me?" I felt angry. "Are you doing charity work tonight? Are you taking care of the handicapped? I don't need handouts and I don't need help." I glared at her. She seemed surprised and puzzled. She took another step backward and turned her head to look back the way we had come. She paused, seemed to think, and then took a step toward me but remained well over an arm's length away.

"I guess you wouldn't understand. Most guys hit on me. You haven't noticed, no, I know you haven't noticed, but every guy in that psych class has hit on me except you. Every one. Do you know how tiring that gets! I'm trying to get guys to leave me alone. And you, the most handsome, the smartest, and the nicest one of the bunch, don't even know I'm there. How come?"

She looked at me. I could see she was annoyed. Then, she shook her head and muttered, "I can't believe it. I can't believe I said all that to you, to someone I don't know!"

She continued to look at me.

"Okay," I said to her. "Let's walk and talk, and talk and walk. Coming?" I took a few steps and looked back at her. She nodded and caught up.

The night was cold but with no wind. Stars shone through the clear night sky. Our breath made abstract characters in the empty air. It was lovely and crystalline.

"We've not been introduced. I'm Jason, Jason Butler."

"I'm Helen, Helen Jones," she said, imitating my phrasing with a wry smile, and she stuck out her hand. I was forced to admit she had a charm and liveliness, a kind of bravado that brought me out of myself. I shook her hand vigorously.

"It is nice to meet you, Helen Jones."

"Likewise, Jason Butler." We were still holding hands, so on a whim, I took a step, and we continued walking holding hands. Her wisecracking irreverence, the irritation I'd been feeling, her forthrightness, and the beer all contributed to loosening my response to her. I had relaxed, stopped feeling self-conscious, and acted spontaneously. It was an intense six weeks with Helen Jones, now Dr. Helen Trent, the widowed, childless Mrs. Rick Volks.

CHAPTER 24

11:55 p.m.

I'm tired. I can't sleep in our bed. To lie next to Deana would be intolerable. But I want just to go up there, hug her, and let her hold me. A terrible aloneness and a pervading hopelessness settle over me. I can't stop myself. I'm compelled to go upstairs. I won't wake them. I'll just peek in.

I creep up the stairs, like a sneak doing something wrong. It is so quiet up here! No matter how I strain my ears, there are no breathing sounds. Has he broken in and killed them?

Heart thumping, braced for the sight of my dead wife, I turn the stairway corner. Though the lights are off, I can search the bedroom with my eyes. Is she there? It is dark. I can't find her. I steady myself with the hallway railing and inch along, hesitant and cautious. I can hear only my breathing. They must be dead; otherwise, I'd hear breathing. From the doorway, the bed is visible. It's empty! I check again. Empty? Yes! I examine the bed carefully. The bedspread is smooth and not folded back. No shadows from indentations. No one sat on the bed. Everything, even in this dim light, looks fine. Check the bathroom. Empty.

Thank God, she's not dead! But where is she? I don't want to turn on the lights or make noise, in case she is up here. But where? She must be asleep in one of the kids' rooms. That's it. Or, like the murder mystery I read years ago, are they all dead in one of those rooms? What a horrifying thought. I control my impulse to run. Instead, I hurry down the hall and find their doors closed as usual. I hold my breath to stifle back a sob. I close my eyes tight before touching the doorknob to Ann's room. That's where Deana would be. I open my eyes as I take a deep breath and turn the knob. Even turning it slightly sends creaks into the night. I crack the door open. Ann's bed is in view as I move the door ajar. She has a night-light so I'll be able to see. A little more and I see . . . an empty bed! Empty! Where is she? I shove the door open. The room is empty.

Visions of all three dead on Mark's floor barrage me. I dash to his door, open it in a panic, and discover it also is empty. *Empty!* How is that possible? Where are they?

Two tours of the upstairs show nothing unusual. Wherever I check, nothing is out of place or gone. Every time I reach for a light switch, I remember the stakeout waiting, prepared for anything unusual in the house. Our night-lights shine bright enough for me to find a body, but subtle clues might be hidden. I probe for evidence. I check the suitcases. They are here. I search for anything that would provide a clue. Nothing. I peer out the upstairs windows. Only the empty road, bright in the moonlight. Nothing moves. I search the dark intersection at the border of the woods for confirmation that the police still wait but there is only darkness.

They must be here! Another horrifying picture strikes my mind. They are dead somewhere else in the house. Our one car was in the garage when I came home; they can't leave without the car. I examine every room in the house . . . and then the basement. No one there. Nothing out of place. At least they are not dead.

What about a note? I've forgotten about notes. We always leave each other notes, but there are no notes anywhere. Check the stove again. Maybe somehow I missed it. None there. The refrigerator? It must be on the refrigerator. I didn't notice it earlier. No. None there either. No notes! They're gone, the car is here, and no notes! I panic. They have disappeared. Not a trace of them.

I pace the study floor but moving does not reduce my alarm. My initial relief when I found no one dead in the house has turned to dread. Where are they? I checked the kitchen, the bathroom, the basement, the bedrooms, the family room, the living room. There was nothing. Nothing out of place. No clues. It is after midnight. Where can they be without the car? My God! They are dead outside in the car . . . or in the yard . . . or they were killed and their bodies whisked away.

I rush out the door into the garage, surprised that I need to unlock it, start to flick on the garage light and stop, stumble down the steps, and yank the driver's door open. The dim interior lights cast dark shadows.

"Deana, Mark, Ann!" To hell with silence. Empty. Empty again. Just to be certain, I check under the seats . . . as if they could fit there. I find it ludicrous but I'm desperate. I search for any clue and find only a wet beach towel and a sandy, red shovel.

I need to explore outside the house. Horrific visions arise: the assassin grabbing Ann as she hopped out the front door, and chasing down Mark and Deana as they tried to escape. I envision one crumpled in the backyard, another face down in the culvert. I get a flashlight from the kitchen's tool drawer and rush to the front door. My knees are shaking. I will venture out for the first time since I got home. I'll be unprotected. Get the brass-handled shillelagh.

I turn the lock on the front door. I close my eyes as I grab the doorknob. Hefting the shillelagh to gather reassurance from its weight, I take a deep breath . . . and freeze. I forgot the stakeout! When I exit the front door, they'll be here in thirty seconds to pick me up. I'm pulled apart by my torment: compelled to search the outside and cowering inside to escape detection.

I crack the door open and scrutinize the front porch. No bodies. Nothing unusual. I relock the door. Since I came home, the moon has risen above the horizon and now blankets everything with its soft, even glow. I step into the living room and without disturbing the curtains peek through the edge. I can observe the whole front yard and the surrounding field that edges the wood. Next to our front sidewalk on the grass, Ann's trike and Mark's two-wheeler lie, handle bars pointing up. The soccer ball we had played with after lunch yesterday still rests next to the driveway, stark white next to its black shadow.

In the moonlight I glance over the terrain, eyes straining to seize any clue. Nothing. No large objects. No bodies. Relief never seems complete tonight. My eyes strain with effort to peer into the dark slash of the culvert. Brush on the far side of the culvert erupts as a raccoon bursts onto the road and disappears on the other side. I exhale, tension easing.

CHAPTER 25

12:20 p.m.

Back in the study. I pace back and forth in front of our book-shelves, crammed from floor to ceiling. I've done more walking in this study tonight than in the previous four years we've lived here. I am seized with suppressed panic. There are no dead bodies inside or outside this house. There is nothing unusual anywhere. With my eyes, I scoured the side and back yards. Nothing! No notes. No explanations. Why is the car here when the house is empty? That makes little sense as we live five miles out of the city, and the kids are too small to walk distances. Somehow they left. Perhaps one of our friends picked them up. But why? Why aren't they home? It's after midnight. I talked to Deana on the phone a little before nine, and she didn't mention leaving. Therefore, they left after that conversation. If it was earlier than midnight, I'd call every one of our friends but it's too late for that now. I don't understand why they left and why Deana didn't write a note.

What if the murderer came here? And kidnapped them? Or found them in town and killed them there? No . . . that would be impossible. The car would be elsewhere, not at the house. Deana would have had to drive to town after we talked, after Ann was asleep and Mark was in bed. She would not do that.

My heart is racing. What happened to them? I need to call the police department to check on them. Seven, seven . . . I hang up. It seems impossible but I'm more distressed now than I was before. How do I negotiate this call to the police? Miller wants me picked up, and that request went to all police agencies. We bought that high-tech call blocker, so the police can't trace my call, but if I give my name or location to anyone, a squad car, the stakeout, will be here in minutes. But how do I find out what happened? I've got an idea.

"Dispatcher."

"Are there any accident reports this evening? For a woman and two children? My wife hasn't come home yet, and I'm worried something has happened to her."

"No, sir. No accidents or other problems this evening."

"Well, thank God. No accidents. Thank you. Thank you so much."

That deals with our local city police department but what about the university's Public Safety Office? That's where Miller works. Their information is the same as for the city police. There's no need to call there.

At least there is no report of their getting hurt or any emergencies or accidents. Hurt? The police would be uninformed were an accident never reported or if they got a ride to the hospital. Wouldn't Deana call here and leave a message? To check, I'll call the hospital, the only one in town.

"Emergency room? . . . Yes? Thank goodness. I'm a frantic husband and father. My wife and two kids aren't home. Has anyone named Butler been in tonight? That's B-U-T-L-E-R. Butler. Deana, Mark, and Ann. That's their names."

Time drags while I wait for the answer. Sounds in the background show he is asking and checking.

"No. No one by that name. We only had a few emergencies this evening. It's been slow."

"You're sure? Absolutely sure?"

"I told you, sir, we had few emergencies. I've been here all night, and that name has not come in."

"Thanks. I feel much better." As I hang up the phone, I notice I'm worse.

I'm relieved there are no reports of their getting injured, but I'm still distressed. I can't keep still, and I wander into the rest of the house. I check behind the sofa in the living room, search every closet, peek under end tables, search for scratches, buttons, cloth, anything at all that could be a clue. Nothing! No one! Where could they be? Why aren't they here? This is crazy! Why would they leave? When I talked to Dee, the kids were here. They were right here, in this house, only a few hours ago, and now they're gone. This is incomprehensible, intolerable. I must do something. I don't care how late it is, I'm calling the Farleys. They go to sleep early since she teaches fifth grade. One ring. Two. Three. Four. Are they there? Did they go somewhere too? Are they also missing?

"Uh?" Her voice is thick. She was in a deep sleep.

"Shirl, I'm sorry. This is Jason. Yes, it's after midnight but I'm overwrought. Are you awake enough to talk? To listen?"

"Yeah, yeah. What?"

"Deana and the kids aren't here. Are they with you? Did they call? Do you have any information?"

"No, Jason. They left hours ago."

"No calls?"

"Nope."

"Was Deana going to do something tonight? Go somewhere other than straight home?"

"Jason, they dragged themselves to the car. Ann was already dozing off before they got to the car, and Deana said she was going right home to put, I'm quoting, 'all of us to bed.'"

"If you learn anything, call me. If I'm not home, leave a message at the psychology department. Okay? Sorry to wake you. I was frantic about what to do."

"Jason, is there some problem?" Now she sounds concerned. She is awake now and processing what I'm telling her. Does she think Deana and I are fighting?

"Shirl, we're getting along fine. There is no reason they shouldn't be here!"

"They aren't there? They aren't at home?"

"No, damn it, that's what I've been telling you! Sorry. I didn't mean to yell. No one's here! Nothing here looks suspicious, so I think nothing happened in the house. It's weird they aren't here. This has never happened before." Shirl is silent for a long time.

"Jason, I don't know what to say. This is creepy!"

"It spooks me too. Thanks, Shirl. Sorry I woke you up. I didn't have a clue what to do and had to ask if you could clear this up. I'll call you tomorrow."

"If we can do anything, call us."

"Thanks. Bye, Shirl."

"Night, Jason."

How is it possible to be more agitated? Their absence is unnerving. Should I call the police and report them missing? But I know what will happen. During my consultations with the police, I learned about their procedures. First, I tell the dispatcher my wife and children are missing and that they should be at home. This is atypical for the early morning and should yield a response. As a result, the next question will be, "What is your name and address?" After that, "We'll send an officer out to talk to you." No, the police wouldn't just talk to me. They would arrest me and take me down to the station. My instincts are to avoid that at all costs. Yet if I can't call the police, what do I do about Deana and the kids? I'm getting hysterical again. I'll call Mom and Dad. Deana might have called them. This will distress them but I need to check. What other options remain?

It sounds as if the phone fell off the receiver, as if someone is fumbling to pick it up.

"Oh, what? Yeah. Oh, yes, hello?"

"Dad . . ." I've got to control this. I'm crying. "Dad? Dad, it's Jason."

"Jason?" I can hear alarm in his voice. "It's Jason," he says to Mom.

"Nothing's wrong. No, I mean, I mean I'm not sure something's wrong. Deana and the kids aren't here. I just found out. They're nowhere. I've searched everywhere. I called the police and the hospital and the Farleys but they're nowhere. Did they call you?"

"No. We talked to you and Deana over the weekend. But not since."

"Damn." I think hard but nothing comes. "No, we are not fighting. I'm aware you didn't ask. Just in case you wondered. There have been no problems at all. In fact, Deana and the kids spent time out at the Farleys to give me a chance to work. I got home late. I talked to Deana on the phone a little after nine. I was downstairs working, walked upstairs a little while ago, and nobody's there! They're gone!"

"Anything out of place? Anything strange?"

"No." I can discern growing frustration. "Nothing's out of place. Not a thing. I checked the house at least five times. That's what makes this so eerie. They disappeared. God, I'm upset. I apologize. I don't want to worry you."

"Well, you already did. I'm damn worried."

"I'm sorry. I had no place to turn and had to know if you had any news. I can't believe they're hurt, or I would have found something here or at the hospital or the police. Try not worry, I'm likely overreacting."

"Overreacting? Your family disappeared."

"I'm sort of under stress anyway. Sorry, Dad. I love you and Mom a lot. Try to get back to sleep. If you hear from Deana, tell her to call me or to leave a message at the department. I want assurance she's okay."

"Jason, do you want us to come there? We can hit the road in half an hour."

"No!" That was too abrupt, too strong. I blurted that without thinking, imagining them walking into the Shra'kufan situation. "Not now, Dad. I can't see how that would help, but your offer chokes me up. Thanks. I'll keep in touch. Thanks a lot. Love you."

"Jason, call us with any news. Call us if there is anything we can do."

"I will. Goodnight."

"Goodnight, son."

CHAPTER 26

12:35 p.m.

Haphazardly is how I pace from family room to kitchen, from kitchen to study, from study to family room. Around and around in futile action. I have, again, become distraught and frantic. How idiotic! I'm pacing again. I can't stand still. I continue to look. To listen. To think. Peep around the blinds. Is he there? Where are they? What's that sound? Is that him? I'm drained; but it's impossible relax.

The texts in my backpack flash to mind. I didn't remove them when I got home. I've forgotten about them, and now I can sense how I'm avoiding those pages. I only read Rick's introduction to the package, so I don't know what's in them. I'll walk to the study and explore them. It's hard to do because of how agitated I am, but those manuscripts are a hidden secret or a tumor that requires investigation. There's nothing more I can do here—I've looked everywhere and can't find answers. I need to relax and think with clarity. If I read the texts, the distraction may help.

What's in these things? Damn I'm tired. And I'm shivering, scared, and overtaxed. Move books and papers aside to create a workspace on my desk and open the first of the eight small packages.

One is yellowed, dark tan parchment. Purple ribbons encircle and tie closed thick and ornamented leather covers. Centered is a five-inch, bas-relief oval; within the oval, colors muted by age, is a snow-topped mountain surrounded by pale blue sky. Ten red dots appear on the mountainside. Arcane symbols decorate the cover. Undo the ribbons and discover what's hiding. The pages fan out and connect. Each page attaches to the next with thread. I've never seen a book designed in this manner; and its script is esoteric.

The next one might be the oldest: parchment, yet bound like a contemporary book. The cover, adorned with that mountain, includes an oval and diverse symbols. I'm guessing these are many centuries old. Two are constructed out of paper, so they are newer. I wonder when paper became available in the Middle and Far East. The books contain similar writing.

Beneath the books, there's a stack of papers written in English. I'd recognize Rick's handwriting anywhere. These are his notes. A few pages have headings: historical overviews, philosophical analyses, and systematic comparisons. He's scratched out sections, squeezed in corrections, and scribbled additions between lines and along margins. I find a to-do list:

—Check on drug action and Shra'kufan rituals.

—Several researchers have looked into chemical action of the drug. Results reported in the press. Extract them. They need translation. Related article in Medical Science, June? last year.

—Follow up on the unique use of language. Examine Baya Z'r's verses, and elsewhere in the manuscripts. Nouns don't function as nouns but as verbs. "Chair," for example, reads as "chairing" or "chaired" or "will-chair." This makes translation and understanding confusing since expected grammatical constructions do not apply. Likewise, from a translator's point of view, which word is the subject and which the verb is impossible to know except from context and that depends on meaning linked to word usage. The usual noun-verb or verb-noun composition of most Indo-European derived languages does not pertain so that "things" (expressed as nouns) are not static objects but processes. Is thinking transformed without rigid concepts for things? How does this form of language relate to the religion? Since the unusual grammatical formation is most prominent in Baya Z'r's writings, might it derive from his mystical experience? Taking a linguistic point of view, not one scholar has unearthed a historical precedent for such modifications of any Indo-European language nor the existence of a language with this structure.

—Record expenses for taxes and reimbursement.

—Send thank-you notes and gifts to Consulates, library officials, newspapers, and the staffs of various hotels.

—People don't speak this language. Why only its written form? I assume, as a result, that the language is used only in the religious context and its rites or initiations. These religious texts must connect to the religious experience.

—A follow-up to an earlier note. Is the verb-form for "objects" or "things" a mirror of the religious experience? Does it point toward something unique happening in the aspirant's consciousness? Does this relate to time?

This list reminds me of Rick. Working with him was frustrating at the time but I now remember his quirks with fondness. His attention darted to this or that, often missing our focus. This list, mixing to-do items with his notes and ruminations, is a perfect example.

When I consider later pages, a goodly number of the translations are illegible. With the scratching out and marginal additions, Rick must have struggled with his preliminary renditions, as if he needed to qualify his attempts again and again. That makes sense in the context of the linguistic complexities.

Blue-sky Seed
Verse I
Kill body(ing); free spirit(ing).

Blue-sky(ed) minding not-earth
Return earth
Spring sky(ing).
Verse II
Bliss(ed) smelting earth(ing)
Mountain(ed) sky(ing)
Bleeding/bliss(ing) conquering fighting
Ever-Blue-sky(ing).

Nota Bene: (1) Tense is obscure, but in most contexts, the object persisting from the past through the present into the future is implicit along with an inherent sense that the object is changing. This opposes assumptions made in Indo-European languages, in which, although the overt form of the object changes over time, its identity does not change within the past-present-future structure of time. Identity remains constant. I do not know whether the conclusion that identity is changing is correct in the Shra'kufan context. (2) The translated word "minding" in Verse I might mean "awareness-ing," which suggests awareness as process (time) as opposed to a static "thing" called "mind" and "thought." (3) "Not-earth," line two and "earth," line three, of Verse I, is not changed into a verb form. Why? Is this an error in the manuscript? Why is "earth" a static thing and not a process? Or, when "earth" is negated and becomes "not-earth," is this the "unchanging absolute beyond earth" (God)?

Although the above translation attempts to be precise about the Shra'kufan language, many meanings emerge from the words. I stumbled on a translation in Urdu of a Shra'kufan text. The translator, a university professor, was found dead! I discovered the manuscript in the archives of an out-of-the-way university library. This was fortunate since the original is amongst those I bought. This rendering established the foundation with which I began my own. Issues arise concerning the accuracy of this first translation; I am gratified to have had such an aide. Otherwise how would I have even known where to begin my own?

The following translation attempts to distill the meaning of these two verses in understandable English although one grants that such an effort alters the original meaning. Because of the unique grammatical construction (most words in these verses are verbs), the correct order of translated words is unknowable. I made different translations of the same two verses. In Verse II, one must wonder about the source of allusions to volcanic activity.

Verse I: Translation 1

Kill the body and free the spirit.
Mind like blue sky is not bound to the earthly body.
Let the body return to the earth,
And the spirit springs to the sky.

Verse I: Translation 2

Free embodiment of the dying spirit.
Earth knows not sky-like awareness.
Earth remains earth;
Sky opens as sky.

Verse II: Translation 1

Bliss transforms the body
As the mountain becomes the sky.
If you transform pain to bliss, you can conquer anything.
Beyond-the-Beyond awaits in the sky, forever blue.

Verse II: Translation 2
Earth glows with bliss,
Like the mountain sky
Which flows like glowing blood
Vanquishing opposition,
Leaving eternal blue sky.

More verses, translated, follow. I assume, due to the antiquity of the parchment, that the author is Baya Z'r. Hundreds more I did not translate. No time!

Verse III
Blue-Sky-Being transforms the every-day,
Transforms Bodying,
Transforms Spiriting,
Knowing all space and time
As One.

Verse IV
Minding trapped in Body-Earthing,
Is solid like mud or rocks,
Yet, when they fall away,
Minding opens as Blue-Sky
And Being-Bliss transforms
Every Thing.

Verse V
Perceiving opening like a flower
Mixing every sense
As One,
Merged,
Waterfall-Cascading,

Mixing you through
Space and Time.

Verse VI
When the truth appears in every land,
The sacrifice of ten hundred years ends;
The Transformer of Truth
Spreads the word to all people.

Verse VII
Minding quiets,
Body slips away,
Sunlight bursts forth,
Barriers gone,
One.

Minding flickering candle-like
Stops
And bodily transformation begins,
Pain wanes,
Healing starts,
And powers emerge.

I see no more translations of verses. But it is interesting to note that some of the verses describe meditation-like states and what can then arise. The next twenty pages are a lexicon Rick developed listing words and their usage. I see he isolated those words treated as nouns and verbs and those that remained only nouns. Few remained only nouns. He filled ten pages with such words, their modifications, roots, and ties to other languages. Other typewritten pages present translations of several Shra'kufan texts.

> The Mountain Record of the Secret Chosen Ones
> The essential secrets must be kept by the chosen because, though the earth can be littered by garbage, the sky remains pure. The perfect can only be known by the perfect; the absolute can only be known by the absolute. Only the pure can or should know the secrets of absolute perfection and, if the impure knows, then it sullies the perfect and absolute. This destroys the purity of the Eternal Beyond ["God"]. Since the essence of "God" is purity, knowledge of "God" by the impure destroys "God."

At this point Rick switches from translating to commenting and summarizing.

To rephrase this in Shra'kufan terminology, since the essence of the Eternal Beyond the Beyond is purity, knowledge of the Eternal by the impure defiles its purity and destroys the Eternal Beyond. Such knowledge is the most horrible of religious threats to a Shra'kufan.

The teachings are doled out as the aspirant "reaches perfection." To be told a "truth" early, before purity is achieved, sullies the Eternal and all Believers. There are twenty-three levels of spiritual growth, each corresponding to segments of a journey up a mountain. The spiritual journey begins in the desert (different stages relate to different deserts), moves to the foothills, up the slopes to conquering the peak and then into the sky itself, becoming part of the Eternal Beyond the Sky. Perfection is defined as the total conquering of the earthly body through privation and torture: suffering pain, going sleepless, enduring fasts, and so forth. It even involves stimulation followed by lack of satisfaction; to work as a cook while starved or to be sexually stimulated yet inhibit any response. This resembles the Karma Yoga and Karmamudra from other traditions. In contrast to the transcendence and ecstasy in those other traditions, asceticism, self-punishment, and pain are central for Shra'kufans. The ultimate test is "swallowing the Blue Sky" (Samatma). When the Eternal, as the "Blue Sky," has been ingested, only the "Godly," pure like the sky and pristine as the Beyond, can survive as a human being. If one is "un-Godly," or impure, then the "Blue Sky" "helps" the person join "God" or the purity of the eternal through death. From what I can find out, this refers to taking a drug (Samatma) called the "Blue Sky" or "Sky Fruit," depending on context. In other portions of the text, allusions refer to the impure being cleansed by the Blue Sky—that, I assume, applies to the ritual and protective murders that characterize this sect. References to "Blue Sky" in this text imply that aspirants take the same drug used to kill others. This is difficult to understand. Why do some die and others live? This must be checked with other sources and cross-validated, if possible.

This must have been part of the evidence that led Rick to warn me regarding the deadly blue poison. Yet it doesn't kill every person. Does one develop a tolerance through repeated usage at low dosages?

The last set of typed pages are stapled together and titled Other Random Texts.

There are six other texts, all short. One is a compendium of Baya Z'r's sayings. "Blood is the path from the valley to the top of the mountain. Pain allows earth to fall away, letting the spirit soar into the sky like a star." There are several hundred of these short verses. Another text describes early history. The second one appears the most ancient of the lot: brittle, yellowed, worn and poorly preserved. It is the most valuable due to its age. It must be the most revered, judging by the number of seals, symbols, and ribbons. The third is a collection of ritual practices, complete with drawings of altars, clothing, and ritual implements such as a dagger, a bell, and a large overturned basin. The fourth, fifth, and sixth, all copies, are writings by other prophets: one following Baya Z'r, the other from the 1200s and one in the last fifty years. This last writer shifted Shra'kufan practice toward active self-protection, what might be viewed from the outside as terrorism. This last text, signed by him, establishes that he was the major force behind those changes. Intriguing is the overt reference to his command of the terrorist sect. The violent and sadistic practices until now inflicted on themselves and unfortunate others were directed toward any threat to the Shra'kufan religion. The textual rhetoric smacks of the evangelical: "kill both the impure and the threat to the pure," and "protect the pure and spread purity." Modern warfare, industrialization, improved communications, increased mobility, and economic changes threatened to destroy the foundation of the Shra'kufan religion and, the text states, "change forever the balance of the earth and sky, the working of natural things." The author refers to the chaos and threat these forces bring to the Devout and the Pure, and then likens this to the world Baya Z'r confronted at the time of his "deliverance from the Earth," and encourages his readers to "listen to the Thunder from the Beyond, which invites them to cleanse the Earth of Impurity."

If one extrapolates from the textual material, social and economic changes threatened the social foundation of the religion and becoming active terrorists solidified, protected and maintained their group, kept the threat external and, by being so effective at inducing fear, incapacitated efforts to eradicate them. Secrecy was no longer enough. Active protection through terrorism became their safety. Their terrorist activities, according to the information I have gleaned up to this date, have worked as prophesied by the third author.

CHAPTER 27

1:00 a.m.

I got so absorbed in my reading I lost track of time and even forgot my predicament. I can't believe the time—1:00 a.m. My plight comes flooding back now I'm not distracted. What a quandary: the assassin and the police and my family. What was I hoping for by reading the materials Rick sent? Reassurance? Knowledge? A way out? There wasn't knowledge in them and no refuge or escape.

I keep dwelling on my family. Where can they be? How can I find them? What search might I do? I don't have a clue. Here in the study, I walk back and forth in front of countless shelves of books and what will they do for me? Do these books help with the most vital issues? How do they help me cope with the fundamental issue of my death and life? Do books help when I'm lying in pain? How do they help when my senses dwindle and my body decays? A few books might, I guess . . . but these do not! In fact, in this predicament, can any book help?

The only solution, a solution that keeps entering my mind, is to learn more about the Shra'kufans. I struggle with my confidence in this plan. Is this a reasonable conclusion? I possess scant information concerning the Shra'kufans, and I assume that if I learn more that will help. Without knowing more, they stay mysterious and unknown . . . a hiddenness that fuels my paranoia. I keep intending—no, I am compelled—to search the library's resources tomorrow. Will the holdings include books and other reference materials on this obscure sect? I'm driven to discover everything possible. Since I'm battling an unknown, the hidden engenders dreadful fantasies and irrational suspicions. I can't cope with what is concealed. Rick referred, without specifics, to journals and newspaper articles. Those might be hard to find. As I consider this, his references to pain, punishment, and self-mortification spook me. They dovetail with my problem managing with pain and punishment. How can this be religion? I'm no expert on religion, but this can't be one.

Books and libraries provided a crucial resource for me ever since I was a boy. Books were my friends, my escape, and my comfort. And many times they helped me solve problems. I've collected stacks of books to read, most kept on the two floor-to-ceiling shelves in the study. They are organized by different topics: anthropological studies on altered states, dissociation and mental health. Upstairs at least ten science-fiction books await my next vacation. I planned to learn new theories in pain management and hypnosis. I had collected fliers announcing workshops and training opportunities. My preparatory work on meditation and how consciousness relates to healing and pain management is useless if I'm killed.

If he kills me, the losses twist my heart with anguish. Teaching fledgling psychologists to do therapy finished. The training model I helped develop with such loving care and effort will go on without me. My treatment of clients never completed. I cringe as I recognize how devastating this will be for the two clients who struggled to trust me. My growth as a therapist, supervisor, and teacher stopped. I finally have an excellent handle on how I want to teach my undergraduate courses. I will never teach again. My delight and excitement at learning and sharing forever ended. All of this thwarted before they can develop and generate results. And, Deana, Deana . . . our plans for a third child. A decision we made less than a day ago. Is this fanatic going to kill me? My plans and dreams crushed. These possibilities taken from me before I can bring them to realization!

I want to avoid this. I'm trying to get away from my thoughts, my feelings, and the things that are forcing themselves into my mind. Uppermost I want to be with my family, except . . . they are missing. Bewildering . . . and challenging. I never expected to stare at my death. I expected to live out my life, grow old with my wife, see my kids grow and marry, enjoy grandchildren. Now this disaster. My life stops. I am anguished knowing, expecting with full knowledge, my death. Not just my death, my murder. And I'm helpless.

I want to stop what is going on inside me. From experience, trying to stop it fuels it. Change follows by allowing it to be, by not fighting it. And then, the state will transform itself. This is the way people work. I am trying to stop this natural progression. I am avoiding. I am avoiding fear. To sit still and to face my fear is formidable.

I remember several clients who battled this dilemma. With one woman in particular, we struggled and struggled. To acknowledge she was without hope and allowing her to experience no escape provided the impetus for change. As had been her pattern, she tried to avoid hopeless, helpless, and awful. She had been trying to avoid those feelings for years by inactivity and depression and alcohol. She had developed a pervasive, entrenched, and protective life pattern to avoid overwhelming, intolerable emotional pain. I did not cooperate in that avoidance and she began to change.

I sit in a blank state, bit by bit returning to the study, realizing, understanding what I had remembered. Fascinating to experience this specific memory right now. The theme connects to my present struggle, helpless and inept. In session, I was there as a therapist, an external person, to confront the issue and to offer support. On her own, she avoided changing. I needed to help her face the experience, knowing she could be different. In my situation, there is no one to force the confrontation. I laugh. But I do! Shit, I do! He is not right here in front of me, but he is lurking somewhere. He might find me later tonight or tomorrow. Is he getting close? Is he waiting? I want to block him from my awareness.

"Awareness." That word echoes in my mind. Awareness is the foundation of meditation. I'd forgotten. How amusing. I'm laughing at myself again. There's comfort in laughing. Years of meditation, trying to be with my inner states, following my experience, teaching others relaxation, and now I'm scrambling to avoid what's going on inside, trying not to think or to feel. I love the irony! This frightening threat has yanked me off balance. Ever since I saw Rick, an inner torrent of emotions has been inundating me. And I've been running and hiding not only from him but from myself. Right in front of me, with me all the time, I ignored what I've been doing. I might as well profit from my years of practicing relaxation and meditation. Do it now. Begin with autogenic training and then following experience.

CHAPTER 28

1:30 a.m.

I remember my amazement when the words I thought and the scenes I envisioned changed the state of my body and mind. Thinking "I am" as I breathe in, "relaxed and at peace" as I breathe out. Repeat this only a few times. Now "limbs" as I breathe in, "heavy, warm, relaxed" as I breathe out. Still, after many years, I'm awed by the response. They feel warm and heavy. I imagine them in the hot sun, feeling leaden. "Heartbeat" as I breathe in, "calm and regular" as I breathe out. Already slowing! A few more times. Notice the sensations along the edges of my nostrils. "Breathing" as I breathe in, "calm and easy" as I breathe out. Now the most powerful one. "It," as I breathe in, "breathes me" as I breathe out. There. The body expands and contracts like a bellows or as if air passes in and out of the pores. This deepens the relaxation. I'm astonished at how the tension is flowing from my body. Now the last phrase, "Forehead and eyes," as I breathe in, "cool and comfortable" as I breathe out. Imagine a cool breeze caressing my hair and face. My mind clears.

I'm more relaxed. I notice the calm flow of my breathing. This is the most free of tension I've been today. Thoughts tumble through my mind and I notice what comes. I am again upstairs. Deana is nowhere; the bed is empty and undisturbed. Images flit by: Ann's room, Mark's room, the car . . . dark and empty; the front and back yards . . . empty except for the moon's silver glow and black shadows; hanging up the phone after empty conversations. "Where are they?" I see Rick on the floor; hear the office doorknob wobble; sense my legs driving into the ground as I run for the moped. I'm flooded with memories, thoughts, and emotions.

I sigh with resignation. I know what's happening. Every time my body and mind relax, whatever is inside gets unleashed. This is massive and powerful, and I must face it. I can't sneak around it by relaxing. Can I confront it? Do I have the guts? Do I know how or what to face? A shiver travels down my spine. I don't know. "I'll try," I say to myself. A part of me knows what that means. Yet I must try. I'll confront this by meditating though I still want to avoid. And I must begin with the experience of avoiding.

Rearrange the straight-backed chair so I can sit without interference. From many forms of meditation I know which I will choose for this state of mind. I'm not sure it has a precise name . . . well, I don't know its name. I intend to follow and to be with whatever arises in experience. I've done this with other problems and concerns. It's like letting a tight, knotted ball of twine unwind, finding the end, or the beginning, and then it's gone. This takes fearless honesty to look, to be with whatever comes. There's no place to hide.

The lotus posture, legs like a pretzel, has been impossible for me to do. I shift to sit on the front edge of the chair. Feet flat. Hands on knees. The most crucial rule is "Don't identify!" It is automatic for us, for me, to own this emotion, this belief, this thought as mine. I've learned, however, that this process is much more subtle. For me to label that creak or that discomfort as a "creak" or a "discomfort" is identifying! As soon as I give any experience a meaning or a significance it is mine. I've got it, and it's got me! I've identified it and identified with it. Oh, how funny! Here I am settling in to meditate, and I am identifying.

What I'm telling myself not to do! Bring my mind back to the meditation.

Spine erect to reduce body tension and free the breathing. Relax. I notice tension in the shoulders, shoulder blades, stomach, jaw, arms, and legs. I can feel their rigid preparedness. Pulled tense like taut wire. Ready to react. Just noticing the heavy, taught preparedness and it changes. It dissolves. Allowing it to change. Breath slowing. Sensations beginning in my belly. Awareness drawn to my back. Stop trying to relax. Don't try. No effort. Just notice, and on its own it will vanish. Don't hold the goal as a goal.

I see the letter I received from my tai chi teacher. I had complained that I was having trouble quieting my mind as I did tai chi. I kept thinking and being distracted. He wrote back, "Human hands cannot still the water. The more they try, the worse it gets." One lets the waves settle. A soft smile spreads across my face. Then, sudden strong facial tension! Powerful and forceful. I want to avoid it. I'm trying to stop it by saying "Relax" in my mind. Just accept the tension. An image of Deana sleeping upstairs, her form dark in the bed, covers rising and falling as she breathes; and then the bed is empty, the house is empty, and the car is empty. A tug at my heart and throat. I miss her! I miss them all! Where is she? Where are they? What can I do? I open my eyes ready to do something, shifting my position.

Startling! I forgot what I was doing. I was pulled into my reactions and emotions. I can do something later. Take a deep breath, hold it . . . let it out. Roll my head in a circle. Just let go. A deep sigh. A smile! Relax my gaze and shift attention back inside. Let it go and allow awareness to shift.

Just notice.

Flowing sensations through my torso . . . like a ripple, a vibration. I feel emotions again. My breathing gets ragged, my jaw tightens. Follow the breathing. At first I'm separate from the breath. I feel one with its rise and fall. Just breathing. Follow what happens. How could I have been so stupid as to forget meditating earlier today? Haven't I learned anything over these years? I'm fine when there is no pressure. Add a pressure, and—poof—the practice dissipates. Laughing at myself again. Another major rule is let go of judging and evaluating. I've been judging myself. While laughing, I'm at least not judging my judging. A smile plays along my lips.

Images appear. Just notice the thoughts, sensations, emotions, and judgments. The murderer stoops over Rick . . . Fear gurgles in the belly and then rage courses through my shoulders and arms followed by sadness that settles in my throat and jaw. The sensations wash through and over like a flood finding its own way, altering patterns and shapes. Heavy tension settles in the front of my throat, and the back of my shoulders rise, becoming hard. I freeze the sensations in my shoulders and throat. I've been here before. I know this. In meditating, don't approach and foster what is pleasurable and don't avoid and stop what is not pleasurable. Just be aware and allow it to continue. My emotions and thoughts are stuck in my shoulders and throat. I've stopped the flow. With the release, the sensations in my throat and back get stronger.

A sharp pain grows in my back. I'm just sitting, I fume, how can I hurt? I want to move. I don't want the pain. It's even sharper now. My jaw tightens against it. Now my butt hurts, and the other pain has shifted from my shoulders to my lower back and is getting worse. Shit! How can I continue when I'm so uncomfortable?

Without thinking, I shift my position, and then I'm aware the pain leaves. I smile. In fighting the pain, I bring it on. In freezing it, it solidifies and doesn't change, doesn't flow away. I brace myself for what will come. I never like this stage. Even my reaction to it is wrong. Damn! There I go judging my judging of judging. I laugh! Laughter helps again. I settle once more. The back pain comes, in the same place, high above the shoulder blades. Be the pain. No separation. Just discomfort. Sharp. Sharper, and then a cutting, a searing. Then the pain fades, softens, melts, becoming warm and spreading, transforming into an understanding I'm afraid. I'm afraid of this murderer hurting me. I'm afraid of what has happened to my family. I'm afraid of the pain. I don't want to feel pain. I recall again the words of my tai chi teacher. "Enjoy the pain," he would say when our legs were burning with fatigue. "Learn to love the thing you hate." Transform, he hinted. Transform your experience and don't get stuck. I hear the word "love" as he pronounced it, "luff." Yet somehow, now, by not fighting this pain, it has lessened, softened, melted away.

Sadness and fear leak out as the sensations flow. Tears wet my cheeks as I feel them inch their way, warm at first, then cool and salty at the edge of my mouth. My body shakes with grief and terror. The picture of Rick's dead body being covered by that green sheet convulses me into a sob. In my mind, I turn around and around, arms reaching out to nothing, screaming as loud as I can for Deana, Mark, and Ann. Panic courses from my abdomen into my constricted chest as I stare at the lethal hand lunging ever toward me. The emotions grow even stronger. *Too much.* I feel them freeze and knot in my body, and then, after noticing this, let them go. Like a huge wave that breaks, it crashes over and around and through me.

I'm uncertain which direction I face or even where I am. My sense of separateness seems to fade in the total merging of sensations within and without. The boundary of my body has dissolved. I know from experience that with movement, my body will re-form. Aware of awareness. I sense my throat gradually tighten, tears well up again, and then crying. Sobs wrack my body. Emotional storms seem to rampage through me. Flow with it. I notice I am separate from the storm, aware that "I" am perceiving it from a distance. Be one with it. Just notice the distance and the "I." Emotions flare up. The body—clenching, sobbing, shaking, tensing—fills my mind. The storm subsides. Tension is followed by release. Stress seems less and less. Almost relaxed.

Now I know why I didn't do this before. No time or safety to let these processes take their course. I did not have to criticize my not meditating earlier. Almost relaxed. Now sad. A dark sadness. The house empty. Coming in the door and yelling, "I'm home," and no answer. Just silence. Suddenly a dreamlike image. A massive black-robed figure towers over me, like a cliff threatening to throw down its boulders, to smash what lies at its base. A knife slashing at my shoulder and throat. Just notice, just watch. Fear. He stabs and stabs. The knife drips blood, but he is deadly silent. He is killing me. Just watching him kill me. No interference. I'm dead. Fear draining away. A new picture forms in fragments and congeals into the memory of a dream. I'm in a bank, sitting on a couch. A man enters. He has a gun! A hold-up! "Stop!" I yell. He turns and shoots. Hits me in the chest. I'm falling back. I'm dying! "This is what it's like to die," I think in my dream. I'm surprised. "But I never said good-bye," I think. Images and more images. Memories of marriage, my children, my childhood, my parents, my clients, my students. Sad, angry…furious. An explosion of emotions. Smashing a fist into the world. Yelling, screaming inside. Jaw clenched. I give up.

My state shifts. It starts with self-disgust, disgust at my giving up. This transforms to loathing the assassin and gets sharper and more intense. Yes. Yes. That's right. Notice it. Notice the hating. Filled with hate, loathing, fear. Erupting like a monster volcano.

Oh no! I've lost myself in the thoughts and experiences. Reacting to them. Planning. Deciding. Not just letting them be in whatever way they present themselves. Accept them. Just let them be. Settle into the feeling of what I have been doing. Protecting, fighting out of fear. Fury. Protective fury. Destroy. Destroy to preserve, to live. I'll kill you to stay alive.

A memory appears: my fear of the wasp that invaded the house. My fury as I destroyed it . . . pure fear, I realized afterward. I'll protect myself. I'll destroy you before you hurt me. Destroy him or he'll destroy me. A flash of nonverbal insight: we are both the same. Both destroyers. I don't like that insight. I want to reject it, to push it away. I don't want that to be part of me. I don't want to know myself as destructive; yet there's more peace.

The image of my dead body in a coffin. Red stains the white satin, and the lid floats down. I jump at the loud, deep clang that reverberates the moment the casket closes. It tumbles in space, one end strikes the ground, and its momentum carries it into a grave. Loose earth falls, falling, falling. Buried. Tears. So much unfinished. Books unread. Vacations never taken. No graduations with my kids, no marriages, no teenager hassles, no grandchildren. No more great times with Deana. Or fights. Or walks. Or sex. So far it's been fantastic and full. Let it be. Let it go. Could I let go of wanting to change this? Just let it be . . . doing nothing? Looking for them everywhere and stopping. Giving up. Tears. Sadness. Grief. Not ready, not ready. I refuse to be ready! I'm holding on to what I have. I want to fight. Sobbing. Angry. Unfair. NO! No matter what happens I will not let him kill me. I do not want to die.

I take a deep breath and swallow. I'm done for now. I stopped it. It's not complete, if it ever could be, but I feel quieter.

How long has it been? Half an hour; it is a little past 1:30. I am cramped and achy. Amazing how much calmer I feel although I still don't want to accept it. Accepting means giving up all hope.

"Yes," I say making my decision aloud, "I'll stay alive." And the thought, "If I can," follows.

Massaging my butt by moving it around on the chair feels . . . refreshing. How ridiculous! Yet there's luxury in it. Circling my head loosens my neck and shoulders. The crickets sound as if they are in the room. A deep breath. A second. The air is cool, invigorating; the house silent. I sense my eyes' relaxation in how I'm seeing. The desk and the doorway appear softer, gentler, and the light benign. Nothing has changed, but I sense a shift.

Stretch and yawn. Almost like waking. Move my toes around. Inhale and rise. My mouth is dry, and I want to drink. As I walk into the kitchen, my whole body seems looser. Sounds are clearer. I notice the slight echo of the water as it gushes into the glass. Coolness floods the front part of my mouth, moving back over my tongue, and sinks with the swallow. I pause and feel the coolness descending the interior of my body. The change from two hours ago is extraordinary. I know from experience that when I am again swept into the turmoil of the everyday, I lose this quiet, deep appreciation. At least I'm getting tired.

Back in the study, I might doze. I can rest in the easy chair. I turn off the dim light and lean back. After I've struggled with a problem, a solution later pops to mind after I've slept.

I bolt upright. Did I lock the front door? I remember turning the deadbolt lock, shoulder pressing into the front door. What about other entry points? I find that I can't sit. I remember bracing the sliding glass door here in the study with a broom handle. Other than the garage, there are two entrances to the house. I checked the windows earlier. Every creak, anything loud, anything at all, I interpret as the assassin: the assassin sliding a window open, the assassin opening a door, the assassin fitting a tool into a lock and . . .

I startle awake. I must have dozed off. What's the time? Ten minutes after two. I went to sleep for a while. Why did I wake up? I'd better try to rest more, if I can. Even with my eyes closed,

I feel alert; I keep listening and waiting. I inhale, tensing and then relaxing my shoulders, hoping to drift off into sleep again.

Buried in my awareness, I now realize that a noise had occurred several times but slipped by my attention. How is that possible given how vigilant I've been? The hair on my neck rises. I reach for the walking stick. I'm glad I turned off that lamp earlier, since it's dark in the study. I tiptoe to the sliding glass door and peek through the slit along the side of the curtains.

It takes all my self-control not to scream. Exposed in the moonlight is the assassin. He works a thin tool into the locking side of the door. I don't think he can unlock it, given the structure of that door. He couldn't open it even if he managed to unlock it because I put that brace between the wall and slider. But he could smash the glass and walk through the opening.

Now what do I do? Do I wait for him to break in and smash his skull with the shillelagh? That is tempting, yet as I imagine it, I know I must choose differently. He will not get in quickly. I have a several minutes but few choices. I must risk being caught by the police.

Put on my coat. My backpack has the texts in it. Zip it— quietly. Keep the shillelagh. Now I feel elated since I can take the car. Because I realize the threat, I know how to escape. I am no longer prey to the unknown. Where are my keys? Right in my coat pocket where they should be. That brings a sigh of relief.

Quietly, I open the back door into the garage. I tiptoe down two stairs to the garage floor, turn, and press the door in place. No time to lock it. Now the car door. It opens noiselessly. I'm in. The car feels safe! Now close the door quietly. That will be more of a challenge. Damn! It didn't close all the way. I need to do it more forcefully. Here goes. That made a loud noise. Did he hear it? Use the automatic door lock on the doors. Start the garage door opener. Shit, I forgot to get the key out! I fumble to get a key out of my pocket and into the ignition. Start the car.

Come on, come on. There we go. Into reverse and back into the driveway. Close the garage door. There he is, coming around the side of the house on the run and sprinting toward the driveway. Get the hell away!

How did he find me?

How did he get to the house?

In the rearview mirror, I see the stakeout's headlights swing onto the main road. My tires squeal as I speed up in the opposite direction. In the bright moonlight I can see what is happening. The assassin has run back toward the house. The stakeout pulls into the driveway and stops at a sharp angle near the garage door. It's too far away to be certain, but I think I saw both doors fly open and two people jump from the car. I glance in the mirror again. One runs down the front sidewalk and the other sprints around the side of the garage where the assassin retreated.

I feel relief knowing the police are chasing him, not me. I am in my car, heading away. I feel safer. What an irony! I felt so safe at home, yet I wasn't protected at all. I was lulled by my illusions. In the car, my back is covered and safe. Now I appreciate another dimension of my relief. Deana and the kids must be safe. If he had gotten them at the house, say kidnapped them before I got home, he would have stayed there, waiting for me. But he wasn't there. He came later. Unless he killed them in town. No, that doesn't add up. My calls to the police and hospital should have turned up three dead people . . . unless he hid them. Why would he do that? Despite my reasoning, I remain disquieted. I know this unease will haunt me until I see them, until I touch them all again.

When I called, I asked about accidents, not murders. There's a phone in the parking lot of a gas station in Brentway, a tiny farm town five miles from here. I can make a phone call without leaving the car. I must, must find out. No cars. No traffic.

I mustn't speed as that would bring me to the attention of the police.

As I expected the town is deserted and the gas station dark. As I turn into the driveway, my headlights illuminate a sign advertising regular gas for 84 cents. I park in the shadows next to the payphone, fish a dime out of the ashtray, reach out the window to get the handle, and slide the dime in the slot. I can hear the dial tone. Now dial the rotor. Most phones in this farming community and the university are now touchtone, but not here in the country.

"911. Emergency."

"Have there been any murders tonight?"

"Um?" I seem to have surprised the dispatcher.

"Have a woman and two children been murdered tonight?" I sound insistent, demanding an answer.

"One moment please."

Now I'm worried. The line seemed to go dead. Are they tracing the call? With 911 they might already know my location, but that was why I went to Brentway, so they wouldn't know or be able to get to me.

"There have been no murders, sir. Who is calling, please?"

What do I say? Do I hang up?

"Is this Dr. Butler?"

Fear courses through me, and I slam down the phone. How could the dispatcher have known to ask my name? They're on the lookout for me. I have to get away fast before they send a car here. I had been planning to go to the library to do research in the morning. I'll park nearby with the doors locked and sleep until seven thirty when it opens. No. The campus police will see the car if I park near the library. I should park somewhere else. And the assassin might explore the campus. He might have my license plate number and know my car. I'll avoid public areas for the rest of the night.

I remember driving by a hill, obscure, out of the way, and far off on a dirt road, at least seven miles farther out in the country and several miles from the main road. I get there by driving on several winding back roads, all dirt. I'll be able to see all around the car. I'm certain that neither the police nor the assassin can find me there. Then, when I drive to campus in the morning, I'll park across campus and walk to the library.

CHAPTER 29

Sunrise

Light shines through my eyelids. The sun warms my face. Six fifty-five. I've slept four hours. Now I have thirty-five minutes to wait until the library opens. Sunrise comes this late? I'm used to it being earlier during the summer. Sunrise must shift later quickly. I'm achy and stiff from sleeping in the car. I'm also a little cold. I wish I had time to rest more. My sleep has been terrible, starting at the slightest sound, dropping off and then startling awake, nightmare pictures of thugs chasing me with knives, trapped in a rowboat with but a single oar in a rough sea, trying and trying to get to shore but slipping farther and farther out into the current and the massive waves.

Dare I slip out of the car and take a leak? I'm painfully uncomfortable. I pick up the shillelagh for protection. Dew has settled on the dry, yellowed growth of weeds that covers the crest of this hill. As I relieve myself, I scan the environment, uncertain what I'm looking for but scared of what I might find.

Whatever I do later today, I must hide from both the assassin and the police. Along the route to town, there's a convenience store where I can buy coffee and an "instant" microwave break- fast. I can park in back and use the pay phone on the side of the building where I'll be shielded from the street. I'll call home again. From there the drive to the commuter lot will take less than fifteen minutes; a lot in which my car wouldn't be parked and where considerable traffic will mask it. Once parked, the walk to the library will take more than ten minutes. Many more students return to campus today and that will engage all the police forces in town to manage traffic, giving me greater freedom. I hop in the car, lock the doors, and start the engine.

I pass no cars going in either direction on my drive. I had wanted to drive by the house to see if there were clues they were back, but I worried about the stakeout seeing me. I pull in behind the convenience store, park, and call home. My hands are shaking. I'm so nervous I can't get the coins in the slot. How many times do I let it ring? That's three. Four. Five. Damn! The answering machine kicked in.

Get "breakfast" and a cup of coffee. I'm starved. I feel trembly and spacey. I hope eating will help. I'll eat behind the store and then leave for the commuter lot.

• • •

As I walk across campus, I have many conflicting impulses: walk on the grass behind bushes and trees that could provide cover, but that would draw more attention; walk on the sidewalk so I blend in with the students who are out and about, but this makes me more vulnerable and visible; walk where I can see the assassin before he sees me, but where is that? I opt for walking among the students, the backpack creating the impression I'm one of them. As I walk, I check to one side, glance to the other, peek behind, and then search in front of me, all the while scrutinizing the out-of-the-way hiding places.

Did he lurk behind the large, abstract sculpture that hints of Picasso? Is he watching me from a doorway or window whose panes are opaque as they reflect the early morning light? Is he hiding inside a large lilac bush or behind some thick-bodied blue spruce? I'm trying to balance protecting myself behind bushes and trees with being as inconspicuous as possible. I ache from the tension.

I hadn't considered his lurking around campus when I parked in the commuter lot. I'm surprised he hasn't caught me. I've developed this belief—a belief based on my experience, not just Rick's historical reports—he can find me wherever I am. I'm convinced that if he saw me, he would approach me.

Open the damn library; it's after seven thirty. I've been too eager, getting here a little early, and that created this problem. It would have been better to get here after it opened, so I wouldn't have to wait outside, exposed and vulnerable. I should have parked closer to the library, and I should have brought that shillelagh. That could be a fatal mistake. I'm doing my best to hide next to the legs of the huge commemorative sculpture in the center of Library Plaza. The base is a cement circle fifteen feet wide. From three evenly spaced points along the circumference, thick steel legs rise to join at the base of a mirrored sphere. From the sphere's upper surface emerges an array of at least a dozen pieces of metal, each a different shape and color.

I remember the dedication ceremony that celebrated the university's fiftieth anniversary and the unveiling of the sculpture. The sculptor named his piece "Exploding." The three legs represent the major roles of a university: teaching, research, and service. The sphere represents the faculty and student body. The metal pieces represent different kinds of knowledge, which explode out into the world. I remember the huge crowd that attended the dedication, the speeches by the university president and the chair of the board, and the caustic comments by almost everyone about its strange appearance and astronomical cost. No one understood what possessed the university art committee to recommend this sculpture.

At last someone unlocks the doors . . . but with agonizing deliberateness. Come on! Open the door! I start for the door before it's unlocked. I glance around to check the plaza, and I'm the only person approaching the library. A few people are going into the Student Union. Only five more paces. Deep breath. Inside!

Before going to the stacks, I need to call home again. It has been half an hour. I can use the free courtesy phone in the hallway. There are so few people in the library it should be available. I remember the countless times I've waited for someone to get off the phone. At those times, I've just wanted to make a brief call, but I have to stand listening to the caller talk on and on, indifferent to the growing line.

Dial home and talk to Deana. What's wrong with this phone? It's ringing while I'm still dialing.

"Accounting. Beth speaking. Can I help you?"

"Oh. I'm sorry. I dialed incorrectly. I was trying to dial an off-campus number, and I forgot to dial nine."

Try again. Dial nine, then the number. One ring, two, three, four. No one's there. I'll leave a message on the machine this time.

"Deana, this is Jason. Where are you? Where have you been? Would you at least let me know where you are? Leave a message at the office. I love you."

What's next? Call the Farleys...if they're home. They should be since it's before eight in the morning.

"Shirl? It's Jason again. Sorry about waking you last night, but I'm scared shitless. Have you heard from Deana since my last call?"

"No, Jason, I'm sorry. Not a word. I wish I knew something but I don't."

"Oh!" I'm sure my desperation is clear in my voice. "I was hanging onto the hope she had called you. If you hear from her, ask her to leave a message at the office, will you? I'm freaked out."

"I know, Jason. I couldn't sleep after you called. Now, this morning, we find out Volks was murdered. I hope they catch him."

"You do not understand how much I'd like him caught."

"I'll bet you do, you being a witness and in the paper."

"My name was in the paper! Oh, God. I didn't know. What did it say?"

"Just a moment. I need to get the paper." I hear the phone clatter, several footsteps, and then the rustle of paper. "Let's see. Rick Volks was murdered at 4:30 yesterday, stated police . . ."

"No, Shirl, about me!"

"Okay, let's see. 'The only witness to the murder was Jason Butler, a faculty member in Psychology, who refused to answer questions.' That's all it says about you."

"Oh, God, no. I asked not to have my name in the paper. What do I do now? What do I do?"

"Why's this a problem?"

"It makes me a target. He might come after me next!" The words tumble out. I feel frantic. "I've got to go! If you hear from Deana, let her know I'm trying to reach her." I hang up.

I was abrupt and rude at the end. *Sorry, Shirl. I had to get off the phone.*

Now I'm terrified. I had forgotten about the paper. He knows my name for sure. Wait. He knows my name anyway. Otherwise, how could he have found my office and my house? I guess it was illogical to think he could find them and still not know who I am. This kind of irrationality, no, it's stupidity, embarrasses me. My name in the paper doesn't give him anything he didn't already have.

I have a sudden insight: keeping my name out of the paper contributed to my illusion of being protected. It was the same illusion of safety in my house . . . and in the car. That's why I feel exposed and threatened now. There is no way to protect myself . . . except leaving town. I know of several remote campgrounds in state forests that would be perfect. But what about Deana and the kids? I can't leave them.

I can do nothing about this right now, so I'd better comb the library. First, grab a place in the faculty reading room on the fourth floor. I'm glad I have the key and a combination locker where I can hide the texts. Since the reading room is private and locked, I'll be protected there.

Take the elevator to the fourth floor. Unlock the door. Look inside. Good, no one is here. That's a relief. Who in their right mind would be here at this hour anyway? Faculty don't use this room before the semester begins. Most do their library research here later in the semester; and preparing for classes takes precedence right now. I'll be alone. Look at that! There are both microfiche and microfilm readers in this room. If I have to use those, I can bring film and fiche up here. The room is perfect. The door is solid; no one can look in. The room is L-shaped, with six long tables arranged along its length and four study carrels in the short arm of the L. That short arm is shielded from the entrance. Drop off my coat and backpack at a carrel around the corner. I'll be hidden from anyone who enters the room. Put the texts in my locker, grab my pad of paper, and take a pen. I'm ready to start; but where do I begin?

Rick alluded to different news stories, but his references were not complete. Better get out the texts and jot down his fragmentary information, so I can track them down. If the library has an index of news stories about the Middle and Far East, that should give me complete citations. And I would need English translations of everything. There is also the special medical report Rick referred to. I must get that. In fact, that report is the most critical item. I don't know where to find that. I'd better start with the reference department. When preparing our grant application, we discovered that those librarians were incredible.

I take the texts out of the locker, record his fragmentary information, lock up the texts, and head for the reference desk on the second floor. Walking down the stairs puts me in the open again. Hesitating at the double doors to the second floor, I push them open, jerk my hand back, and then let them close again while I scrutinize what lies on the other side of the entryway glass. The white-tiled, open floor extends at least twenty yards to the reference desk. Thirty banks of card catalogues create rows behind and to the side of the reference desk. Only two patrons, students, are working at open drawers of cards. I'm glad I know the librarian who's working this morning.

"Hi, Susan," I say while I'm still a long distance from the counter. "Can you help me?"

She nods, mouths, "Good morning," but studies at me. Then, after continuing to stare, she says, "Sure," as if she realized she had said nothing in response to my question. Do I look that bad? I haven't shaved, but her look communicates something more. Even under the press of her continued stare and silence, I delay, agonizing over the words I am about to say. These words are a public declaration of my knowledge about the terrorists. Dread reinforces my silence. The awkwardness between us continues. I try to break out of my immobility by moving my mouth and licking my lips, a curious action and Susan raises her eyebrows. Clearing my throat frees me to talk. I take a deep breath and start.

"What do we have on a Middle or Far Eastern terrorist group called the Shra'kufans?" I blurt out. There! I've said the words! My legs get shaky as adrenaline surges through me. I find it difficult to concentrate or hear Susan. My heart pounds and my ears seem filled with a rushing noise. I swallow and retrieve the auditory memory of what she said.

"Let's look." She stands and walks to the public computer a few yards to the side of the reference desk. I watch her walk away and then realize I should follow. I shuffle after her but can't hear her question from the terminal. She inserts a five-and-a-quarter-inch disk into the drive and pushes a few keys. The computer loads the disk. She turns toward me and repeats her words. By now, I'm close enough to hear.

"How do you spell that?"

I mumble the name, finding I cannot say the sounds right. Using one of the library's stubby pencils, I write "Shra'kufan" on a slip of paper, amazed at how my hand trembles and how my coordination requires exacting effort. Susan's expression reminds me of someone who ate a lemon. She types the word and presses return. "Not found" flashes on the screen a short while later.

"Let's try something else." She makes five more tries and gives up. She next looks at the contents of two additional discs. "It's not a book title or a subject anywhere in any library in a ten-state area," she reports. My heart sinks. "Do you want to try searching the Library of Congress?"

"Um." I have trouble knowing how to proceed. Her expression is souring again. "Yes," I say, realizing it makes no sense not to try. She flips through a pile of discs in a plastic box and loads a new disc. After a little typing at the keyboard, she shakes her head.

"Nope," she says. "Not there."

I remember the notes I jotted down from Rick's materials and glance down at them. "How about a journal called *Medical Science*?"

She loads a new disk and enters the title.

"We don't have that journal, but we show that a few libraries in the area do. Burrel State does. That's close, so you might have good luck there. State also has the journal. You could try interlibrary loan."

"I'll go to interlibrary loan next." I stall and, on a hope, ask, "But let me ask another question. If I want to get news reports out of the Middle and Far East, what do I do?"

"Let's see." Again she types and examines the screen. She writes call numbers down. "We have the Middle and Far East Abstract and the Oriental Index. That title," she adds in lecture style, "is a hold-over from the cultural attitudes when the Index was first created in the late 1800s. Oh, and there is the Index of Contemporary Asian News. If none of these have what you want, you could try the indexes to the *Washington Post, New York Times,* and the *International Herald Tribune.* Those are all in that large area at the other end of this floor with the psych abstracts." She points across the wide open lobby to table after table of double-shelved abstracts and indexes. I realize I can hide between the tables once I get there. But first I'll make my way to interlibrary loan.

"Thanks, Susan. I appreciate your help." As I turn away, Susan clears her throat, and I pause, glancing at her.

"I saw the story in the paper. I don't know if you know this, but you look like hell. Are you all right?"

"I'm okay, I guess."

"Well, it's terrible." Her voice has dropped to a loud whisper but her speech is quick. "What happened? Did you see it? Who did it? And is this terrorist group involved in Dr. Volks's murder?"

I groan inside. "Susan, I wish I could talk about it. Not now, okay? I need all my energy to follow up on this stuff." She looks disappointed, but nods with understanding. "And, I'm not up to talking about it right now."

"I can understand that. But I had to ask. I don't think we've had a murder in town. Ever."

"Thanks for being understanding."

As I enter the interlibrary loan office, the librarian looks up.

"Hi! I need materials we don't have here," I say.

The librarian sets down his cup of coffee and swallows. "Well, that's what we do. You're in the right place."

His gray hair is brushed straight back, and he wears black-framed glasses that make his eyes appear owlish. His skin is gray-tinged and made more noticeable by his red-striped shirt. I'm dismayed that I don't know him, though he looks familiar.

"I sure hope you can help. There's an article published last year in *Medical Science*. We don't get that journal, but Burrel State does." I'm repelled by the sound of my voice. The pitch is high and nasal, and my words seem to rush out. "I don't know the exact title, and I don't know the author." My voice is pleading, and I hope I'm not alienating him. "Is there any way you could get me the table of contents so I can see what's there and then request the article itself? And, hope upon hope, do it today? Maybe even this morning?"

"No problem." Relief. *But there's got to be a catch.* "You're lucky you got here early. We've just opened and so has Burrel. I'll fax the request promptly. The ILL there, that's the interlibrary loan librarian, is cooperative. We send stuff back and forth all the time. If he's not sick, we should get a response within the hour. One thing, though: there is a charge for rush orders."

"That's fine. I'll pay double if that would help. Here," I say, handing him the paper with the journal name. "The article is in one of last year's volumes." I pause. He says nothing and picks up the paper. "Thanks heaps. I'll be in the abstracts if it comes in soon." As I turn to leave, he nods while looking at the paper.

The rows of abstracts and indexes stretch out in front of me. An aisle runs down the center. I drift along the aisle looking right and left for the volumes dealing with the Middle and Far East. Here they are. I can start my search. The more I focus on the task at hand, the less I'm aware of my internal state. And that's a good thing.

CHAPTER 30

10:45 a.m.

Thank goodness for reference librarians. I wouldn't have known where to begin without their help. I have been here for two hours and so far my own search has been fruitless. I take a break from the indexes and consult with the librarian for Religion, Philosophy and Anthropology—a woman I don't know—and ask if she has any books that might give me information about an obscure religion.

"I do," she says, beaming. She leads me to a shelf of books and pulls one out. "This," she says, "is the gold standard, *The Encyclopedia of Religions*. It is the most up-to-date publication on religion. Revised this year." She hands me the heavy tome. "There you go," she says with a big smile, eyes twinkling with satisfaction.

I turn to the index, and I'm exhilarated to see it includes Shra'kufans. I flip through the book until I find the right page and read.

SHRA'KUFAN(S) The religion is based on the teachings of Baya Z'r, a poor desert nomad born in the mountainous regions of the Far East. He proselytized his beliefs in the fifth century B.C. and began agrarian reforms. The adherents of this religion live in the region where Baya Z'r spread his teachings. Little is known about their beliefs, but experts assert modern adherents are few. Some contend that the religion is extinct. The derivation of the name "Shra'kufan" is not clear but most authorities agree that the group was a band of desert nomads who herded camels, hence the origin of the name.

The entry is inaccurate and incomplete though the book was just published. This makes me wonder if I already know more about them than is available anywhere. I'm going back to the faculty reading room to find the passage Rick wrote about the etymology of the name Shra'kufan.

Back in the room, I flip through the manuscript pages looking for Rick's explanation. I know I saw it last night. Last night? It's only been twelve hours since this mess began. At last I find what I am looking for:

A variety of sources clarify the etymology of "Shra'kufan" as a name that evolved from the contraction and blending of two words. "Sahra" or "shara" meaning "desert" and "kaufa" meaning "mountain." Over time, the two sounds shifted to "shra" and "kufa." The anglicizing of the word added the final "n" and the English name became "Shra'kufan." In effect, this name denotes the region from which this religion came, "the desert-mountain," or the foothills. As Baya Z'r's new religion flourished, it became known as the religion from the foothills: Shra'kufan.

Some scholars, not privy to either this information or the original texts and attempting from their limited perspective to understand an obscure and dead religion, have assumed that the name "Shra'kufan" referred to a group of desert nomads. They infer this by interpreting the "kufa" as "kaofa," which means a "camel's hump." Thus, they suggest the name means "desert camel" referring to desert nomads who used or traded camels. This interpretation is inaccurate and captures largely the extent to which the Shra'kufans are misunderstood and unknown.

Of additional interest is the impossibility of pinpointing the precise origin and current location of the Shra'kufans. The geography of the Middle and Far East shows an almost continuous series of mountains, most bordering deserts, from Turkey to China, traveling along or through Iraq, Iran, Afghanistan, India, and Tibet. A branch of these mountains reaches up toward Russia. The Shra'kufan's origin could be anywhere along those mountains, and the current adherents live in small enclaves scattered across a thousand miles of foothills.

After reading this, I realize that current religious scholars would be of little help to my understanding of the Shra'kufans. Standard references will not be useful. I must do my research on my own and creatively.

I try searching the two computerized databases the library acquired. After what feels like an eternity, the first disk loads, and I enter my search terms, one at a time: Middle East, Far East, terrorist, Shra'kufan, Baya Z'r. Neither database proves useful.

I go back to searching the paper indexes, focusing my attention on one I had ignored, the Index of Contemporary Asian News. There are sixty volumes to review, a big job. I start with the newest volume and look up the heading "terrorism." I scan every one of its subheadings, but Shra'kufan never appears. I repeat my search for the past 15 years, but still no mention of Shra'kufan.

The interlibrary loan librarian turns into my aisle. I jump in surprise and I can feel my face turning red. He grunts in response to my reaction, stops moving for a second, peers at me, furrows his brow, and then, easing forward, stretches out his hand holding a fax.

"Thanks. I'm not sleeping well...jumpy..." My voice trails off as the words fail to come. He shrugs, after a perfunctory

"S'okay," and turns and leaves. I skim the fax, find the title I want, and follow him back to his office. After my reaction when he showed up, I feel awkward being around him.

"Fill out this form and I'll fax it right away," he says. I complete the form standing next to his desk, eager to get back to the indexes. When he takes the form, he glances down, puts it in a filing basket, and then brings it closer to his glasses to peer at it.

"Were you . . . ," His voice trails off. He peers at me. "That murder yesterday. Are you?"

"Yes. That was me. I was there. That's why I'm sort of jumpy."

"Oh, yeah. I would be too." He sits with a thoughtful expression on his face. Before he can ask any more questions, I turn to leave.

"Got to get back to it," I say on my way out the door. But then I pause, turning back. "Is it possible to get that article quickly?" He nods and stands up, turning toward what I think is a fax machine.

"Thanks. Thanks a lot," I say as I start back to the abstracts and indexes.

Throughout these past hours, my background worry has nagged at me. Where are Deana and the kids? I've called home every half hour! No answer. As I look for specific books, journals, and microfiche, my family has been a constant preoccupation. Where are they? Are they safe?

I called my office for messages. There were none. Then I called my secretary to find out if Deana had called. "If she calls," I asked her, "please have her leave a phone number and ask her if she is okay? If the kids are okay?"

"I saw the story in the paper. Are you okay? Are they okay?" she had asked. I avoided her question by saying I had to rush off, but before I could hang up she said, "Wait. One more thing. The police dropped by earlier. They looked in your office and asked questions. They wanted to know if you had called. I'm not sure . . ."

"Got to go, PJ. Thanks." I decided not to call her again. I had also stopped calling the police but called the hospital again. I don't care if they're bothered. I need to know! As before, they had no information that was helpful.

No messages at Deana's job either. Not even a call saying she would be late or was sick. This can only mean she can't call because she's injured or being kept from the phone.

The five different friends I contacted this morning knew *nothing*. Nobody has heard from her. And Mom and Dad didn't answer. I'm sure that means they are on their way here. I've got to let all of this go and return to learning about the Shra'kufans.

I change tactics and pull out the microfiche for "The Source: Where East and West Meet Daily." I check the annual index for the past ten years, the entire run of the newspaper. Nothing! No articles reference Shra'kufans. Talk about frustrating. Dismayed, I turn to religion journals, even though I am convinced I will find nothing. After a fruitless search, what other options do I have but to return to the paper abstracts and indexes? I glance at my watch and see what time it is. 11:25. I've been so engrossed I've lost track of time.

I'm giving up hope of finding anything and out of desperation and stubbornness, search indexes that summarize English-language newspapers, a resource I had considered irrelevant. At last, I find a single reference to Shra'kufans, over six years old, in the *Middle and Far East News Service*, a newspaper that writes for a British and American audience. We have the complete works on microfiche. I find the story on the fiche and read.

SHRA'KUFANS ELUSIVE
Today's efforts to trace the headquarters of the Shra'kufan terrorists who assassinated two elected representatives proved

futile. "An extensive search for their base in the mountains yielded no results," stated a government official. In frustration the search party burned and destroyed what remained of a camp, believed to have been set up by the Shra'kufans.

Attempts to get information from local residents provided nothing useful. Informants who did not want to be identified stated that people fear Shra'kufan retaliation if they talk with reporters. General Kohtue said, "No one will even talk to us. The terrorists definitely threatened the locals with severe reprisals. Shra'kufan spies are likely standing right here among us, listening to what everyone says, including myself. Under these circumstances, no one would be foolish enough to talk." The search for these terrorists continues, but a spokesman said they are not hopeful.

I've found information, scant though it is. It echoes Rick's warnings about how dangerous the Shra'kufans are. I take my collected materials back to the faculty reading room. When there, I'll check the newspaper's microfiche for other stories on Shra'kufans. I select books, journals, magazines, microfilms, and other microfiche, stack them on a cart, shove it onto the elevator, and travel up to the fourth floor to go back to my makeshift office. On the way, my mind turns again to my family and my safety. I've been able to block out my fears as I operated in academic mode. The story I read makes that no longer possible. I want to make another call to someone, anyone who could give me information about my family, but I've already tried everyone I can think of, and right now I need to focus on my library search.

Back in the reading room, I start with the microfiche of the *Middle and Far East News Service* and go through each paper, page by page, scanning every article in editions dated three months before and after the one referencing the Shra'kufans.

Success! I find three articles: the earliest is dated a few days before that first abstract with "Shra'kufan" in the title; the other two are dated afterward, perhaps a week or two. I read them attentively.

FANATICS KILL SENATORS DECIDING THEIR FATE

During yesterday's parliamentary session, Senators Makshoh Rubizyr and Hopol Saifell were assassinated in front of their elected colleagues as they urged the routing and destruction of subversive and violent Shra'kufan terrorists. This new terrorist group had come to the attention of the parliament following the destruction of an electricity generating plant, almost ready to produce power, which would have stimulated this country's flagging economy. To the horror of all present, two zealots ran from the hallway at the front of the chamber while being chased by guards, guns drawn but unable to shoot given the crush of people. They pressed lethal blue pellets against both senators' necks. Each died a short while later. Only moments after the assassinations, now having clear shots, guards opened fire and killed both assassins. This is one of a recent series of atrocities by Shra'kufans that have alarmed government officials here.

Given the severity of the atrocities, I'm baffled why the group has not attracted more attention, but at least I have found something. It confirms what Rick wrote. I had been hoping Rick was wrong. I had been hoping that what I found here in the library would put a different spin on the events; that the Shra'kufans would not be as determined and as lethal as Rick concluded. This is not good news. I'd better read the other two stories.

DEADLY CHEMICAL, USED BY ASSASSINS, ANALYZED

Unofficial reports from the medical school here show that chemical analysis of the blue substance found in the lethal pellets used by Shra'kufan fanatics to assassinate political leaders last Monday contain both neurotransmitters and site-specific hormones, related to endorphin inhibition. Neurotransmitters are the chemical messengers that travel between nerve cells to excite or inhibit the transmission of nerve impulses. Endorphins are the body's self-generated opiates and often work as anesthetic or mood enhancers. Analysis was difficult since the compound is unstable when exposed to air. The fluid possesses remarkable transfer properties. It passes through the skin and into the body on contact. What remains in contact with the air breaks down into harmless chemicals. Researchers were fortunate to find substance still trapped inside one pellet used this past Monday. Further research is being done by Dr. Joag Saifell to clarify the precise action of the chemical within the body.

NOTED PHYSICIAN DIES UNEXPECTEDLY

Dr. Joag Saifell died yesterday, suffering an overall systemic breakdown while working alone on an experiment in his laboratory. He had been working day and night to understand the chemical makeup and activity of the lethal drug used by Shra'kufan terrorists to assassinate his brother, Hopol Saifell, one of this country's most respected politicians. Physicians at the hospital said, off the record, that his death was out of the ordinary in that a recent, routine checkup proved normal, and other than a few colds, he had not been ill in several years. Those interviewed admitted that a healthy physical exam did not prevent his dying soon thereafter. Some conjectured that he had gotten it on his skin. Others remarked on the cardiovascular ruptures found at his autopsy. A hospital spokesperson said it was as if his blood pressure and heart rate had gone out of control, leading to the eventual rupturing of the vascular walls not only of his heart but throughout his body. Several physicians, unwilling to be identified, feared that he had been assassinated.

Reading these materials has taken longer than I expected. It's already 11:45, and I still have much to review. I shouldn't be surprised that this is a slow process: poring over indices and abstracts and reading articles. I have something, but it's scant. It seems to corroborate Rick's claim governments and media know little about the Shra'kufans. They have remained hidden and outside the mainstream.

I'm exhausted right now. This has wrung me out. Well, I got little sleep. I will be tired. And this is stressful. When I rub my face, I feel the stubble from not having shaved. I'll take a break, go to the bathroom, wash my face, get a drink of water, call home for the umpteenth time, and check with interlibrary loan to see if the article from *Medical Science* has arrived.

Bathroom, here I come.

• • •

After pushing through the restroom doors, I walk by a long mirror that stretches across three sinks. I glance at myself and can't believe how awful I look. I have stubble growing above and below my beard; swollen, bloodshot eyes; and disheveled, greasy hair. The face doesn't look like me. It stares back at me, open-mouthed and unfamiliar. My appearance is visible evidence of the toll this has been taking. That must be why these librarians and many patrons keep shooting me sidelong glances and avoid looking at me when we talk. I look down at the sink. I turn on the water, wait for it to get warm, and then wash my hands and face. Scrubbing my face seems to invigorate me, yet when I look in the mirror, my appearance disturbs me since my face seems distorted in some confusing way.

As I walk toward the interlibrary loan office, I reflect on the absence of any new information from my phone calls. No messages. Nothing new. It's like my family has disappeared. When I enter the office, the librarian nods, beaming, and waves a greeting with several sheets of paper. He must not be too appalled at my appearance if he is greeting me this way.

"You got the article! Fantastic. You've saved my life. I worried it would take at least a day. Thank you, thank you, and thank you. What do I owe you?"

"We'll bill you. Everything we need is on the form you submitted." He hands me the papers, and I head back to the faculty reading room.

"Let's see," I say to myself as I walk to the elevator, "who wrote this article? It's … it's …" I'm dumbfounded. G. J. Saifell. Wasn't that the researcher in the newspaper story? The one who was killed? As soon as I get to the reading room, I flip the fiche back into the reader and check the news story. Yep, it was Saifell. But it was a Joag Saifell named in the article, not G. J. Saifell. Are there three Saifells: Hopol, Joag, and G. J.? Are they related? If so, is one still alive? And might he be a source of information? I don't know how to figure this out right now, but if one's alive, that's important.

I glance down at the article and notice it is in the Brief Research Reports section of the journal. In the journals I'm familiar with, these are less formal and detailed than peer-reviewed research articles and often submitted for quick publication to disseminate important results. I scan its pages, and I'm dismayed to see it is technical. I hope I can understand it, since I'm not a medical doctor or pharmacologist. I settle back into my chair to read "Compound E-X8—Hormone, Neurotransmitter or Biochemical Unknown" by G. J. Saifell, M.D. The summary at the beginning says:

This pilot study examined the chemical properties and physiological action of a lethal compound used by terrorists to assassinate politicians. Blue pellets discovered in the assassin's

BLUE SKY DEADLY SECRETS • 223

clothing were analyzed. The researchers assigned the name E-X8 to the compound, which passes through the skin and the blood-brain barrier. This compound killed rats in four out of five experimental conditions. E-X8 seems to act on the body in a heretofore unknown way, and so far, researchers could not develop an antidote.

At last I've found something I could use. The blue pellets must be the Samatma, the Blue Sky, Rick referred to in his writing. And this must have been what the assassin tried to put against my neck as I was falling in Rick's doorway. Lethal and no antidote. All right, onto the next section.

Researchers have discovered that E-X8 enters the body through the skin. Since the assassins killed by placing the blue pellets against the neck, the researchers used dermal contact as one of the experimental conditions. Rats were randomly assigned to five groups, 20 subjects per group. All subjects were administered E-X8.

Group 1 was administered E-X8 via dermal contact.

Group 2 received an injection of E-X8.

Group 3 was given a tranquilizer 30 minutes prior to an injection of E-X8.

Group 4 was given reserpine, a drug that inhibits all bodily movement, and then injected with E-X8.

Group 5 was given a general anesthetic making them unconscious prior to the injection of E-X8.

All rats were monitored for muscle tension, blood pressure, heart rate, rate of breathing, and oxygen usage. Blood was sampled at 15-second intervals from 10 minutes before the administration of E-X8 until 20 minutes post-injection or until the subject died.

So far, so good. I can follow the article. I understand the five groups: the first and second were in a normal, undrugged state; the third was calmer than the others due to the tranquilizer; the fourth group was awake, but couldn't move due to reserpine which, Saifell indicated, immobilizes the subject while allowing them to remain conscious; and the fifth was unconscious and "slept" through the whole experience. I wonder why he chose these options. Did he do preliminary work with other rats to figure out the best conditions from which to gather data? I wonder if that was when he discovered the Samatma would go right through the skin.

> Group 1 and 2 rats, E-X8 only, died in 20 to 30 seconds.
> Group 3, tranquilized rats, were the slowest to die, dying in 40 to 90 seconds.
> Group 4, reserpine-treated rats, were the fastest to die, dying in 10 to 15 seconds.
> Group 5, unconscious rats, did not die.

My mind is going a mile a minute. How can you explain these results? What do they mean? And what does this mean about Samatma's effect on humans? I assume it is slower because the human body is so much larger than a rat's. Read the next section.

> Results: Muscle contractions, blood pressure, heart rate, and blood oxygen.
> All subjects in all groups showed increasing contraction of the skeletal muscles eventuating in almost complete rigidity of the body. For the unconscious subjects, all of whom survived, the rigidity lessened over 10 to 30 seconds once heart rate and blood pressure dropped.

Looking at the following pages, the article is getting more technical, and I'm sweating, both literally and figuratively. If I remember my physiology course, the skeletal muscles connect to the bones and allow us to move. That's why I can pick up a pencil. The study results focus on skeletal muscles and show that the drug leads to full-body contractions and immobility, which clear up in the unconscious group.

All right, what's next? It's getting technical, and there are graphs. Glancing at the text, I see the words "exponential increase." I can see that all the graphs, except for Group 5 (the unconscious subjects), follow an exponential increase in heart rate, blood pressure, and decrease in blood-oxygen level, which stops when they die. Group 5 levels off and then drops back to normal. Why does the drug work differently in the unconscious group?

I don't understand how all of this fits together. Where is Harry Brown when I need him? Harry is a tall, lanky fellow with receding hair and bulging eyes. He is a physiologist, runner, and all-around pleasant guy. We often run together, and I enjoy hearing him talk about the new discoveries in his field. He would understand the article and could answer the many questions I have.

Saifell continues with more research results in which he measured two different chemicals in the blood that are triggered by stress. These graphs are almost identical to the earlier ones, including the unconscious group, which never has an exponential increase.

As the article goes on, the text is getting yet more technical, referring to different brain regions, hormones, and neurotransmitters. There's a lot in this part I don't understand, but I understand Saifell's statement that E-X8 penetrates the blood-brain barrier. That means it can influence what happens in the brain. And

Saifell writes: "E-X8 blocks the usual feedback mechanism that stops the release of stress-activating hormones." He continues with the following passage:

> We hypothesize that E-X8 acts synergistically with epineph-rine to exacerbate the stress response. This stimulates the release of more adrenaline. Once the new adrenaline is in the bloodstream, this increased level seems to interact with E-X8 to increase the release of even more adrenaline. This hypothesis explains why there is an initial stress response, followed by an exponential increase in all physiological stress measures when the synergistic cycle kicks into action. (However, the muscle contractions and low oxygen levels cannot be explained by this hypothesis.) The intense, abrupt, and enormous increase in the stress response propels the body to "burn itself out," to destroy itself with excessive activation.

That's it. That's the end of the article. And look at that! At the bottom of the article, where more detailed information is listed, the author's name is "G. Joag Saifell." Is this the same "Joag Saifell" referred to in the news story? Was he called by his middle name, and the news story followed suit? Is the author of this article the same man who was killed in his laboratory? If the university affiliation is the same, I'll be certain. The different names would then refer to the same person. I check the newspaper article again, this time having the foresight not to take it out of the microfiche reader. It's the same university! It's the same man. There must only be two Saifells, not three. The Saifells, whoever they are, must have been trying to stop the Shra'kufans. The consequences are what Rick forewarned; both are dead.

I'm dumbfounded and overwhelmed by what I read. I couldn't get all the technical details but I could understand the methods and conclusions, which frighten me: death is fast and unavoidable. I now realize that in the back of my mind I had counted on finding a way out, but from what I can tell this drug is impossible to counteract. If I have it right, the drug increases heart rate and blood pressure, constricts the muscles of the body so it is rigid, and drops oxygen in the blood to lethal levels. Damn. I try to avoid noticing the slight but undeniable shaking that has crept into my belly. Damn. My hands and feet tingle; adrenaline must pump in my system. What do I do? What can I do?

Death occurred in twenty to thirty seconds. Burns itself out. These sentences from the article force themselves back into my mind. I came to the library to get information on what to do and how to survive. Instead I found out there's no way to survive if the assassin gets near enough to put Samatma on my neck.

CHAPTER 31

12:25 p.m.

One day! Less than one day! And this has happened. Unbelievable. At least I can discern the drop in my adrenaline. For an unknown reason, I find myself better and less frightened. Although I'm confused as why.

I walk back and forth between the door and the long vertical windows that could offer a view of the sculpture in front of the library's main door. My pacing has been a major way I've coped this past day. The venetian blinds angle to stop anyone on the ground from seeing in. I pull aside the edge of one slat and look at the plaza. The sun shines on the yellow-green grass and reflects off the sculpture. I'm surprised no one is walking along the path next to the library. This is in stark contrast to next week when students will scurry back and forth to classes. I drop the slats. What do I do now? I shrug as I turn away from the window. I might as well collect the reference material and return it.

Stack up the books. The microfiche, as much as I dislike them, are much easier to gather than the heavy volumes. *Body reactions.* Those words keep coming to mind. I assume because the article discussed them. And over this past day, I have been experiencing strong bodily reactions! I sense a connection. What does the article mention regarding physical reactions? I pause, holding a stack of fiche above the cart; a gut reaction grabs my attention. I recognize what this reaction means: There's something here! Keep going! Stay with it! What did the article say? Where is it? I put the stack of fiche on the cart and, still standing, pick up the research article again. I scan the text, looking for the passage.

> Researchers were puzzled that rats under a general anesthetic showed bodily changes such as increased oxygen use, blood pressure, heart rate and constricted muscles, but did not die. Reserpine-treated rats died more quickly, and tranquilized rats, though awake, died more slowly than non-tranquilized rats.

Bodily reactions! Maybe. Maybe that's the key. If a rat knows what is going on, epinephrine gets released since the rat experiences fear or stress. That kicks off a strong bodily response. An unconscious rat, knocked out by an anesthetic, does not react. Since it is unaware what's happening, it will not respond with fear. If it were afraid, its body would release epinephrine. But it's not afraid; as a result, no epinephrine. Since no epinephrine is released, it does not trigger the synergistic cycle with the drug and the rat survives. A tranquilized rat reacts more slowly. The tranquilizer keeps the fear in check, so the release of epinephrine is slower than for a rat that was not tranquilized. Once epinephrine is released, the synergistic cycle starts, the process goes haywire, and the tranquilized rat dies. A rat unable to move because of reserpine must be terrified, so it dies more quickly. The terror leads to a hard-wired fight-or-flight response, which the immobilized rat can't activate, leading to even more fear, increasing epinephrine. Since that rat already has high epinephrine in its bloodstream, when you add Samatma the rat dies in ten to fifteen seconds.

I'll be damned. It fits! The secret of staying alive is not to react with fear. Now I know what to do. These years practicing tai chi, meditation, and mind-body activities can save my life. I create these bodily responses myself, by my perceptions, by my thoughts, by my expectations, by my beliefs. This past day emotions have swamped me: terror, grief, and rage. It is time to confront the whole of it. Time to stop. To stop . . . what? Fighting the inevitable? Fighting time? Fighting the future? Thank goodness few use this room this early in the semester. My teacher's words flow through my mind.

"Yield and be preserved whole. These are no idle words."

"Lose the battle, but win the war."

"Transform your emotions; do not resist or encourage them; without effort, they transform themselves."

Last night I was dismissing these exact words. I didn't believe them. Yet, here and now, I understand how they might succeed, how they might, in fact, work in this impossible predicament.

The door remains locked. Though some people have a key, I can expect to stay alone and can confront this. I know where I need to focus my meditation: my death and my fear. Last night, I sensed this precise focus, though I didn't confront it. Now I need to plunge into and through it. Can I overcome my fear of death? I might never know. No. Wrong. I will know if I succeed . . . and I will apprehend my failure as I die. Thinking this, saying the words to myself, my stomach hurts.

First, settle. Spine vertical. Notice breathing. Notice what appears. Where are Deana and the kids? Where can they be? Are they safe? Did they call home and find I wasn't there? Or call the office? Are they frantic about where I am? I'm frantic about them. My God, I haven't called home again. I'll do that before I start. Otherwise, intrusions will come next time I try.

I lean forward, roll onto the balls of my feet, and, as I rise, swivel toward the open room. I have learned that, as my mind relaxes, whatever is bothering me bubbles up—my motivations, worries, discomforts, any unfinished business. I open the door, checking my pocket for the key. The intrusions become a telling pointer to my state, who I am at that moment, since I am exposed to myself. But now, as I begin to meditate, the next thing I do is to avoid the whole thing by walking to the phone. Ironic. I push through the doorway leading to a librarian's telephone. Am I avoiding what is frightening me? Am I too agitated to focus my mind? Perhaps. But I'll never find the answers since I'm avoiding the situation . . . and here is the phone. No one is at the desk. I put my hand on the phone and take a deep breath, now reflexive. Dial. The phone rings three times and clicks as it shifts to the answering machine. I shake my head in bewilderment, lower the phone, pause, and let it drop the last inch. I stare through the empty stacks of books, waiting for an answer, a solution, a direction, to come from an unknown place. I call the hospital emergency room and hear again that there have been no accidents and no emergencies involving two children and a mother. Resigned, I start back to the reading room.

When I get to the chair in the reading room, I slip off my shoes. I wiggle my toes, their movement helping me relax. Now try to meditate again. Sit on the forward edge of the chair, feet flat. Let tension go. Let my posture straighten and relax. I'm glad I called. No accidents, no hospital emergencies, no information. That means they are okay. Although as I consider the details further, my conclusion might be an error in logic. Despite my conviction (or my wish) that they are safe and healthy, no answer at home still creates uneasiness.

I need to do a focused, problem-solving meditation. I've been avoiding this. I've closed my eyes to the issues. That is understandable: why would I want to focus on my death? Yet that is what I need to do! I can hear a counterargument: whatever needs to come up will emerge. No need to restrict your mind. But this agitated energy needs focus. I know without question I must confront death. Even the phrasing is avoidance: "confront death." I must confront *my* death. I'm troubled at facing it and at hiding from it. I'm caught either way.

Once I'm relaxed and my breath even and smooth, I have to let my mind settle on an image of my death. By holding the image, emotions, thoughts, and sensations will erupt, and I need to let them be until they neutralize. Repeat the process again and again. I don't want to do this. I want to avoid this but I must. I must.

Let the tension go … notice it and let it go … then transition to breathing. Just notice. Let it … go. Calmer, more even, smoother. Body light. Almost no sense of a body. The I-sense becomes central in awareness. Let the self go. Let the watcher and the watched join. No distance. Let whatever happens happen.

Light. Flowing. Nothing to grab. No thoughts. How long have I been in this state? An instant? An hour? Time is irrelevant. I am settled, open, relaxed. I'm ready. Ready to focus the meditation.

Imagine that the murderer finds me. See him. Greasy hair and garlic breath. He snarls … a wild animal ready to attack his prey. Nearer. Ah, the body tightens. Sense it. Let it tighten. Experience the fear. Expand it. Don't hold on. Be the tightening. Be the fear. Let it be as it is. It transforms itself—as energy. He pops up, close. Increased fear. Yet swiftly neutralized this time, transformed into expanded energy. There is almost a joyfulness. A smile plays at the corner of my lips. I can do it! Startled: he's next to me! Shoulders and neck scrunch down. I'm tightening. Spread it, expand it. Let it go … let it be. It's tight. Aware of tightness in my mind. Kernel of resistance. No. NO. NO! Become the "NO!" The world is shrieking "NO!" In a flash, I understand. This is the "NO!" I've screamed at life's unfairness. This "No" motivated me to be a helper. No, I won't let you do this to me! I'll fight you at every turn. YOU WILL NOT DO THIS TO ME! I REFUSE! With a snort, I find the thought, "I won't let nature play its hand." Laughable. I won't let experience go its course. Go MY way!

ONLY MY WAY. I refuse. I refuse to let experience, to let life run its natural course. I will only allow it to unfold MY way. I refuse to die. I am fighting the inevitable. I am fighting the way it is. I want it to be different than it is. Yes. Ah, a shift ... the stirring of relaxation ... deepens ... slowly ... more ...

Quiet peacefulness.

He walks, slow, squeaky steps with his dirty mauve tennis shoes, yet each step brings him no closer. He holds a noose, smiles, exposing a cracked tooth, and throws the rope. It misses the first time. The next slips through my neck, falling back toward him. The third time I notice it land on the back of my neck; and he throws it again and again. Each time I sense it land on my neck. Abruptly he is lying on the ground and, foot on his neck, I'm ripping my fingernails into his throat below my shoe, pressing hard against the solid resistance of his windpipe, and he gags as I pull on the rope around his neck, foot against his chin, eyes bulging, blood trickling from the edge of his mouth. I pull tighter, stronger, using my legs, my strength, until he dies.

I wish it were finished. I know there's more. A thought surfaces: be careful not to grab for the relaxation, for the release. If I reach for that state, I create more blocks. Without judgment or interference, let experience present itself. The next thought appalls me. "Be him." My gut answers, "Yes. That's it. Be him!" Trying not to exert, trying to be receptive, I imagine that I am my murderer. My consciousness splits: killer and killed the same. I am stabbing and cutting. I stop my mind, knife poised in the air. Frozen. I cement the "NO!" I fear my violence. Run from it! See myself, observe myself dashing away. I'm shaking my head from side to side, smashing aside obstructions. I have to get away! I have to escape! Nothing will stop me! I'm smashing, bulldozing huge walls. "Out of my way!" I scream. My massive tractor is tearing up gardens and flattening fences. Pedestrians scramble and trip trying to escape me. "I'll destroy you if you get in my way!" It stops for an empty moment, and I shift from escape to intentional destruction. I want to destroy you, killer. If you don't get away, I'll destroy you! We are the same: both destructive, both violent. But I am afraid. You are not. He is here, hands on my neck, putting increasing pressure on my throat. Can feel the start of "No!" choked off by his stranglehold. My neck tightens. Pain shoots through my right eye and jabs above the right kidney. I want to stop the pain. I shift away from his hands, and the pain subsides. I'm hyperventilating. Sadness builds in my throat. I fear pain. I don't want to hurt. I don't want to hurt. His hands dig into my throat, and pain stabs me in the back. NO! Now I know I MUST confront the pain. Let it be! I'm sad, and I'm in pain. A sob starts the tears rolling down my cheeks. I'm in pain. I'm in pain. There is only pain. Notice it. No resistance. My neck is a loose joint. The head flops unconnected to the body. I am dying. I am dead. He is exultant. He kicks my body over and dances on my torso. I rebel again. No! No one can do that to me. I refuse. Never. NEVER! No one has the right. Still he gloats, kicking dirt and spitting on the dead body. My raging subsides, and I accept my indignity. I'm dead. In celebration, he gets out a knife and cuts off my head, drains out the body's blood, gouges out my eyes, cuts out the tongue. He cuts the body apart with relish and abandon. He slits open my abdomen and yanks out my intestines like a long, thick rope he swings and pulls until it snaps out of the body. His is a terrible joy. He did that to me! Sadness rises and falls, like an ocean swell that passes. Nothing left. Maimed. Destroyed. Blood covers him. Parts of my body are strewn around, like garbage ripped and scattered by dogs— bones, muscles, entrails scattered where they fell. He licks his fingers, spreads his arms, and yells triumphantly into the blue sky. Tears, real tears, drop from my cheeks onto my arms. The coolness startles me.

A little at a time, coming back. I believe I can accept this and confront my death. This room has been a friend, the table scarred by pens and this chair worn threadbare through use. The setting has been comfortable. I need time before I get moving. I need to return to here, return to now. Move my head around. Stretch. Take a deep breath. Look around the room. Okay. I'm back. Mostly. I move slowly, dazed.

Collect the journals and books I brought here and lock up the texts. Do that now. The thought comes that if I survive, I will still have the texts, I will still know about the cult, I will still know Rick was murdered, and I can identify the murderer. If I live, I wonder what the Shra'kufans will do. I'll deal with that later, if I survive.

CHAPTER 32

1:10 p.m.

Even though the sun illuminates everything, bringing edges into sharp relief, the air remains cool. What a crystalline day! A single cloud hangs in the sky to the east. I delight in the gentle breeze. The air smells fresh. This simple, clear purity blossoms, dawnlike, as the world stirs, wakes, and stretches itself glowing along the horizon. My steps are springy as I stride along the sidewalk.

Do I get the car or walk to Kramer? They are in opposite directions. I'm excited to be outside. There is a freedom I've not had since yesterday. Even my back moves with more comfort. The tension has slipped away. Birds chirp to each other. I think I'll walk. I'm eager to get to the office, and this will be faster.

When I get there, I must reach Deana. Where is she? Where are the kids? I torment myself with this nagging concern. What if...?" I ask myself, followed by no answer, followed by empty silence while the world, heedless, busies itself with activity. Deana and the kids in a field miles from town; Deana and the kids locked in a basement; Deana and the kids trapped in a vehicle speeding along a highway. By dwelling on these thoughts, I've unsettled myself again. Damn! I loathe these changes in my emotional state. I want to recapture that pleasant state and shift to pay attention to my present experience. I tune in to my body. To walk is fulfilling in itself, to appreciate the solidity of the sidewalk under each step, to inhale the air and experience it moving through my nose and filling my lungs.

The light is extraordinary, playing with the trees and flowers to illuminate them with a glow I never detected, a glow that embraces them like a halo. Even the dull sidewalk, in its gray cement-hard commonness, possesses an arresting beauty. The earth now appears vibrant, alive, radiant. This alteration in my experience is profound and magical. Am I perceiving within a different paradigm? Am I different? Changed? If so, I know what happened. My dealing with death had an effect.

My feet freeze to the spot: only one day ago, I saw Rick push his way through that entrance to the Student Union, the door not thirty yards away. Impossible to believe what has happened since then. As I walk past the union and approach the administration building, an insight surfaces. I've returned! As if I've arrived home from a trip, I now view as pristine and fascinating what I accepted as everyday and ignored as commonplace. There is truth to that observation. I have been running, feeling scared and as though I was fighting for my life. That has encompassed my whole awareness since I saw Rick yesterday. Though I'm back, I recognize a shift—changed by what I've experienced. Kramer and my office, now visible from where I'm walking, are waiting. Bright green ivy splashes its color across Kramer's red brick and hundreds of birds have found their home in its thick foliage.

My view shifts to the north edge of campus, a hundred yards away, where at least ten trucks have satellite dishes sprouting from their roofs. I've seen nothing like this. The clamor of generators echoes from the buildings surrounding the grassy mall. Figures mill around the vehicles, television network logos on their sides. A block away, a small crowd of people form a semicircle around a woman holding a microphone out to an interviewee. A cameraman takes a step closer. The microphone cord leads to a thick, orange cable that connects the camera to a truck.

I stop while I consider walking closer to the crowds. Last night I ran by that street and not a single truck was there. Every one arrived today. They must be here to cover the murder. And as I reflect on it, that is the last place I want to show my face. I don't want to answer questions, in particular on national television. I'll have plenty of time to learn about their activity later, when I see their broadcasts.

To my right, a huge oak patterns the sidewalk with lovely, changing shadows; a lattice work of light plays across the ground. Cars clog a metered parking lot, twenty yards away and across the street from Kramer. It should be busy; registration for classes is taking place right now.

There he is! In the metered parking lot! I've stopped dead. I'm in the open; he's looking the other way. Where can I go? Behind the oak tree. Hide! I let my breath out when the trunk supports and hides me, its bark rough against my right shoulder. Why risk discovery or be foolish? Slide the backpack from my shoulder and place it behind the tree. Heart is beating fast. He cannot see me but I can peek at him. His shadow rests on the side and across the hood of a red station wagon. What do I do? Not half an hour ago, I readied myself, worked through these issues, completed my preparation, and now I discover I am not set. I'm hiding again. *Damn.* A vast melancholy settles over me like a black cloak. My shoulders are leaden and my throat constricted. I'm squeezing back tears. I've failed. I know I have failed.

His shadow moves over the roof and now stretches along the asphalt pavement farther into the lot, away from me. Thank goodness. I move back, close my eyes, and take several deep breaths. I glance back and can't see his shadow anymore. I search the lot as best I can, able to see only the section to my left, half of the lot. He is not visible. I keep searching, frantic, and then see his mauve tennis shoe take a slow step onto the sidewalk at the edge of the parking lot, the sidewalk that runs ten feet from this tree. I shift back, heart pounding. He is moving in my direction. The tree blocked my view while he went around a car to get to the sidewalk. Did he see me? How could he? How could he know I'm here? Whether he does or not seems moot. I'm trapped! Trapped again . . . and even more imperiled. Do I run? Do I fight? I left the walking stick in the car. A foolish oversight. I sink into insignificance and vulnerability. This confrontation has terrorized me. Is it? Is this the end? I find no answer. Is there ever an answer to this question beforehand?

Just in case, I had better prepare myself in the time left. A heavy tiredness settles over me. Focus on sensations. Expand them. Focus on the tiredness. As it expands and fills me, I sink, weary, sad, and defenseless. It twists to fear. I'm filled with fear that quakes in my belly. Let the fear out. Expand the sensations. Just let them be without influence or judgment. Let them go. Let them transform. Stomach flutters. Expand the sensations. Let them spread outside my body, rippling outward to fill the world and further. Rushing, rippling out. Awareness goes to the breath. It's tight. Just notice. Expand the tightness. Fear rises again from below my stomach. I'm fighting the fear. Let the fighting be. Do not fight the fighting. "I am relaxed!" I say in my mind, and experience an immediate drop in tension, followed by quick fear. I see myself dead, hurting. Good-bye! Good-bye, family! Good-bye, world! I love you. Time to face my death. I DO NOT WANT TO FACE IT! No, NO, NO! But I have no choice. Yes. Yes, I have a choice. I could run. I could make that choice. I have yet another choice. I could wait for him to go away and then I will be safe. I could roll along the side of the oak hidden from him as he walks along the path. Yes. I do have choices. But the only real choice I have is confronting this . . . facing him . . . falling into the unknown.

Time to let go. I realize I did not resolve my death or my murder in the library. Death lurks in the shadows. The fury that being murdered evokes gathers power. Murdered! Murder, even an accident, was not in my life plan. How ludicrous! Getting killed does not happen in my world . . . or to *me*. It does in many parts of the world. And now my emotional reactions could lead to my death. I must attenuate the strength of my rage, the power in my fight, the intensity of wanting to run. Could I let go of wanting to fight, to control, to live for just a few seconds? A continual inner scream reverberates through my mind: "No, No, No . . ." This asks too much. I cannot, I will not stop fighting.

I peek around the trunk, careful to stay hidden. His shadow moves closer, closer along the path and disappears into the shadow of the tree. Ten yards from the tree? I can't guess his distance. Is he sidling up to the tree? I shift my weight to ease the tension in my back. The rustle of the breeze whispers in my ear, cools my neck. I see the grid of gray cement holding together the brick of the administration building twenty yards to my left. Red-flowering Candy Oh! rose bushes hug its foundation. Black shadows, played with by the wind, ripple along the wall. I'm light-headed. The ambient illumination brightens as if the sun came out from behind clouds. Across the mall, a man and woman walk hand in hand, swinging their arms. She hugs him.

The scrape of a single step near the base on the other side of the tree seizes my attention. I hold my breath, trying not to make a sound. I pull my head and shoulders inward to make myself smaller. My feet stick to the ground, yet my thoughts are racing. I need to run. He'd never try to kill me out in the open! *Fool!* These people don't care about themselves. I could knee him in the balls as soon as he's close. I realize with surprise I'm struggling with whether to attack or to run. My struggle stimulates adrenaline, which will kill me if he is using that blue poison! Should I try to escape? But if I survive by escaping, someday one of the Shra'kufans will locate me and murder me with the blue stuff. I must confront it now. I have to! And I'm terrified.

I don't want to face it. I'm afraid I'll fail. My heart pounds in response. It pulses out of my eyes and bursts in my chest. Breath sharp and quick . . . How long have I been waiting since that footstep? Minutes? Am I losing track of time? My legs wobble. I've decided! I'll slide out and expose myself so he can see me. Tears well in my eyes. This is IT! Sadness tugs at the edges of my lips; heaviness sinks into my throat.

The cool air through my nostrils calms me. I inhale, closing my eyes. What's that smell? His breath? It's garlicky and acrid. I know he is close. I can hear the whisper of his clothes, which stops. Silence from the other side of the tree. Not moving? Heart pounding. "Relax! Heartbeat calm and regular." One last breath and I am ready. I will move first. Inhale.

His face jolts me as it springs before my eyes. He moved before me and stepped around the tree. The instant freezes. His brown eyes dilated and glazed, wide and staring. The pock marks on his face and the scar near his right eye have a violet cast. The thought intrudes, "Why violet?" Black hair, disheveled, parted on the left, falls over his forehead. The bark is rough against the back of my right hand and through my shirt. Body tightening, neck stiff, shoulders raised, taught and ready. Two impulses frozen together—turn and run or smash his face and strangle him. Frozen. Stopped. Unprotected.

A suppressed snarl erupts from him. His lips pull back in a sneer and his right arm snakes up to the left side of my neck, unprotected by the tree. Is he going to hit me? I flinch in apprehension but no blow falls, only sudden pressure on my neck. His face is close. Smiling. No, leering. A leer of triumph? My burst of rage brings with it a question: Does he expect to enjoy my pain? My death? Another question tumbles forth: Am I distancing myself right now? Yet another question: Is his a religious interest?

Spittle has dried in a line along his lips and collected at the edges of his mouth. A front tooth angles and has a cracked edge. Another is brown and crosses its neighbor at an angle. I'm surprised to sense in him a frantic panic. My wish? A reality? I realize that these thoughts and perceptions have flashed through my mind in an instant.

As his hand presses, my neck numbs, and I slide to my knees. I shrink and pull my body inward. Inside I yell, "Run. RUN! There is still time!" I answer, "No! He's here. It will make it worse. You know that!" I tighten and at once know I'm resisting, I'm fighting. "Relax." Just notice. I discern an alteration in awareness. Heart beating in a different pattern, breath slowing. Ribs press inward, a constriction. Fear creeps through the body discharging a subtle shudder. Oh, no . . . the adrenaline! It tingles in my feet. I need air. Relax. Just notice. Observe. Fear. I sense the adrenaline rush along my arms and legs, the churning in my belly. Attend to breathing. In and out of the nostrils. Relaxing. Breath more constricted. Just bare attention. Heart beating quicker. Body unfeeling and more constricted. Muscles tying up. Paralyzed. Want to fight, want to stretch, to oppose the constricting muscles. Even the slightest impulse fails. Muscles tighten more in reaction. Helpless. Trapped. I am caught in this bodily prison and can only witness.

Time unfolds itself in an extraordinary progression. Expanded. Insignificant details unveil profound meanings: the clean smell of the breeze; his dirty, mauve tennis shoes; the stain on his faded blue canvas shirt; the ripped pocket. Most portentously, my internal state slows and becomes tranquil. Has it been only a few breaths since he first appeared? Attention shifts to the breath, and it catches in my throat.

"Relax. Calm," I say. My heart hammers against the inside of my chest. The pounding slows. Yet I can't stop my fear when my body is reacting bizarrely and I'm in agony. Insight! I'm trying not to experience my feelings. Not experiencing is impossible. I can only let them be; I can only let them transform. In the library, I learned that I could survive by not reacting with fear, and, if I experience fear, I must not fuel it; let it fade away. Fear and pain are inevitable. Just let them be. Slowing, calming. A subtle calm descends, a gentle wash of rain. Consciousness changing cryptically. Not inhibiting. Observing, attending, yet letting be. Distant yet absorbed.

A pristine and uncharacteristic knowingness is...don't know what it is, where it is, or how it is; it simply is. I can decide to get upset or to be afraid because I can't breathe . . . because I might die. Uncanny, the awareness I can decide. A flash rivets attention. Of light? Of understanding? I want to change the way things are. A similar insight came in the library; but this time a power grabs every facet of my being and conceives new inter-relationships. My whole life I've wanted *this* to be different, *that* to be different. "This isn't going the way I want it to, expect it to, NEED it to . . ." And then the anger, the disappointment, the frustration. Change it. Change me. Make it different. And now, here is unavoidable pain. I want to change it. I don't want to die! I want to change *that*! I want to live!! And now I'm engulfed in an ironic paradox: to live I must not want to live; to live I must not fight death. In this state of mind, a transformation emerges. All struggle drops. No more resistance.

Now discomfort comes—no, not discomfort, a pressure on both sides of the chest. A burning develops—no, a hot and buzz-ing sensation in the throat and upper abdomen. I notice and, coincident with this awareness, the realization appears that awareness is without an "I" in it. Sounds. Sensations. Sights. A profound awareness: an "I" could surface and could live or die. It is. That is all.

He wrinkles his forehead. "Puzzled" enters my mind. Movements in slow motion. His Adam's apple sinks; he parts his lips and inhales. Fascinating how slowly he moves. He sucks in his breath. It starts soft, getting louder, the strain and effort sticks high in his throat. He tries to startle me. Just watching him try. It is a curious yell, starting confident, full, then pushing itself, rage filled, battering, trying to bust in, and ending scattered and doubting. The time of a single yell expands and unfurls over what seems like minutes.

His expression has changed. His eyes even wider. Surprise? Brighter and brighter. Heart slowing more. Laboring? There is only observing whatever presents. Insight: a different aware-ness would stimulate strong emotions. Am I dying? There is distance from everything. Detachment? Yet I'm more a part of what's happening too. He is trying to kill me, and I'm just looking. Crazy? Neurotic? Suicidal? Laughter bubbles from the center of the body, but no laugh comes. Muscles fail. Smiling inside. Crazy response that connects as true. He moved away. His mouth drops open. He looks shocked. He stares, eyebrows narrowed. He yanks his hand away from my neck and scruti-nizes it. A blue fluid rests in a scarred indentation in the center of his palm. He pinches the liquid between his thumb and index finger, grinds them around, and smells them. Then he glances at me again, leans forward, peers at my face, my eyes. As he bends toward me, his shirt opens and a small, circular medallion hang-ing from his neck swings forward. My view is brief, but it looks blue and brown—a large, sharp brown tooth with a bright white tip surrounded by blue.

Inside the mind glows as light permeates the skull and then spreads through the body. Experience presents itself as wondrous. No words. No images. Experience no longer fixed but flowing. This tree, this man, this moment are fluid and open. The oak is growing; the earth is shifting inside and tumbling. Awareness knows these processes, knows this motion has no beginning, has no end. Only changing. The tree, the object we call "tree," is a slice of change made static, made into an object. Death is not a static end point but another part of ceaseless change. Rick's translations flash to understanding: nothing is static like a noun; everything is a verb; everything is process. Static words cannot capture this; it is beyond words, beyond concepts. The totality of all that is, is flowing. No barriers. Each barrier, each wall, each concept rigidifies inherent flow. Light and love permeate this knowing; are this knowing. How has this profound and exalting transcendence twisted into violence?

Brilliance floods everywhere inside and out seeing around and above with eyes closed. There is "seeing" all around . . . and on the other side and the inside of buildings. A red sedan turns into Kramer's parking lot while a squirrel climbs to the topmost branch of this oak tree; at the library a brunette woman wearing white sandals and shorts stops to search her pink bag; inside the administration building a bookkeeper pushes the enter key on his computer and the printer chatters. . . . Myriad details present to awareness. The body labors, heavy with its burden, and tries to sink further, trying but unable to drop to the earth. Amazement shows in his eyes. Seeing through his eyes as he holds my body up. *The Blue Sky lives in him!* His thought? Is this an illusion? Elation cascades around me. Success! I've done it! I'm not responding as expected. The aftermath of elation burns through my lungs. Elation kicks off the drug's action. Must not respond any more.

Light radiates. Is this the light people see when they die? Images of childhood and adolescence. A computer dumping its memory banks to clear its programming? Is this good-bye to life? Am I dying? My body aches—constricted, starved for air— and wants to drop of its own accord. But he still grips my neck. Hours appear to have passed yet I know only a few minutes have elapsed. Remarkable. Even though these words come to me, none capture this unprecedented quality of mind. No established concepts or ways of thinking plumb the depths, complexity, and profundity of this state. Seeing, hearing, feeling, and knowing have transformed so whatever presents itself arises as magical and whole.

A flash of insight brings with it ecstasy, flooded with love, gratitude, and the upwelling of compassion. I am aware again that this man has helped me. This poor, angry, twisted man has helped! I want to thank him. I discern the roots of my fear, my violence, my resistance…and his. My violence and his violence grow from fear. Fear serves to protect me and mine. My life. My body. His ideology. His religion. I am laughing inside. As laughter and joy bubble up, it does not aggravate the drug. Smiling. We are both, the both of us, *life*!

The completeness commanding, nearly overpowering, as it washes over and through, losing increasingly consciousness of self until just light. Simple awareness there, effortlessly, no struggle. Awareness neither inside nor outside, neither here nor there, yet both. Peacefulness beyond gentleness, devoid of conflict and opposition.

Awareness touches the tree touching the body, moving the leaves with the wind caressing the hair and grass, gentle bobbing flowers. Serenity mixes the stabbing ache beneath the ribs to the skin and surrounding air bathing the space blue sky, floating a white cloud above the oak tree. Noticing, noticing golden chirp, glow voice saying "Hello," fresh-breeze all mingled in the mind while cars park at the meters, two bodies one standing a neck holding the hand down by the side. Time blends: he stands next to the oak, and he walks from the parking lot to the tree, and he marches along the side of the building tucking something beneath his shirt, and people run from Kramer Hall.

People float along the sidewalk with exquisite slowness and precision, as he reaches inside his shirt and removes a six-inch knife, the blade tinged in blue, stained and scratched. Curved to a point. He brings it to his face. He breaths on it, then mutters. Talking to the handle. "Hello, handle!" Thinking strange. Who am I? What am I? The radiance shines, increasing. He stops . . . talking . . . to the knife. Holding in both hands presses the knife toward my face, my eyes, to above my nose. Cut nose? Gouge eye? Kill with knives? Drilling a third eye? Presses knife and cuts straight down. Stops. Stings. Cuts sideways. Stops. Now on the diagonal. Again other way. Confused. Where's the pain? His warm breath gasps across my face. Faint scars trace the center of his forehead, just above his nose, creating a pattern, similar to a quarter-inch star. Blood stinging eyes blink. He rests his forehead on mine. Two stars touching?

Time slipping between cracks, between one moment and the next. Series of kaleidoscope images superimposed. All happening together separately. Star still touching star / he stands replacing the knife / he is in a crowd, arms reaching forward, palms up, then out to the side, ring finger and thumb create circles, hands come together at heart, circle over circle, fingers pointing away, up over his head, slides downward to forehead, slight bow, to center of chest, palms open to side / night, a large room with a dirt floor, five weathered men facing dancing fire, at the same time all perform the same motion / at first ten, then thirty, a crowd, row after row, stretches away standing on packed dirt craggy dry valley, all perform the same motion / . . .

More light light-headed sense the body slipping, sliding down the tree. No longer can hold clear awareness . . . slipping. The light is blinding as the body teeters. . . . From above, seeing, the body on the ground. He still holds the knife. At his feet, the body lies crumpled on its right side as if folded over on top of itself. Blood drips on the right arm and dribbles along the inner edge. He slips the knife back under his shirt. He kneels, grabs the backpack, and dumps the contents on the ground. It scatters over the legs. He shakes it. Checks the interior. He tosses it away and hurries along the grass next to the administration building. People have stopped on the sidewalk, staring. A woman stands up from her bench, book dropping to her side, takes several steps toward the oak. Detective Miller runs from the door of Kramer Hall, across the street. He gestures with his right arm, and a uniformed policeman follows him. Deana then bursts out of Kramer, trying to catch up with them as they slow to cross the street. A mixture of emotions bubble up. Relief and joy at seeing Deana; apprehension and fear at seeing Miller. She is safe. People gravitate toward the body, covered with the discarded backpack, strewn with papers. The light is blinding. Brighter and brighter awareness loses itself in the light. Only brightness everywhere.

CHAPTER 33

1:55 p.m.

A spontaneous reaction forms, tries to and then finds wordless, imperceptible expression, meaning, "Go away! Leave me alone!" The throat, the tongue, the lips, frozen. I can't move, and my reaction coalesces as a powerful, inarticulate grunt.

A distant sound hurts my head. A gulf separates me from the intrusion, but the sound is too powerful. I try to widen the distance from me, yet the assault continues. It endures, creeps in, at first remote, then invades, persists, sharpens, and pierces into my mind as the inescapable shrill of a siren. My face winces. I can't stop the noise; I can't block the sound, but relief comes on its own: it stops. Silence!

The darkness confuses me. My body jumbles discordant: the parts don't fit correctly. I can't understand what is happening. There is an ache in my right shoulder and a sharp pain in the center of the right rib cage. Where are my legs? Did I lose them? I scrunch my eyes shut and flicker them open for an instant. Too bright! My right eye opens as if gummy and my sight blurs. An "Oh!" comes from nearby and then, "He moved!" Something touches my hair, pushes on my forehead, and slides toward my eyes. I yank away. Don't touch me. Leave me alone.

"Shush. Just lay there. Don't move." The concerned male voice is authoritative.

Thoughts of this past day and the Shra'kufan assassin flood back. I'm alive. I'm alive! I did it. I want to jump, to dance, but my body is inert. I struggle to shift my position. A groan.

Surprised it comes from me. My right leg crumples under me, the hip and thigh scrunched up into my body. I try to roll to my right and can't. A wall? I'm baffled by the sensations since pushing shows it's neither smooth nor flat. Puzzled, I relax into it, and the answer pops into mind. I realize I am slumped against the tree. The pain in my rib cage sharpens. I straighten the right leg, scraping it along the ground, and roll to my left, trying to lie on my stomach. Pressure on my left shoulder stops me. I now recall the sensation, yet not perceiving it this whole time.

"Hold it. Don't move. I need to check you over. I'm an EMT."

"Is he . . . ?"

It's Deana's voice. She sounds alarmed and panicked. I realize she is okay. She is alive. A smile breaks out on my face. I try to croak out my first words as the EMT takes my wrist. I squint as another EMT forces a light into my eyes. I want to keep them closed.

"Yeah. I'm . . ." I have to swallow. My throat is dry and tight. I inhale through my nose. I relish being able to breathe again. The air is cool, and I can smell the earth. A deep breath clears the mind.

"I'm okay. I did it," I mumble. To talk takes enormous effort. A spontaneous sigh. Though the ache in my side deepens, each breath strengthens me.

"Sir, what happened to you?"

Someone's moving my arm and palpating my neck and upper back. I ignore my treatment, of being moved and treated as an object.

"Sir? Can you talk?"

"Umm. I . . ."

"Jason, that man attacked you!" Deana sounds panicky. "Are you certain he's okay?" she asks the medic. "I'm his wife."

"So far, he appears okay. But we need to be sure."

"Ma'am." It's the voice of the other medic. "What happened to him?"

"The only thing I saw was a man attacking him ten minutes ago. Miller and I, well, Miller thinks it was the same man who killed Rick Volks yesterday. We could see them struggling here next to this tree. When we got here, he was crumpled against the tree, and you got here at the same time we did. That man got away."

"So no one knows what happened in the attack," the other medic states.

"Well, I have no idea."

"Okay then."

My attention swings to remembering this past day and gets stolen by what they are doing. I flinch as tightness builds around my upper arm and then realize he's taking my blood pressure. Intrusions distract me: first, nodding in response to questions and probing; then hands checking under and around me. Where do you hurt? Don't move. Neck hurt? Can you move your head this way? Can you move your fingers? Your toes? Back? Abdominal pain? What's your name? How old are you? I grunt out answers. I want them to leave me alone so I can understand the last twenty-four hours. And I revel in the relief that Deana is okay.

"I'm Detective Miller. How is he?" He sounds worried.

"I was telling his wife that so far he comes out okay."

"So, he's not dead?" asks Miller.

"Not at all."

"Good news," says Miller. "Folks, did anyone witness this attack?" As I listen for responses, I recognize there had been a cacophonous buzz of voices in the surrounding area.

"I was reading on that bench over there, and a strange noise came from the tree. I thought it could have been a yell, but the tree barred my view."

"I was in the parking lot and saw a man riffling through his backpack and tossing papers."

The thump of footsteps retreating. Miller's voice, now a distance away. "What did you see?"

As I tune in to the mixture of voices, snatches of conversation drift to my hearing.

"Dr. Butler . . ."

"What happened?"

"That's his wife . . ."

"Fell or something . . ."

"Someone told me a stroke."

"Well, somebody over there told me he has a drinking problem."

"Ma'am?" My attention shifts back to the EMT kneeling next to me. I still keep my eyes closed. "Ma'am!" he repeats.

"Wha," Deana says, surprised.

"Does he have any allergies?"

"Well, ragweed always makes him sneeze."

"Any other allergies?"

"No. Nothing."

"Is he on any medication?"

"No."

"Does he have any illnesses? For example, diabetes?"

"No. He's healthy. Doesn't get sick."

I flinch from a stinging sensation on my forehead.

"Sorry. Should have warned you. I'm cleaning up these cuts." Something cool rubs, then burns into my forehead.

"Keep your eyes closed, please." He dabs something cool and moist on my right eyelid, rubbing it, and then proceeds along my nose and cheek. He returns to work on the lower edge of the right eye. I conclude he is washing off the blood and checking for cuts. Then he starts on the right arm.

"Nothing wrong with his arm," the EMT says to his partner. "The blood came from his forehead." He presses a soft pad that might be gauze against my forehead and tapes it in place.

"Nothing more we can do here. He checks out fine. Let's get him to the hospital." The rustling of the medic's clothes signal he stands and walks away.

I open my eyes a slit and find that the light isn't as painful. The two blue-suited EMTs roll a stretcher from the open back of an ambulance parked on the grass. A uniformed officer stands nearby, legs spread, one arm on his hip, the outline of a pistol showing at his side. Behind him, a crowd jostles to gawk. Two people have microphones and interview spectators. A video camera, a small red light gleaming, pans from the interviewer toward the medics carrying the stretcher. I close my eyes because they ache from the effort of looking around me.

"Move back, folks! Let us through!"

Hands go around my neck and hold it steady as they lay my body flat on the ground. I figure out that my body had crumpled downward along the tree trunk. My shoulder rested against the rough trunk, and my rib cage crossed a large root that grew several inches above the ground before disappearing into the earth. Now, with a firm hold on my neck, they roll my body on its side, shove a board under me, and then roll me flat onto the board. Straps tighten across my torso and legs.

Memories kaleidoscope through my mind: the murder, the texts, and the assassin jumble together. Through my half-open eyes, I see Deana from the waist to feet. She fiddles with her ring, rotating it without pause, first one way and then the other. The hands lift the board to the wheeled stretcher. I'm thankful to find that the pain in my side has gone. A sigh of relief comes from my mouth. I stretch to take Deana's hand, but she is not close enough to reach. I want to touch her, to have tangible evidence she is here.

"Deana." I can only mutter the words. No reaction. With effort, louder. "Deana!"

To my relief, she reacts, steps closer, and grasps my hand. It brings another sigh to find her squeeze my hand back. I don't have to worry about her anymore!

"Jason . . . ," she says. My name catches in her throat. I can tell she's stifling the impulse to cry. She isn't convinced I'm all right. I want to reassure her.

"Deana, I'm all right. I'll be okay." I intend to put strength and confidence into my voice, hoping they will communicate health; but the sound alarms even me as I croak out the raspy words. I squeeze her hand to reassure her, but her fear is palpable.

"Kids?" I rasp.

"They're fine."

"Ahhhhh."

"Mrs. Butler, we're taking him to the emergency room. Can you get there or do you want to ride with us?"

"Yes. Yes, of course." Deana sounds distracted. From our years together, I understand that her repetition shows she wants to go in the ambulance but can't. "I've got my car. It's behind Kramer. The drive to the hospital is only ten minutes. I guess I can do that. Yes. That's right. I'll meet you at the emergency room. Take care of him!" She squeezes my hand. I grip her hand, not wanting her to leave, not wanting her to go out of my reach or sight.

"We'll take care of him."

They roll the stretcher, and I refuse to let Deana's hand loose, forcing her to walk alongside, until we reach the ambulance doors. From behind, Detective Miller's voice fills the surrounding space.

"Folks, please stand back. Osgood, inspect the ground around the tree for evidence. Johnson, did you apprehend the suspect?" I see the yellow tape surrounding the oak tree, blocking the sidewalk and extending in a large square. Then I can't make out what he says into his handheld radio.

Something's different. The experienced-world has rearranged itself and reshaped intangibly. I can't figure out what. I toss around in my experience trying to locate what is happening; it is diffuse and pervasive; slips out of reach. The world manifests strangely, almost transparent. People interact with depth as if layered within experiential strata. And, I now realize, the grass and trees, even the ivy gripping the exterior of the administration building, have been orienting and reacting, been alive. Is it my mind? Yes. Yes, I'm aware it is. Consciousness does not work as it did an hour ago. Is this the aftermath of the drug? Will it wear off or has the experience changed me in a profound way? I find it curious that I'm not unsettled. A profound peacefulness pervades the most trivial. Despite my discomfort and tiredness, the change permeates every aspect of experience. Each happening sparkles crystalline and pure, exquisite in itself, as if possessing an inherent loveliness and value.

The ambulance doors slam shut. The sound reverberates in its complexity and depth within and without me. Awareness locates itself outside yet includes the body and mind. I remember, the instant before being slid into the ambulance, the billowing edge of a white cloud captured behind the edge of the ambulance's roof, framed in iridescent blue. The sun glistened as a brilliant circle on the curved edge of the roof. Radiating through this simple experience is the essential wonder and totality of existence. Even now the hurried care of the EMT, stabilizing the stretcher in the ambulance, checking me for life-threatening changes, is natural and perfect. He places a brace around my neck and starts an IV.

Deana and the kids are not injured. They are protected. I can at last relax regarding my family's condition and whereabouts. A vivid fantasy blooms in my mind. The kids are watching television, lying on a bed in a motel room. A large woman whom I've never seen, her brunette hair pulled back in a bun, sits on a straight-backed chair reading a newspaper, glancing at the kids. Next to her is a white Styrofoam cup that contains coffee, and she wants to smoke but cannot do so in the room. I recall Deana's last words and her distracted and agonized decision to drive to the hospital. She worries I'm injured.

Another fantasy pops into my mind. Deana is getting into the car behind Kramer. The door remains open, and she sinks, sobbing, into the driver's seat. She supports herself on the steering wheel as her back spasms with her crying, tears falling on her beige skirt. She rises and reaches for a tissue, tears and black mascara blending along her cheeks. There are dark spots on her white blouse and skirt. She wipes her face and puts the key in the ignition. She glances at the steering wheel, sees the spots, and slaps at them with the tissue in her hand. Then she turns the key to start the engine.

More memories of the last twenty-four hours pop to mind: seeing Rick at the Student Union, finding the package he sent to my office, walking in on the assassin, hiding in my office, exploring parts of the package, escaping, finding the house empty, fleeing the house, and searching the library for what I needed to survive. I'm okay now but the threat of the Shra'kufans is real. I am still at risk. I know they exist, and I have the texts. What, it occurs to me, was Deana doing here? And Detective Miller? And how does she have the car? I parked it across campus, not behind Kramer. More unsolved mysteries.

A multitude of distinct modes of experience interpenetrate, as if many films are playing at once, each unique yet simultaneous. Even though the films advance, the individual frames are present at once. It is seeing a whole movie in each frame while the movie continues. Everyday experience continues as usual, as do my natural reactions, emotions, and perceptions. Underlying is a peaceful, open totality that shimmers through the surface. It is looking at clouds, which pass and change shape while seeing the whole, glorious blue sky from above and below and within, at the same time. Each moment sparkles with a magical wonder.

It is amazing how the mind clears, although the body recuperates in slow motion. Did I pass out? If the victim does not panic when the Blue Sky first hits the bloodstream and releases adrenaline, and when the body tightens and breathing becomes ever shallower, then after a time, the person passes out from lack of oxygen. Saifell's article didn't state this, but it is a logical conclusion.

Since I am recuperating, the drug must have metabolized, allowing my lungs to work. My thinking is clearer, and I am better. Are there aftereffects from the drug?

That I've survived does not solve my problems. What do I do regarding the Shra'kufans? What do I tell Deana? And what do I tell Miller? Although I've escaped this attempt on my life, I am not convinced that the Shra'kufans will leave me alone. Since the Blue Sky didn't kill me, will they try another method? I still have their sacred texts, and I assume the assassin knows this. They want them. Will I be able to keep them secret? How will they search? More chillingly, what are the implications for my family? Will they search only for me, or will they include Deana and the kids? If they kill me, will they also kill them?

I thought surviving would solve the whole problem, but it only postponed it. Another thought: If they planned to kill me, why didn't the assassin use the knife? He cut my forehead, but he did not kill me. I couldn't have protected myself, so killing me was easy. Dare I conclude they won't try again? And what to do with the texts? And, now I consider it, why did he cut my forehead?

The ambulance ride will be over soon. Another vision fills my mind. The stretcher rolls from the back of the vehicle through large doors and into an examining room. Four six-foot-tall, green, banded cylinders stand along one wall. Three white-suited people surround me, one taking my blood pressure and another listening to my heart. One wore a navy blue sweater over her white uniform with a stethoscope sticking out of the right pocket; another, with a small mole on her cheek, wore a large silver watch with a black face and large white numbers; and the third was short, pear-shaped, and, in contrast to the others, wore black shoes rather than white. Deana walks in the door and cries, sitting down on a chair next to the door, one arm across her stomach, the other across her mouth and nose. After the staff leaves, she approaches the foot of the examination table and asks how I am. The vision ends.

I realize, once others are around me, that I must answer questions, questions from Deana...and from Detective Miller. How do I approach this? At the least, I can assume that I'm no longer a suspect.

CHAPTER 34

2:30 p.m.

"Dr. Butler, our examination reveals no abnormalities."

I don't like having to crane my neck to interact with the emergency room doctor. He is behind me and to my right while I lie on the gurney. The top of his head is bald, leaving a crescent of black hair above his ears. His round face is slightly puffy. He is tall and stoops from the shoulders up, perhaps to mask his height. He takes his glasses off as he talks, puts them on again to glance at the chart, and then takes them off, resting them next to his mouth as if he might chew the end of the stem. I want to get up, but he has advised me to lie still for a while. I'll accept his recommendation, but I'm fine. His voice drones on as he puts on and takes off his glasses.

"When the paramedics took your blood pressure and heart rate, they were both elevated. They normalized quickly. By the time you got in the ambulance, they had returned to normal and remained that way since you got here. The blood and urine samples are all negative. And, as you keep telling us, you also are fine. The only physical problem I've found are the cuts on your forehead, but those are superficial and will heal. We urge you to stay in the emergency room so we can evaluate you. We can't figure out what happened to you, and we prefer to err on the side of caution."

"I'll stay, but I have no problems now." He grunts, frowns and steps toward the door.

"Well, okay," he says. "I'll check on you later. Ring for the nurse if anything unusual happens." He nods as he leaves, then pauses, hand on the open door. As I follow him with my eyes, I recognize the four six-foot-tall, green, banded cylinders that stand along one wall. I remember again the images that popped up in the ambulance. These are identical. In fact, the mental picture of the three white-suited people that checked me over as soon as I got in this room were the same, including incidental details right down to the blue sweater and the black shoes. Another of the mental images foreshadowed how Deana walked in the door and cried, sitting on a chair next to the door. The dark spots on her dress and blouse matched what I saw in those images when she sat in the car. As I recall the mental pictures, the accuracy is eerie.

All the times during this past day I wanted to hug Deana, to hold her, to be with her, coalesce into a single urge. That is all I want. I want to be with Deana. I haven't even talked with her. I'm glad the doctor left.

As the door closes, Deana and I blurt in unison, "Where have you been?" I stretch out my hand, but she doesn't move closer.

"You first," I'm able to say. "My anxiety about you and the kids last night was intense. I called the cops and the hospital and Mom and Dad and the Farleys and your work and friends but no one had any information. So many questions flooded my mind. Where were you and why was the car in the garage last night? And how did the car get to Kramer when I left it in the commuter lot? And, how did you and Miller get to the administration building in the nick of time?"

My words tumble out; I stop talking. I regret I didn't ask her to come closer. Why is she so far away? At last, she steps near me. I was holding my breath and exhaled.

"All right. You win," she says, frowning as she sits down next to the examining table, taking my hand, and then smiling.

It is not the deep smile that brings her dimples alive. She is too far away, and I tug on her hand, urging her to move closer. Now I don't want her to talk. I want to examine her so I can be certain she is here, that it is her. I squeeze her hand and rub her arm. As she closes the distance, I put my arm around her waist and nestle my head against her stomach. It's awkward but I don't care. She strokes my head. I'm choked up, crying. It is so wonderful to do this. A multitude of times over the past day I expected I would never hug her again. Now she's with me and I can hold onto her, I will not allow this moment to pass. A sudden, strong longing wells up to hold the kids. I yearn to hug them, too. Gripping her arm, I push her away to peer at her. Her eyes open wide in surprise at the sudden change.

"The kids? The kids? You said they are okay. Are they? All right?"

"They're fine!" She seems to laugh at my irrational distress. "They're at a motel with Mom and Dad and a police woman. They ate a fast-food breakfast and are watching television. I talked to them before I came here and told them you were okay. They wanted to come too, but I realized they should wait. I wasn't sure what would happen, and if you were injured. Jason," she sounds serious, "are you healthy? For real?"

"Yes. Yes, Deana. And I'm righter and righter all the time." I check to assess whether she believes me. She can't accept it yet but shrugs. Her smile seems forced. I want the attention off me and back to her and the kids.

"Tell me everything that happened. Why are Mom and Dad here?"

"After you called, they wanted to learn for themselves. When they got to our house after five this morning, police met them, which terrified them as you might imagine, and Miller brought them over to the motel. The police have been fantastic."

Her change in expression startles me. She clenches her jaw and pulls her eyebrows down and in. She leans forward, and punches me, a little hard, on my arm.

"Why? Why? Why?" She punches my arm with each *why*.

"Why didn't you tell me about Rick when we talked on the phone?" Last punch.

"Ah, I struggled with that. My rationality got scrambled. I somehow assumed I was protecting you. And, the way I analyzed it, I needed to figure out what to do before upsetting you."

"Well, your logic borders on stupid! I'd find out soon enough. And how do you think I felt knowing you didn't tell me?"

"I struggled to figure out what to do. And I panicked about the assassin coming after me. I frantically tried to stay alive and to keep all of you alive. Oh, I can hear it. The words you might say bang in my mind. 'Telling us would help us stay alive and not telling would put us at risk.' No defense. You're right."

She sits back, the storm clearing from her face, but her arms cross over her chest. After a while, she sighs, leans forward, and puts her elbows on her thighs. I wait, tracking her to find out what she'll do. I'm about to ask a question when she talks again.

"Detective Miller called the house last night to reach you. He said you called him, fearing for your life because you witnessed the murder and can single out Rick Volks's murderer. Poor Rick. I am so sorry for him and for Helen. But, when Miller called, that scared me. He tried calling you at the office and you didn't answer. When I talked to you half an hour earlier, you were in your office waiting for a client. Miller said that seemed fishy. He didn't used that word. 'Suspicious' is what he said. 'It didn't add up,' he said.

"Well, Miller worried about me too. He found no information about the murderer except the connection that Rick just returned from Asia and the Middle East. Through the FBI, he learned about several dangerous terrorist groups in the countries Rick visited. He couldn't get firm intelligence, but said the murderer might belong to those groups. He went to Rick's house during the evening, after Helen was informed about the murder. She took it hard. Who wouldn't? I would! She became hysterical, crying and repeating, 'I knew we should have called! I should never have listened to Rick!' Rick refused to report a break-in at their house the previous evening. He forbade even a mention of it to anyone. A screaming match about it ensued. Helen presumed that Rick would be alive if the police had investigated. Because of what happened at the Volkses, because you feared for your own safety, he contacted me."

A nurse's aide comes in. "How are you both doing? Do you need anything?"

"Yes," Deana and I say in unison.

"I'd love a cup of coffee. Black," says Deana.

"How about some ice water? I'm parched."

"Be right back. It's around the corner." As the door closes, Deana continues.

"Where was I? Oh, yeah: Miller's call. He told us to lock all the doors and not to answer the phone. If anybody knocked on the door, we should call the police. The house should appear normal. And above all, no notes. If the murderer broke in, clues as to our whereabouts must not remain. Not even that we left for our safety and would contact you later. He wanted to take no chances."

We both glance at the door as it opens and the nurse's aide gives us the drinks. I drink, as does Deana, who takes a cautious sip of her coffee.

"Thanks. That hit the spot," I tell the aide on her way out. I pause until the door closes. "Well, that explains why nothing was out of place and no notes. No sign you had been there except for a towel in the car. The normalcy freaked me out." I glance at her, hoping she will continue. She obliges.

"When he picked us up last night, he said he drove by Kramer Hall and your office light was off. I told him that didn't seem right since you were working with a client. He took us to the Wheel Inn where he registered us as the Smiths and whisked us into the room. Only he knew where we were. He wouldn't even tell the dispatcher where we were staying so if the murderer called, the information couldn't slip out. Orders to the 911 dispatcher were to contact him if you called, but they never got a call from you."

"Wait. I called all the time. I tried to find out if you and the kids were safe. So Miller should have known I was alive."

"I don't know what to say. Someone messed up somewhere. Anyway, Miller mentioned, when he picked me up this morning, that the police figured out you were alive around two fifteen in the morning. A stakeout monitored our house, waiting for you to come home, to bring you to the motel, but somehow you got home without their seeing you. Then a car zoomed backward out our driveway."

The memory of what happened flashes into my mind: seeing him trying to break in through the slider, my anxiety about making too much noise when I closed the car door, timing my exit from the garage so I didn't hit the door, that abrupt stop on the main road to shift from reverse to drive to escape.

"They couldn't see who was driving. Given the speed it backed down the driveway, they thought the murderer was driving, but as soon as a man started chasing the car down the driveway, they figured you were the driver. When the stakeout pulled onto the road, the man ran back toward the house." Deana takes a sip of coffee before continuing.

"From what they observed, he fit your description of the murderer. The stakeout debated whether to follow the car or the man running; they opted to chase the man on foot. They didn't get him. That's obvious—since he attacked you an hour ago.

Miller claimed it was you in the car. They had an APB on you, but you probably parked out of the way."

"Wow, I didn't consider all this going on. I thought the police wanted to arrest me."

"No, not you. They were looking for Rick's killer."

I can't help but wonder how the night would have gone had I known that.

"I kept waking up and called Miller every hour. Poor guy got no sleep, what with my calls and everything else he was doing, but he invited me to call whenever I wanted. Around five Miller checked out our house, and someone had broken in. Nothing stolen, but papers were strewn about in the study; books thrown off the shelves and drawers pulled out of the desks. Miller speculated whoever broke in was a professional searching for something specific. That led to all kinds of conjectures. And a curious question: why would this man search our house?"

The texts pop into my mind: the texts locked in the library, the texts he searched to find. I can't say anything right now. Think through what to do. I'm very thirsty and take several large gulps of the ice water.

"When Mom and Dad got to the hotel, they agreed to watch the kids, and Miller and I went to your office and then the house. He hoped I might find anything that was unusual. A few things were strange. On your office desk was a copy of the *Tao Te Ching*, half opened as if you were reading it. And the Greens' book on biofeedback and several other books on meditation were nearby, which confused both of us. Why were you reading those books at this time? There was a broken picture on your office floor and papers strewn about, files open, and drawers dumped. The mess is unbelievable. Do you have any idea how much paper is in your office? Your briefcase was also on the floor, open, with its contents littering the floor. That was strange, I told Miller, since you always carry your briefcase back and forth. I didn't tell him," Deana smiles, "you take it on vacation."

I think back to my decision to take the texts with me. What would have happened had he found the texts in my office? Would he have left? Would he still have tried to kill me?

"In the center of your office floor, we found brown paper which had wrapped a large package. It laid flat on your floor as if he had examined it. The outside had your name and address on it, and the top corner where the stamp goes was ripped off."

It never crossed my mind I shouldn't have thrown the wrapping into the trash can. I was so preoccupied with the texts and the assassin, it never occurred to me to take the outer paper with me.

"At home, there was a half-eaten sandwich on the kitchen table, one empty glass next to the sink, and all the . . . "

"Oh, that's right. I never threw that away. I couldn't eat. I was hungry and then, so upset, I walked away from the table without thinking about it."

"Well, I wondered. You hadn't gotten into bed, since everything was untouched upstairs. And all the shades were down. Miller had called our answering machine last night asking you to call, but you never did. The message remained on the machine, and you had listened to it, and . . ."

"As I told you, I thought the police wanted to arrest me. That's why I didn't call."

"But we found lots of messages from you trying to find out if we were alive. When I listened to all those messages, your upset and confusion were palpable. I'm sorry you had to go through that." Deana takes a drink of coffee and, still holding the cup, looks over at me and says, "Your messages let us know you were alive during the morning." She puts her coffee down.

"Miller checked Rick's office and that also had been broken into last night. The door remained sealed with police tape and appeared undamaged. How the guy broke in keeping the seal intact is a mystery. Again papers littered the floor. We had a very busy morning, and a little after eleven thirty, Miller decided we should go back to Kramer and wait there. P-J told us you had been calling all morning to find out if we were okay. But we had no clue where you were or what you were doing."

All of my frantic calls swell back to mind. I had been so awash with worry, and they had been protected the whole time.

"Miller and I waited in Kramer Hall with police backup. We were getting worried because we hadn't heard from you. And then, just a short while later, maybe eleven forty-five, a police officer found our car across campus in the commuter lot. Miller drove me over to the car so I could look at it with him. I was a jittery wreck, worried you were dead in the car. The engine was cold. Miller guessed it stopped over three hours ago. Before eight o'clock. Otherwise it would have been warm. Nothing was amiss inside the car. No blood or signs of a struggle. And no notes. Why no notes?"

As I started to respond, Deana broke in: "Never mind. I'll ask you later. Miller wanted me to look the car over since I might see things he didn't. I found the walking stick, right down next to the driver's seat. I'm not sure anyone else would know the significance of that walking stick. I remembered that we bought it for protection. So I figured that was why you must have taken it."

"I forgot it. I meant to take it this morning but left it there. I'm glad I forgot it . . . in the long run. But there were times I wished I had it with me."

"Well, we guessed you had it for protection. And, since there was no blood or 'other evidence'—those are Miller's words—on it, we, well, more he, concluded you hadn't used it. We figured that if you left it there, you must have felt safe."

"Nope. Forgetful."

"Well, since I needed the car, Miller told me to take it. He hoped you'd figure it out . . . if you came back. He also put the commuter lot on frequent spot checks by local and campus police. They'd swing by every half hour. Since you weren't at home, were somewhere around campus and now didn't have transportation, Miller decided Kramer was the best place to wait. We were about to give up and leave when a call came on Miller's handheld radio that two men were struggling outside, near the admin building.

"We ran across the street. I've never been so terrified in my life. I could see your body on the ground next to that tree and had visions of you dead, with a knife in your chest or a gunshot wound to your head. I could see a man dressed in a pale blue shirt rummaging through a backpack that looked like yours. When he saw us coming—well, Miller yelled, and a police car behind Kramer started its siren—he jumped up, walked away, and then ran along the outside of the administration building. As soon as Miller saw you on the ground, he called for an ambulance and it arrived in less than two minutes. When I got there, you were lying crumpled on the ground. I was certain you were dead. I wanted the crowd and the television cameras to go away and leave you, leave us, alone."

"Why were TV crews there? Because of Rick's murder?"

"No. Fall kickoff party. It's a big news story, and all the networks are in town to cover tonight's 'riot.' So far it's quiet, and the injunction still stands." She pauses and studies me. "I still can't get rid of my fear you were dead. I don't remember a night this long."

"To me . . . " I don't know what to say. What words can capture this? "To me . . . it has felt like a lifetime. I'm so relieved that you and the kids are not hurt. I envisioned many disasters. I saw him breaking into the house, of you and . . . " The door swings open and interrupts my words.

"Dr. Butler. Glad to see you're well."

"Detective Miller. Good to see you. Deana has been telling me about all the things you did this past night, including calls every hour. I appreciate it. I only wish I could have told you more." Miller is again wearing his brown corduroy coat, but today he sports a pale green tie. As I expect, his left hand is in his coat pocket.

"I need to ask you some questions, but first you need to know the murderer has not been apprehended. I observed the suspect walking away from the location of the attack. He escaped into the administration building, and witnesses report seeing him exit the far side of it. Local, state, and campus police and the FBI have been searching the area and still have no clues as to his whereabouts. I'm sorry. I wish I could tell you he was in custody."

"You might find this difficult to believe, but since I've survived his attempt to murder me, I am not concerned. He could have killed me with the knife he used to cut my forehead. He didn't. I'm confident my life is not in danger, at least not right now." Deana flinches at the words "right now" and stares at me.

"I'm not so convinced," Miller says and takes out his small pad of paper and a stubby pencil. The eraser is worn away. "I have several questions."

• • •

"Detective Miller, I don't know how I'll do answering questions right now. I'm not feeling great." Will this give me an excuse to skirt questions I'm not ready to answer?

"Let's do the best we can. We need to apprehend him to protect other innocent, potential victims. He is a danger to the community. Okay?" He looks at me, eyebrows raised, but his tone of voice communicates there will be no discussion. I don't want to talk to him, but I will. Resigned, I nod.

"Was the man who tried to kill you the same individual you saw leaning over Dr. Volks's body yesterday afternoon?"

"Yes. There is no doubt in my mind. It's the same man."

"Would you describe him again?"

"Detective Miller, I told you what he looked like yesterday." The irritation, if not disgust, that crosses his face stops me. "Okay. I'll do it again. Let's see, I guess I noticed more about him. I'm surprised as I think about it that there are additional things I can tell you. Last night I couldn't sleep and was pacing around near the study. Something alerted me, and then I heard a scraping sound outside the sliding glass door. I peeked around the curtain, and he was trying to force his way in the door. If I had been asleep upstairs, I never would have heard him."

"Jason!" Deana gasps. She stares at Miller as she continues. "If you hadn't checked us in at the motel, he would have been in the house while we were asleep, and we might have been killed. We could be dead right now!" Miller nods. Deana hugs herself, her face blanching.

"I escaped with the car after I saw him at the door. From what Deana told me, he must have broken into the house sometime later." As I continue delaying, I realize that I must respond with more detail to Miller's question about the assassin.

"I got a good look at him. He was close. He had acne scars on his face." Miller writes. "And his hand, the hand that held something against my neck, it had a scarred indentation. He held something blue in that hand and, oh yes, he also had a scar right above the bridge of his nose that looked like a star. His teeth . . ."

I kept talking and told him all I knew.

CHAPTER 35

2:45 p.m.

"Detective Miller, if more comes to mind I'll call you. Thanks for protecting Deana and the kids and trying to find me. You went above and beyond the call of duty." He smiles, pleased that his efforts are appreciated and, putting his left hand into the pocket of his jacket, starts toward the door. I'm relieved that Miller has not asked about the brown paper on my office floor or about any information concerning Rick. He is focusing on the assassin and has no reason to suspect other information from me. I feel guilty withholding information, but I can't yet risk telling anyone what I know.

"Detective Miller? Some questions continue to niggle at me." He stops, midstride, looking over his shoulder at me. "I had the impression you considered me the most likely murderer. But, that must have altered when you protected Deana and the kids. Am I still a ... I don't know the word ..."

"A suspect?" he says. He takes a deep breath and looks upward. He has turned halfway back toward me and stopped with his side facing me. He nods several times and then turns the rest of the way and steps toward us.

"You are no longer a suspect, although on first questioning you were the prime suspect. Something about your interrogation aroused suspicions. No witness reported seeing someone else enter his office, only you. No witness, other than yourself, confirmed an individual running from his office. You might be fabricating your story. But witnesses reported seeing your legs on the floor of the hallway; the rest of your body also had to be on the floor in Dr. Volks's office. Although that supported your statements, you might have killed the victim, bumped your own head, and then fallen to the ground, to make it appear you had been attacked."

"No, I didn't bump my head and fall; I was trying to get into Rick's office, and the murderer pulled open the door. That caused my fall."

Deana is wide-eyed and moves closer. She fingers the sheet of the hospital bed, next to my head.

"You think Jason killed Rick?"

"No. Not anymore. Several of the other witnesses we interrogated described him," he gestures with his head toward me, "as having an excellent relationship with the victim and a reputation for resolving conflict. The shift in prime suspect hinged on the break-in at the Volkses. You were still a possible, though more unlikely suspect, as you might have performed the break-in. When I questioned the victim's wife, she reported that Dr. Volks brooded about the B&E, and he was thankful they had been out of the house when it occurred. She quoted him as saying, 'I'm so worried you will get hurt. I never should have done it. Now your life is in danger too.' The wife reported that he referred to terrorists but was not specific about them. The B&E scared him, and he feared for his wife's and, I would assume, his own safety. He made reservations at a local motel for yesterday evening so they would be out of the house. He died before they got there. As I considered all the evidence again, I concluded the threat to you and your family was real. I then became concerned about your family's safety. You had expressed that same concern when we talked on the phone last night after you reported he was pursing you in Tower Hall."

"Jason! He chased you?" Deana grips my shoulder.

"No, hon, if he was chasing me, he'd have caught me. That was my paranoia. But later he tried to break into my office while I was there."

"Although you were supposed to be at your office," Miller continued, "it was dark, and you didn't answer your phone. You had recently talked to your wife from your office, so why weren't you there? I drove by the office with your wife, and the moped was not in front, which meant you had departed."

"Deana, I forgot to tell you I now park behind Kramer, not in front."

"I had a stakeout put on your house to keep an eye on it and pick you up when you got home. I expected you would call when your family was missing. But to be on the safe side, I left several messages on your answering machine to call me. Any message I left about your family's whereabouts or notes they might have left for you, placed you and them in danger. So, although you were a prime suspect at the start, that is no longer the situation." Miller takes a step backward, turns, and leaves. Silence spreads through the sterile hospital room.

"Jason," Deana says, taking my hand, "I had no idea! I'm so relieved you are okay." She drops my hand and moves toward the door. "The doctor said we are free to go anytime. While you get dressed, I'm going to the bathroom, and the receptionist said there was paperwork for me to sign before we leave. I won't be long."

"Okay, sweetie."

The body is lighter and more supple; the head clearer. Miller's questioning tumbles over in my mind. The events with the Blue Sky at the oak tree re-create themselves. The picture of his leering, wide-eyed face and of his arm against my neck flashes again and again. It is like a still photo that remains frozen and unchanging.

Several thought-streams, discrete yet co-present, flow through awareness. Miller's doubts about my safety resonate with one aspect of awareness. Is the assassin still looking for me? Am I safe? Are Deana and the kids safe? And yet another aspect of awareness is peaceful, profound, and secure. With the layering and mixing of awareness comes wonder at the workings of the mind. The clarity and simplicity of mind evoke a gentle smile.

As I swing my legs off the hospital bed, the door opens to admit a male nurse.

"Dr. Butler, the paramedics took this pendant from your neck when they first found you. They didn't want it to interfere with their procedures. I wanted to return it before you left."

I glance at the medallion, which hangs from an old, worn leather strap. The leather is smooth and shiny, discolored from use, and the width varies down its length. The medallion penetrates my consciousness. I gape at it. I never, ever wear anything around my neck. It looks like the medallion I saw around the assassin's neck when he was trying to kill me. I examine it now: about an inch in diameter, with several bright red dots on the side of a brown mountain just below a jagged snow line. The mountain's two sharp peaks stretch into a blue sky in which blazes a single eight-pointed sun. The surface feels smooth, like enamel. I flip it over, expecting it to be blank. Instead I find shiny silver is inlaid flush to a smooth, gray surface. The pattern is abstruse and beautiful. From the top of a large outer circle, two identical arcs swing down to the outer edge. In the exact center, a second, small circle touches those two arcs, and within the small circle is an eight-pointed sun created by four crossing lines. The pendant is simple and elegant.

"It was around my neck?"

"Yes, sir."

"Are you sure? My neck? Not on the ground?"

"I guess so. Ken?" he calls out into the waiting area. "Ken, did you find that thing around his neck or what?"

"It was around his neck," he answers coming to the door. I recognize him from the ambulance. Looking at me, he continues, "Didn't know what it was. But I wanted to get it off you in case it became a problem. It was the first thing I did on finding you."

"But it was around my neck?" I ask again. "My neck. On me?"

"Yes." He seems irritated. "Yes. It was around your neck."

"You see, I don't . . ." I stop midsentence. "Thanks. I appreciate it."

CHAPTER 36

3:15 p.m.

We rushed down the motel hallway to where the kids were. Deana couldn't keep up with me. My mouth opened in surprise when a large policewoman with her hair in a bun seemed about to stop me from coming into the room. Her appearance was exactly like the person in my mental picture an hour earlier. I pushed around her and picked up both kids, hugging and holding them tight. I cried with joy and relief. We laughed and joked and kidded. Deana watched teary-eyed, with a gentle smile playing along her lips, her dimple coming and going with the depth of her smile. I sat down with the kids on my lap. We talked some about what they had done, how the policewoman had brought them breakfast and sat in a corner of the room the whole time (except, they said, when she went outside to smoke a cigarette or to get a cup of coffee), and they watched cartoons on television the whole time. When they tired of talking, I spent time with Mom and Dad, thanked them for coming down, and apologized for waking them. As we talked, I kept walking over to the kids to look at them, to ruffle their hair, to make any kind of contact. I guess to verify that I had survived.

The possible solution had come to me during the five-minute drive from the hospital to the motel. My course of action was evident and now that I had seen the kids, I could do it. I picked up my backpack and started to leave without saying a word. As an afterthought, I paused at the door to yell, "See you all later." I was exiting to the parking lot when I heard Deana yelling somewhere behind me, "Jason? Jason?" I yelled back, "See you later, Dee." I had to leave quickly. I backed the car out, turned, and accelerated when she burst out the door. The shock on her face was heart-wrenching. I stopped the car and opened the window.

"It's okay, Dee. I'll be back."

"But where are you going? Why are you leaving? What's going on?" With each sentence, she took a small, hesitant step toward the car and then stopped.

"I must do something. Then we will all be safe. It will be over." As I pulled away, I could hear her scream "Jason." She stood on the black pavement, mouth open in dismay and bewilderment, trying to reach out to stop me. As I drove to the library, I had to force the image out of mind to rethink my solution to this impossible predicament.

He killed Rick to get the texts, but he didn't get them. Rick didn't have them. He continued searching. He searched Rick's office and home, and my office and home. He tracked me down, at my office and home. He searched my backpack after I survived his attempt to murder me. My surviving the drug did not send him on his way. He will continue his search. Yet what Deana told me about finding the brown paper is most disturbing. My conviction that he couldn't know I had the texts is wrong. That had granted me a measure of protection, now gone.

He had examined the brown paper that wrapped the texts. Why did he leave it like that on my office floor? Why did he remove the stamps? I assume he searched my office and, finding nothing, looked in the wastebasket as a last resort. He discovered crumpled, brown wrapping paper, took it out, and flattened it on the floor to examine it. My name, address, and the postmark were visible. The size of the paper and the creased outline would make it obvious that Rick sent the texts to me. He knows I have them. And they are locked in the faculty reading room of the library. I avoided discussing the texts when Miller questioned me. I assume he is correct that I am still in danger. Can I ever be free and safe?

Secret! All of this must stay secret. I cannot talk about it because I place the listener in jeopardy. By maintaining secrecy and by creating fear, the Shra'kufans remain protected and immune. The secrecy maintains itself, and any individual who learns about them will remain silent out of fear. This stops any efforts to respond to Shra'kufan terrorism. What is the social, political, personal, and financial cost of their terrorism? Will it spread around the world? That is an ironic question. A Shra'kufan terrorist is visiting Terrace Hills, in the middle of the USA, right now. What can a lone individual do to make a difference? What can I do to keep them from killing me and my family?

One foundation of the Shra'kufan belief in secrecy rests in the texts. A nonbeliever must never view them. To destroy them would not solve my problem, since the Shra'kufans now realize I have the texts. They are sacrosanct, and they are intent on retrieving the copy I have.

Before I act on my solution, I must analyze it. I hope I'm right, but I'm also convinced I can't return the texts to the Shra'kufans. I can't hand them to the assassin, since he would see me holding the texts. Could I return them anonymously? I have no idea where to send them, so this isn't an option. To return them would not solve my dilemma. Since I have seen the texts—and they know—they would kill me. This creates a life-threatening problem for me and for my family.

This is the problem I believe I am about to solve. I don't want the texts. I'm in this dilemma, not out of my choice, but because I was thrown into it by Rick and by the actions and beliefs of the Shra'kufans. My solution to this insoluble dilemma might work. Otherwise, I'm dead.

Alongside this logical mentation, alternative layers of experience unfold. Together with confusion and distress are clarity and simplicity. The most incidental event glories in itself. What I would have called significant remains significant. Yet every event is of equal importance to any other. Fewer differences manifest, although each is more distinct. Peace settles. Deep quieting. The state of mind is like autumn leaves dropping without plan, blanketing the ground.

Within another layer of experience, questions and doubt arise from vestiges of earlier beliefs. These older, lifelong habits still operate and amuse and intrigue me. Coincident with them, interpenetrating through and within them, are ways of perceiving, of knowing, of being, which are . . . inexpressible. Within this open and new awareness, action, though a gamble, remains clear.

I recall pacing the floors of my office and study last night, and I recall my contempt of the useless books arrayed shelf upon shelf. How ironic that books showed me the way. Previously I viewed them as ends in themselves. Yet books create possibilities. Books did not save my life. What I did with and through them saved me. Words point beyond themselves, like a finger leading to a flower. Words create the trellis for the tenuous and fragile beauty of a yellow rose, trembling in the gentle breeze. Often scholars read only the words and miss the intimations beckoning beyond. They miss the birds perched on the bobbing vine. Look through the vine, look through the trellis, and an exquisite landscape unfolds its green and brown texture, rolling into the haze, which mixes sky with earth and earth with sky. The encompassing context is present, giving meaning to the whole experience, beckoning, inviting, all the time.

• • •

It's now early evening, about six fifteen. I am walking from the library to the edge of campus where the television news crews have parked. I'm carrying my backpack, the same one the assassin riffled through this morning. It's not heavy, and I have it slung over one shoulder. I am attuned to having it with me. And I am hypervigilant about the assassin. I am not confident I'll ever be safe but I must give this a try.

Alongside the worry is a pervasive peacefulness, a kind of knowledge that everything is fine just as it is, even if I die. This new, multilayered presentation of experience complicates, confuses, and reassures. He is nearby, and I apprehend the he is poised to act in whatever way he must. Part of my mind is terrified by what he could do. At the same time, I doubt the accuracy of what I sense about him, wondering if I'm making it up. This provides no reassurance. It's a complex mix I don't understand. I experience a massive sense of chaos and excitement, an indescribable swirling turmoil. I can't capture the fluid appearance of this previously solid world. Everything is stationary yet moving at the same time. Words cannot capture the experience.

The evening is warm, almost balmy; the sky is cloudless. A gentle breeze comes and goes. The sun is low in the sky but still above the horizon. A block from the library, only a few people are out walking. Traffic is light. The huge, old oak, where I confronted the assassin, is in the shade of the administration building. I walk along the street that travels between that building and Kramer Hall. I pass the parking lot where I first glimpsed the assassin this afternoon.

About thirty yards in front of me is Baldwin Avenue, the street that divides the campus from the city. The scene here is different. A policeman directs traffic, and cars cram the streets. As I approach Baldwin, foot and street traffic jam together in all directions. Several large sawhorses barricade the entrances to the streets intersecting Baldwin to my left, where large numbers of students live. The sawhorses leave room for only a single car to pass. Uniformed police stand clustered at every street corner, and other police roam the streets, carrying two-way radios. Wherever

I glance, I find a police car. A cameraman accompanies some-one down the street in front of me. A large box, connected to the camera, hangs by a strap from his shoulder. Along Baldwin, where traffic is gnarled and slowed, at least four medium-sized trucks park on the grass bordering campus. They have satel-lite dishes on their roofs and network logos on their sides. The television crews, the police, and the barricades seem to act like magnets attracting this crowd.

In sharp contrast to the jammed street bordering campus, the blocked ones are devoid of cars, with only a scattering of pedes-trians. A policeman adjusts a sawhorse, allowing a single car to turn onto a street, and then stops the next car, walking to the driver's window to talk.

Gawkers and sightseers and pedestrians clutter the sidewalks and the street. I recognize network runners by the logos on their polo shirts and their clipboards. They stop cars and walkers, jotting things down.

The clamor of the generator from the closest news truck increases as I walk closer. Will the reporter listen? Will the reporter even consider talking to me? It is not about the kickoff party but, from my point of view, my story is significant. Will a reporter agree and broadcast it? How do I reach the news crew? If I get one interview, I'm certain it will spread to the other networks, and I will have accomplished what I want. That first one is crucial. I don't want to wander about, though I've not seen the assassin anywhere. He is here somewhere despite the heavy police presence, but they would not stop him. If he sees me being interviewed on television, will he retaliate? Will he kill me on the spot despite police in the vicinity? How careful do I need to be? When I glance across the street to the lawn along the edge of campus, I spot an interviewer talking to a student. People mill about, jockeying for the best view, and, when they part, Detective Miller is talking into a microphone.

Unexpectedly, I am swept into the sensations of being carried along in a current or strong wind. I stop, sensing it try to move me, and search around to find its source. No one else seems to experience it. Its direction leads to the interviewer. I clutch the backpack in front of me, thread my way between cars, and walk along the side of a network truck. The generator drowns out the raucous noise of the traffic and pedestrians. Thick, bright-orange cables run along the ground from the truck for at least a hundred feet at which point they enter the crowd. I assume they lead to the camera. I need to get in there.

"Excuse me." I push by one bystander, then another. "Excuse me. Coming through. Excuse me. Can I get by, please? Thanks. Excuse me."

I break through the front of the crowd. I'm not ten feet from the interviewer and Miller.

"Detective, do you have any leads on the murder yesterday?"

"We have information but no suspects in custody."

"Is there a connection between the fall kickoff party and the murder?"

"We suspect these are unrelated events. We have no motive for the murder and no leads to follow."

"I do," I yell, sneaking under the elbow of a guard who is holding his arms out to his sides to keep the crowd back. I take several quick steps toward the interviewer. "I know why Dr. Volks was murdered. I have the evidence right here, and it has nothing to do with the fall kickoff party!" The interviewer turns to stare at me. His expression communicates doubt and caution. He pulls his microphone back and places it beneath his armpit. He furrows his brow and scrutinizes me. Miller looks surprised and takes his hand out of his left coat pocket. The interviewer is someone I recognize, though I can't recall his name. Howard something, I guess. I step even closer to the microphone.

"A terrorist tried to assassinate me this afternoon, but I survived."

"Are you the fellow attacked this afternoon? Over there?" He gestures to his right, toward the administration building. Relief floods me. This is my entry card! This is my validation! But I have got to keep his attention or I might lose the interview.

"Yes, but I lived through the assassination attempt. A religion professor was murdered yesterday by the same terrorist. That's the story I'd like to talk about." His eyes have opened wider; he licks his lips. He steps toward me and puts the microphone a few inches from my mouth. I glance at the cameraman and notice a red light shining on the front of the camera. The light is much smaller than I expected. A long, thin wire connects the microphone to the camera. I notice with surprise I am peaceful. Miller is paying attention to me, unsure whether to stop me. The interviewer pushes on his ear, looks to the side as though listening, and then nods. As his hand drops, I notice he has a small earpiece there.

"Who are you?"

"I'm Dr. Jason Butler, a psychologist here at Eastern State. My friend and colleague, Rick Volks, a professor of religion, was murdered yesterday by a Shra'kufan terrorist. Rick had bought some sacred texts in the Middle or Far East. He sent them to me as a safety precaution." I peer out and search the crowd. Then I continue, saying, "I'm worried that the assassin is here and that he will try to stop me."

Before I unzip the backpack, the portentousness of what I am about to do strikes me. Though there are doubts, this action might save me and my family. I reach in and remove the most ancient text, holding the rest in the other arm. I let the backpack drop off the texts, revealing them all. I flip the pages so the arcane writing can be in a camera close-up. I can tell from the angle of the camera and how far out it has zoomed that he is getting shots of the texts. I can sense the words inside my mind ready to tumble forth. I don't want to give the interviewer a chance to stop the flow of my speech. I must spurt it all out.

I glance from the interviewer to the crowd. I scan them and stare into black eyes in a pock-marked face at the rear of the crowd. The stony-faced assassin stares back. Can he hear me? Does he understand English? What will he do? Is this my death? Without warning, time shifts and unfolds mysteriously. Time slows. The multiple layers of experience, like separate strands, proceed on their own and separate courses.

The crowd acts unaffected by his presence. Everything but the assassin seems to stop. His movements appear unhurried, and as he performs them, they seem familiar. The whole time, he does not shift his eyes from me. He reaches out in front and to the sides at waist height, palms upward. The motion appears to be both reaching out and welcoming. He brings his hands together in front of him, both palms still facing upward. The index finger and thumb of both hands connect to make circles. The hands fold over, one circle on top of the other, remaining fingertips together pointing away, right at me. He raises both arms above his head, lowers them to right above his eyes, inclines his head, and brings the hands to his heart, fingers still pointing upward. Then his hands open, extend outward as if releasing a gift, and drift down as he lowers them to his side. A shiver of recognition travels along my spine to the top of my head. I saw this exact scene after he cut my forehead this afternoon.

Time snaps back. The multilayers continue, as does understanding that Miller will try to stop me from talking, and the FBI and CIA will step in. My gaze shifts to Miller, and when I look back, the assassin has disappeared.

"Miller," I yell, "the assassin was right there in the crowd." I point to where I had seen him. A murmur of concern comes from the individuals in that area. They search about, voices panicked, and scurry to leave. I see cameramen moving in while police surround the group to contain it.

"Miller," I yell even louder. He turns. "He's already past the administration building, almost to the parking lot." Miller pulls out his two-way radio and runs in that direction.

The reporter debates following Miller but instead turns his attention back.

"Dr. Butler, what is happening?"

"Dr. Rick Volks was murdered yesterday and I was, sort of, a witness. Rick was murdered by someone who wants these texts. The man who was at the back of the crowd," I point to where I saw him, "tried to kill me this afternoon. He is part of a group that will kill anyone who even knows these texts exist, let alone anyone who has seen them. These," I hold up the texts, "are ultimate religious secrets for this group. I want the whole country, the world, to know this complete story . . . and to show the texts. That will undercut the power of their secrecy and protect me and my family and reduce their power to intimidate people in other countries."

"If these texts are secret and sacred, why would you expose them?"

"You know, I've asked myself the same question. Would this act on my part be equally destructive from their point of view? That might be the case. Yet they are terrorists."

"Aren't you risking your life to do this?"

"That is my greatest fear. I yearn for the opposite: speaking out might keep me and others safe. In addition, the broadcast will not place others in danger, and it should save many lives. When finished, it is my hope that I, you, all of us will be safe from these terrorists.

"I'm speaking out of compassion and concern. I love peace and believe, from my heart, that life is precious. Violence can only breed violence. It solves nothing. It is fear that provokes violence. These past twenty-four hours I learned, learned in my gut, that violence functions to protect: to protect 'me and mine,' to protect ideas, religion, country, and ways of life. The motivation for violence is fear. This kind of self-protection and fear breeds further violence, conflict, and hate, which threatens the very thing protected.

"We are one humanity on this planet. To view ourselves as better, to believe we alone have correct ideas or to impose our political or religious dogma leads to conflict, which creates the potential for violence and war. A refusal to negotiate or to dialogue protects ideas and beliefs and betrays the hidden fear they are insupportable. Secrets separate one group from another, but secrets cannot work when the entire world knows. When secrets come to light, they lose their power and get tested on their own merit. It is from this heartfelt conviction I am here." The interviewer is getting restless with my rhetoric. Ideas are not so exciting or newsworthy. I can tell he is listening to someone in his earpiece, and his nonverbal behavior shows he is about to shift away from me. I step closer, forcing him to attend to me.

"One more thing. Dr. Volks was murdered because he bought these texts. I have made copies and sent them to newspapers and government officials in the United States, the United Nations, and many countries abroad, including the Middle and Far East. I will give the originals to the police, though I urge their return to the Shra'kufans. I have no wish to keep them. They are not mine; and they belong to the Shra'kufans." The interviewer stares at me unblinking, lips separated. "I hope I will survive."

CHAPTER 37

Twilight, 9:45 p.m.

After everything I went through this past day, I want my family as close to me as possible, and all four of us are piled on the bed. So many times I concluded I would never touch them again. Four pillows raise my back and head so I can watch the television. Deana, raised by her own pillows, rests on my left arm and snuggles against my side. Ann has draped herself over my chest and is sound asleep, her head resting on Deana. And my right hand and lower arm hold Mark, who is fidgety and looking at a book. Mom and Dad are down the hall in the spare room.

Like ocean depths, my state is peaceful and profound while the surface swirls. There has been a transformation. People and objects arise alive and vibrant, yet the mind glows translucent and sharp with few distinctions. Is the drug lingering in my system? Has my encounter with the Blue Sky exposed an obscured potential of the mind? Has it forced inner capacities to develop?

The multilayered state of consciousness soothes and jars at the same time. I must delay reactions to figure out an appropriate response. I no longer consider what comes into mind fantasies, but I'm muddled about how to distinguish reality from imagination. When I focus on certain things, such as a sensation or what is going on outside me, these inner happenings seem to shut down, and I'm aware of the focus of my attention. Then, as I relax, the multiple layers appear again like the sun emerging from behind clouds.

As we watch the news on TV, engaging in small talk, reveling in being together, I "know" that Dad and Mom are getting ready for bed talking about how worried they are since the assassin is on the loose. What would happen if I got killed? How would Deana support the family? Do we have enough life insurance? How would she manage?

Dad worries about his shortness of breath that started last night, a concern he has not yet shared with Mom. He is not uncomfortable but reacting to worries piqued by colon cancer diagnosed in one of his longtime friends. Ann is dreaming about playing soccer with a green mouse, the same character she watched in cartoons at the motel. Deana struggles with the image of me, crumpled on the ground, the assassin kneeling over me. Each time the image returns, she presses more into my side, sometimes angling her face up so we can kiss. Her hand grips my knee, a way to hold on so I don't slip away. A vision comes. I can't locate it. I view Deana's back and side. She wears a loose top, pulled up to free her breast, and she nurses an infant. The image is discomforting since she is alone. My attention switches. Mark struggles to stay awake, to stay with his mom and dad. Despite his young age, he sensed that something had been wrong during the day: his routine turned on its end; his parents not close, and even when present, would disappear; and he could sense our anxiety and preoccupation. Before I can reassure him that life is back to normal, he drifts off to sleep. Deana stiffens and lifts a shoulder so she can glare at me.

"When you left us at the motel, I was furious." The sharp edge to her voice has dulled but still cuts.

"I'm aware of that, Dee."

"I don't understand why you went away like that! Yes, you've explained it, and, yes, I watched the news report, but it still seems, I don't know, wrong. I was so worried the whole time you were missing. Do you realize how long it was?" She is gathering emotional momentum, getting afraid and angry all over again. "You weren't out of the hospital an hour before you disappeared. And you were missing for over four hours! You have never done that before, Jason. And the way you did it. And the circumstances."

"I'm sorry. I might have been wrong, but I did what I believed was best."

"Please, please, never do that again. At least tell me something, give me some warning, or call me to say you're okay. But don't disappear like that." I can hear the tears and desperation behind the words, the frustration and the fear.

"All right. Never again."

She continues to stare at me, as if to check the truth of what I've said. She inhales sharply, nods, and, as she leans back, looks at the TV.

"It's coming on, Jason."

I turn my attention to the television in time to hear the announcer say, "Coming up, in Terrace Hills, surviving a terrorist's attack. We have a special report from our correspondent, Mel Howard, who is on the scene and interviewed Dr. Jason Butler, who lived despite the attack." The screen shows the paramedics working on my crumpled body and then a commercial comes on.

"Jason!" Deana turns toward me and raises herself on one elbow. Our faces are only six inches apart; her eyes opened wide. "Do you realize what you did? You talked on television . . . to a national audience. You were natural and weren't anxious at all. You were great."

"My god, Dee, you're right. I had missed it. In fact, I hadn't noticed until you mentioned it." I search inside for what had been blocking me for so long. I recall the clear and unrestrained way I acted during the interview. To my amazement, I can't find a memory of any tension or distress. What I discover is freedom.

"Whatever it was, it's gone, Dee. It's not there anymore."

She beams, her eyes twinkling, her dimple appearing. She leans closer and presses her lips to mine. Tenderness suffuses the room. When she rolls back to her previous position, she sighs.

"You recognize," she says in a matter-of-fact way, "we need to work on project number three . . . but not tonight." She turns her head to wink at me, a suppressed grin showing at the edges of her lips. I can't help smiling in reaction.

"What happened with Drake Chemical?"

"Oh, nothing much. Spent the day looking for a missing person . . . and during the afternoon, missed a found person. This impeded work. But I called Jack to advise him what was happening. He understood. Two weeks until the first presentation. We're in fine shape."

She looks back toward the television, and, distracted, asks, "Do you expect they'll do anything to you?"

"Who?"

"The courts, of course."

"No. I anticipate no action. Why would they?"

"You withheld evidence."

"I had good reason. And I solved the crime . . . and they now have the evidence."

"But the FBI and CIA are involved." She turns to peer at me.

"I don't foresee it's a problem."

She raises her eyebrows in a way that communicates I suffer from terminal naivety and turns back to the television.

"I hope you're right," she says.

The commercial continues. As I anticipate seeing the news report, recollections of what led up to the interview come back into my mind, but I'm startled when the screen shows Helen bursting through the front of the crowd. She runs up and throws her arms around me, sobbing and crying. She clutches me, her head moving side to side on my shoulder as she weeps. I could feel my shirt getting wet from her tears. I reached around to hold her, still gripping the texts in both hands. This scene remains on the television screen, while in the background the commentator says, "Dr. Helen Trent, wife of the murdered religion professor, grieves over the loss of her husband, Dr. Rick Volks." The camera moves in for a close-up of her sobbing on my shoulder.

I'm uncomfortable as Deana and I watch this portion of the news broadcast. I wonder how she is reacting. It takes no time to find out, as she blurts, "I have such mixed reactions to this." She moves her head back and forth, like a diminutive "no" as she talks. "This scene and the one with you against the tree, they play over and over. I feel so sorry for Helen. What a terrible thing! My heart goes out to her. But your embracing her, over and over, is troublesome to view."

"I have the same reaction." I am filled with compassion for Helen but a deep and abiding love for Deana wells up from deep inside. "But I love you, Deana. I want to be with you. You alone. Don't feel threatened by her. There is no threat there."

I feel her snuggle into my side, and I squeeze her against me. I feel her relax with my words, and I can see that her eyes are closed and she has a gentle, serene smile on her face. Her breathing is settling down. All of us are exhausted. With the remote control, I turn the volume down low, wanting to keep sound in the background for company. The lights are still on . . . but I think none of us will mind if we sleep in the light. I can tell by the sound of her breathing that Deana has already drifted into sleep. I imagine kissing her forehead and find my eyes closing. As I slip into sleep, light shines through, brighter and brighter.

•   •   •

The horde of the future
Marches relentlessly
Crushing
Plant and animal,

Earth and water,
Even air.
Nothing untouched.
Churning,
The burgeoning horde
Attacks itself.
We have loved the desert of the past;
Despite its emptiness, it fosters life.
Fear the desert of the future;
Collapsing, life twisted, what remains?
The thief steps from the mountain
Across the sea.
From the bearer of truth,
The word flies, touches fertile soil
And scatters like seeds
Everywhere . . .

The Prophecies of Baya Z'r, Verse 1

The End

ACKNOWLEDGMENTS

This book would have been impossible without the support of my family. Our fifty-year marriage has been a source of profound growth and satisfaction. In particular, I am grateful to my wife, Carole, who's loving, consistent, wise and honest way of being has inspired me to confront and grow in ways I had not thought possible. Her sharp-eyed editing strengthened the novel in significant ways. My children, Jennifer and Jonathan, both of whom provided editorial commentary on the manuscript, have enriched me and prodded me to grow in yet other ways.

Mr. Hubert H. Lui, my Tai Chi teacher for over twenty years, has been an inspirational example of living on the Tao. The books and teachings of Tarthang Tulku Rimpoche have confronted my assumptions and provided transformative practices. This book could not have been written without their influence. I thank Dharma Publishing for permission to include a quotation from *Knowledge of Freedom.*

Finally, many people over many years have provided feedback about the manuscript which I began writing in 1983. I thank David Lascu, Liz and John Schweitzer, Joel Darby, Therm Looman, Walter Lesiak, John Robertson, Michael Gainer and Meg, Cecily and John Haeger, and Joyce Carter. In particular, I thank Brenda Lovegrove-Lepisto who provided feedback on several drafts. In the middle stages, I also thank Stephanie Repasky and Matt Echelberger for their help. In 2017, when I was finally preparing the manuscript for professional editing, Beth McLeode, and Matthew Hile provided invaluable feedback. Katherine Pickett provided professional editing that was sensitive and careful, always matching the thrust of the story. Peggy Nehmen provided invaluable help about publishing and created a fantastic front and back cover.

DBB, 2019

REFERENCES

Green. E., & Green, A. (1977.) *Beyond Biofeedback.* (2nd ed.) New York: Delacorte Press.

Hartley, I., Hartley, E., & Green, E. (1975.) Biofeedback: The yoga of the West. VHS Tape. Hartley Film Foundation, Cos Cob, CT.

Horowitz, T., & Kimmelman, S. with Lui, H. H. (1976.) *Tai Chi Ch'uan: The Technique of Power.* Chicago: Chicago Review Press.

Tarthang, T. (1984.) *Knowledge of Freedom: Time to Change.* Berkeley, CA: Dharma Publishing.

DEAR READER

Thank you for reading my book. I hope you enjoyed it. If you did, please tell your friends.

I love hearing from readers. Please email me at DonCardonBooks @gmail.com and let me know what you think and how my book affected you. I'd love some feedback.

And I would appreciate your writing a review on Amazon or Goodreads. Those reviews help other readers find my book.

Don